An Au Pair to Remember

A Male Housekeeper Mystery

by

Stephen Kaminski

For information, email Cozy Cat Press, cozycatpress@aol.com or visit our website at: www.cozycatpress.com

COZY CAT
PRESS

ISBN: 978-1-946063-70-0
Printed in the United States of America

10 9 8 7 6 5 4 3 2 1

For my Babcia (grandmother) who turned 100 years old recently. She's a true inspiration.

Don't Miss the Damon Lassard Dabbling Detective Mysteries by Stephen Kaminski

It Takes Two to Strangle (Cozy Cat Press, 2012):
 Winner of the 2012 Reader Views Literary Award—Mid-Atlantic Region

Don't Cry Over Killed Milk (Cozy Cat Press, 2013):
 Winner of the 2014 Murder & Mayhem Awards for Best Classic Cozy
 Winner of the 2013 Reader Views Literary Award—Mid-Atlantic Region
 2013 Chanticleer Media CLUE Awards Finalist

Murder, She Floats (Cozy Cat Press, 2014):
 Winner of the 2014 Reader Views Literary Award—Mid-Atlantic Region
 Winner of the 2014 Reader Views Global Award—Caribbean Region

Chapter 1
Thursday, September 17

"What kind of person steals coupons?" Cam Reddick asked through gritted teeth. He plunked a pair of sturdy, reusable grocery bags on the spotless, wooden floor of his mother's kitchen. Raising himself upright, Cam swatted at a bead of perspiration tickling his brow as if it were a mosquito.

"Thanks." Darby Reddick stood on her tiptoes and pecked her son on his cheek. "I don't know—someone who can't get a pry bar under a hubcap?"

"Or got outwrestled by a baby for a lollipop," Cam said.

Darby snickered. "Desperation causes people to do crazy things. Earlier this summer, there was a story on the news about a couple from Lake Orion who was pilfering the inserts from Sunday paper vending machines."

"The dark underbelly of extreme couponing."

"For sure. I think the police arrested them. Did you see something at the store?"

"Nothing like that." Cam poured himself a cup of black coffee from a timeworn pot and sat at the kitchen table. "I had a stack of coupons in my shopping cart."

"Manufacturers' coupons?" Darby began to unpack nonperishables into the pantry tucked behind carved wooden doors.

"Nope, hubcap coupons."

Darby laughed.

"Yes, mostly for cereal and bread," Cam said. "But I had a rewards coupon from the store, too—a flat five dollars off. It printed out with my receipt when I was there on Tuesday doing my own shopping." He sipped, the coffee blistering the tip of his tongue.

Darby swiveled a hard-backed chair to the front of the pantry and stepped onto it with a carton of chicken stock in hand. Strands of graying blond hair touched her middle back as she craned her head to slip the box between a jar of olives and a canister of dried plums on the top shelf. Cam considered her pantry management approach to be laissez-faire rather than slipshod.

"Let me guess," Darby said, turning to face him. "You left the five dollar coupon in plain sight and walked away from your cart."

He grimaced. His mother was remarkably astute at recognizing his foibles. Not that leaving a coupon unattended was indicative of a character flaw. "I had a pile of them in the upper basket, on a container of strawberries. And yes, the five dollars was on top." He stretched his long, bony legs under the table. Ostrich limbs.

"Rookie mistake," Darby teased.

Cam grunted. "I left the cart in the frozen food section to run back and pick up taco shells in another aisle." He pointed to the guilty box—Old El Paso proffered no defense. "The cart wasn't out of my sight for more than two minutes. When I came back, poof! My five bucks were gone. I guess I'm not the brightest bulb in the shed."

Darby tittered. "You remind me so much of your father when you mix your metaphors."

Cam grinned. "I do it on purpose, you know."

"So did he. It made me laugh every time." She slipped down from the chair and smoothed her pleated skirt, then stepped over to a cabinet and pulled out a roll of paper towels and lemon-scented Pledge. Darby started wiping down the kitchen island's black granite.

"That countertop is already spotless," Cam observed.

"Just a force of habit." Darby had spent almost forty years as a professional housekeeper—the first ten working for a large agency in Bloomfield Hills, and the last thirty as the owner of Peachy Kleen. After Cam moved back to Michigan, Darby had transitioned all operations of the small business to him. "I'll pay you back for the groceries," she said. "You should have saved the five dollars to stock your own fridge, anyway."

"That's not the point, Mother." Cam sipped his coffee. It had cooled to a manageable temperature.

"No, I suppose it's not. What it is, is a sad example of the distress that's hit so many of the folks here."

Cam had come back to the village of Rusted Bonnet, Michigan—his boyhood home—six months earlier, after spending half of a decade floundering in a Washington, DC, suburb. Rusted Bonnet hadn't changed much during those five years, or the last fifty for that matter, but Cameron Reddick had.

It wasn't the first time he'd returned to the quaintly eclectic village thirty miles north of Detroit. After graduating with an engineering degree from Michigan State, he went home to live with his widowed mother and pursue his high school sweetheart, Kacey Gingerfield. Kacey had joined the local police force, and Cam landed an operations manager position at a nearby Vlasic pickle-packing plant. They married just weeks after he turned twenty-four and had a daughter two years later.

Then Cam left. To be more precise, he ran. Not ready to tackle the responsibilities of adult life head on, he and Kacey divorced just after Emma's first birthday and he fled east, abandoning the only people who ever loved him.

Only now had Cam begun to treat Kacey with the respect he felt she deserved and become a visible part of Emma's life.

"Are you going to tell Kacey about the stolen coupon?" Darby asked.

"Tell the police that someone swiped a few bucks from a shopping cart? No, I don't think so." Kacey had been promoted to deputy chief of the Rusted Bonnet Police Department a year earlier.

Darby dipped her hand back into a grocery bag. "Did you happen to pick up any corn niblets? I want to make tortilla soup tomorrow and you know I like to go heavy on the corn."

"I did. Remind me again, how many ears are in a niblet?"

* * *

"I feel like a hot mess," Kacey Gingerfield Reddick said, wiping grit from her forehead. She was perched cross-legged on the edge of a sandbox.

"How did you get so much sand on yourself?" Cam asked, standing above her. The blazing September sun beat down on their heads. A clutch of recently planted saplings failed to provide much-needed shade at the community center playground.

Kacey pointed surreptitiously toward their daughter. "Miss Emma thought it would be fun to sprinkle my hair with *pixie dust*," she whispered.

Cam brushed sand from the sleeve of his ex-wife's police uniform. He noted a faint scent of lilac perfume.

"Thanks," Kacey said with a smile.

When Cam returned to Rusted Bonnet, Kacey had been cordial but understandably guarded. Their conversations were purely functional—coordinating drop-off and pick-up times and hashing out a division of costs to cover Emma's needs. But Kacey had allowed him to reenter both of their lives and, it seemed, she was gradually relaxing. She hadn't reverted to high school flirtations, but her playful and tender demeanor reminded Cam why he had fallen hard for her so many years earlier.

Kacey tilted her head toward the ground and raked her fingers through her thick waves of dark hair, freeing specks of sand. Cam's eyes lingered on the honey-colored skin along the arch of her neckline.

"Daddy!" Emma shouted and raced toward the sandbox from a nearby jungle gym. A bob of blond hair bounced as she ran. Emma wrapped scrawny arms around Cam's waist, her egg yolk yellow T-shirt pressed against his midsection.

"Hi, sweetie," he said.

"Mommy, can I tell Daddy the joke? Can I, can I?" Emma asked, the words surging like bursts of rifle fire. She clutched Cam's hand with her right and reached out toward Kacey with her left.

"Of course," Kacey said. She stood and took Emma's hand, aligning the three in a human chain.

"Okay, Daddy, I have a joke!" Emma bounced on the balls of her feet with excitement.

"I'm all ears." Cam unlinked his hand from hers and wiggled his ears with his fingertips.

Emma laughed. "A cat had kittens in the road." She paused for dramatic effect. "She had litter!"

Cam erupted in a belly laugh despite having no idea what Emma meant.

"Wait, wait, I told it wrong," Emma said after a moment. "Mommy, how does it go?" She turned her cobalt blue saucer eyes up to Kacey and tugged at her pant leg.

"A mama cat had baby kittens in the road," Kacey said patiently, then after a beat, added, "she got a ticket for littering."

Emma squealed with delight.

"Listen, sweetness," Kacey said, bending at the knees, "I have to go to a meeting for work. Daddy will take you to his house for dinner, then he'll bring you home in time for your bath tonight." She had school—first grade—the following morning.

Emma lived with Kacey in her 1950s bungalow, but spent every Sunday with Cam. And he had offered to take her any time Kacey was needed at the station outside of school or aftercare hours. Fortunately, the sleepy village had a well-staffed force: Chief Bernie Leftwich, Kacey, four junior officers, and a pair of dispatchers.

"Can I feed Bait?" Emma asked Cam. "Can I, can I?"

His goldfish, Bait—a "rescue" he saved from a local tackle shop—listened to Cam better than any therapist money could buy.

"As soon as we get to my house," Cam said. "And I bet he's hungry."

"He's always hungry!" Emma shrieked.

"That's true. Why don't we let Mommy go, and play here for a few more minutes." He looked around the playground. "I see an open swing with your name on it."

Chapter 2
Friday, September 18

Black sludge plastered Cam's fingernails—a Gothic manicure. At nine o'clock in the morning, on water-wrinkled hands and aching knees, he was losing the war on grout in a two-person shower.

The McRaes' master bath outsized his kitchen. Rusted Bonnet was largely occupied by those of modest means, but a handful of affluent neighborhoods had cropped up—commuters to Detroit and its environs who sought a bucolic setting for their McMansions.

Greta Astor lingered in the bathroom, her knees bent in yellow skinny jeans, her back flush to the doorframe connecting to the bedroom. She had brought Cam coffee and set it on the vanity.

"Pay close attention to the soap dish," Greta said in a mischievous tone. "Mrs. McRae can't stand scum."

Unsure of the thrust of the barb, Cam asked, "Where are the twins?" over his shoulder. Greta served as au pair to a pair of four-year-olds—Nicolas and Sophie. The McRaes were one of Peachy Kleen's every-other-week regulars. Wealthy clients who could weather economic turmoil were the bread-and-butter of the cleaning company's livelihood, Darby had explained to Cam: They never miss a payment and run in social circles with others who can afford housekeeping services. And in small towns, word-of-mouth referrals dwarfed the value of even social media reviews.

"The twins?" Greta waved a hand in the air flippantly. "They're watching a Disney movie. I'll lug them off to the park in the double-wide stroller after you and that cantankerous woman downstairs are finished."

Greta sure has a firm grasp of the English language for a German au pair, Cam thought. Cantankerous was as good of a word as any to describe Samantha Krause, one of Peachy Kleen's full-time cleaners. The beefy older woman didn't take criticism well but relished dishing it out. Samantha had been less than pleased when Cam took over the business from his mother, not because he was thirty-two years old or male, but due to his status as a divorced father. "It's not right, leaving a young woman to fend for herself with a child," Cam had overheard Samantha saying to Tabby Vazquez, another of his three housekeepers. He hadn't let on that he was wise to Samantha's protestations of his "objectionable" marital status—plus, he *had* made mistakes. And if his penance included enduring the occasional whispered disapproval, so be it.

"Do you need any help in there?" Greta asked, with a teasing lilt in her voice. "There's nothing sexier than a man on all fours, up to his elbows in Scrubbing Bubbles."

Cam grinned. To get a feel for his clientele, he had spent time in the homes of each of Peachy Kleen's regulars. After meeting Greta, he assigned himself to the McRae household as often as possible. The twenty-five-year-old knockout with high cheekbones and alabaster skin hailed from the outskirts of Dresden, near Germany's border with the Czech Republic. Greta had recently explained to him that an au pair could spend one to two years "in country," and she'd been with the McRaes for nine months. It was her second stint— according to her, an arrangement with a family in Cleveland hadn't worked out. Greta never explained why, and Cam hadn't felt it was his place to press her on the point.

From his perspective, Greta delighted in shoveling innuendo in Cam's direction. And he enjoyed playing along. He didn't relish cleaning, and spent as much time handling Peachy Kleen's operations—scheduling clients, ordering supplies, and balancing the books—as he did scouring grime. But with only Samantha, Tabby, and Nombecko Blom on staff, when a day's appointment book was full or the McRae house was scheduled, he dirtied his hands.

Samantha didn't approve of his flirtations with Greta. "A professional shouldn't speak with a client or their help unless it has to do with the cleaning," she told him months earlier, "*especially* au pairs and nannies—can't lead to anything but trouble for a young man such as yourself." Cam had nodded in agreement, then tried in earnest to pair himself with Tabby to tackle the McRae house. But today, Tabby was chaperoning a school field trip for one of her daughters and Nombecko—Becka—had called in sick.

"How's Reynold?" Cam, now unclogging the drain, asked Greta. Reynold Cornell, a bartender at the Stagger Inn in Rusted Bonnet and according to Greta, her lover, had neck muscles thicker than Cam's biceps.

"He's not fun like you, just a big hairy gorilla," Greta said and touched her tongue to her upper lip. "And you, Cam, have such a lovely baby face."

Cam groaned. His youthful appearance was both a blessing and a curse when it came to women. "I haven't shaved for a month, and I still only have a two o'clock shadow," he joked.

Greta laughed and left the bathroom—the McRae twins were crying out for breakfast.

* * *

Moving boxes stacked five feet high greeted Cam on his front porch when he arrived home at six o'clock, exhausted from a full day. His townhouse sat in the center of a strip of seven matching units. Despite being built thirty years earlier, the homes were still in relatively good condition and Cam's had been fitted with new appliances before he signed a two-year lease. He looked at the label on one of the boxes—Elena Ramp. Her address matched a unit two doors down from his.

"The moving company unloaded on the wrong porch," Cam heard.

He turned to see a young, athletically built woman on the sidewalk, her thin auburn hair tied into a side ponytail. She wore a red, moisture-wicking running shirt, Lululemon crops, and sneakers.

"No problem," Cam said as she mounted the three steps to his narrow porch. "Are you moving in?"

"Yes. I'm Elena." She extended a hand. The polish on her nails matched her hair color.

He shook hands. "I'm Cam." Despite his fatigue, he added, "Can I help you with these boxes?"

"Would you mind?" Elena gave him an inviting smile. She had an angular face that exuded confidence.

"Not at all." Cam apologized for his sullied clothing, then explained how he had spent his day—cleaning a house in McLean Gardens followed by two homes in upscale Bloomfield Hills.

"Which house in McLean Gardens?" Elena asked as Cam hefted a box marked "dishes" onto his shoulder. "I have two decorating jobs in that neighborhood—Dr. Bowles and the McRae house."

"Small world. The McRaes are one of my clients. That's where I was this morning. Interior design?"

"I have a degree in design, but this is more of a decorating job. They're technically not the same, but sometimes you take the work you can get. I must have just missed you, because I got there shortly before noon," Elena said as they approached her front door. She opened it to let Cam pass through.

He set the box of dishes down on the laminate floor in an otherwise bare kitchen save for an opened bag of gummy bears on the counter. "The McRaes' au pair didn't tell me Dutch and Tatum were having the place redecorated."

"Dutch?"

"Hank McRae. My mother tells me everyone calls him Dutch. There was a character from the *Karate Kid* with that name—one of the bad guys. Apparently, Hank looked like him as a teenager and the name stuck."

"One of the Cobra Kai, right?" she asked with a smile.

"That's right." Cam strode out of Elena's townhouse to retrieve another box from his porch. She followed. "Where are you from?" he asked. "I can't place your accent."

"Switzerland. But I've been in the States for the past nine years. Since I turned eighteen."

"So you went to school here?"

"At the University of Cincinnati. They have a pretty big program. After graduation, much to my parents' dismay, I took a position in Chicago rather than latching on with a firm back in Lucerne." She hesitated, then added, "I moved to Michigan to follow a man I was dating. The relationship didn't work out but my business did. Even though times are tough here, I've been able to get enough work."

"So why Rusted Bonnet?" Cam asked, plucking a light box from the stack.

Country stores, village saloons—of both the ice cream and drinking variety—and antique shops sprinkled among faceless complexes serving the automotive industry provided Rusted Bonnet an inkling of charm. On one edge of the village, union workers manufactured engines for F-150s, Mustangs, and Crown Victorias, and on the other, ninety-plus miles of track wound through the Ford proving ground—a four thousand-acre plot nestled among corn and lavender fields.

"Let me take that one—it's just towels." Elena scooped the box from Cam's arms and cradled it in hers. "Why Rusted Bonnet? The lease on my apartment in Rochester ended and I was looking for a place with more space at a cheaper price. Tatum McRae invited me to see her home a couple of weeks ago and afterward, I took a drive around the village. It seems pleasant enough."

"Well, I think you made an excellent choice," Cam said. He spent the next ten minutes carrying boxes for Elena, exchanged phone numbers with her, and then returned to his townhouse for a scalding hot shower and a bowl of reheated linguini. He dropped off to sleep three hours later on the sofa in front of a Hitchcock film.

* * *

Saturday, September 19

At two o'clock in the morning, Cam's telephone shrilled. He shielded his eyes from an infomercial touting a "revolutionary breakthrough in exercise science." Cam squinted at his watch, then reached for the phone on the coffee table. Kacey's name gleamed up at him. His heart lurched as he jabbed at the touchscreen.

"What's wrong?" he shouted. "Is Emma all right?"

"Yes, yes, she's fine," Kacey said through labored breath. "She's asleep but I have to leave. It's an emergency. I'm so sorry to ask you at this hour, but could you come to the house right now? I'd bring her to you but I don't want to wake her."

Cam shook his head, freeing the cobwebs. "I can do that," he said. "What's happening?"

"Greta Astor has been murdered."

Chapter 3

"How did she die?" Cam whispered. A single lamp weakly lit Kacey's front parlor. Cam had dressed, shoved a change of clothes into an overnight bag, and raced to her bungalow in ten minutes flat.

"I don't know for sure. The chief phoned me just before I called you. According to Bernie, Dutch McRae called 911 and reported that his au pair was lying dead in a heap at the bottom of the stairs. The 911 dispatcher contacted an ambulance, then the chief. Thankfully, Bernie arrived before the paramedics could clear away the body." Kacey sat on the edge of a white, wicker chair and pulled on a pair of Magnum boots. "He said he saw something that made him suspect that Greta hadn't fallen accidentally. No time to speculate, I have to get over there right away." She whipped the laces into double knots, stood, and touched Cam's elbow. "Thank you for coming so soon. I'm not sure who I'd turn to if you weren't here."

Probably my mother, Cam thought. Kacey's parents lived over an hour away. He said, "I can't believe Greta's dead. I just saw her at the McRaes' yesterday morning."

Kacey blinked rapidly. "You cleaned their house yesterday?" she asked.

"Samantha and I did, yes. Does it matter?"

"I don't know, I've never investigated a murder before." She slapped a set of keys into Cam's palm and bolted out of the house to her cruiser.

* * *

After surviving a Saturday morning filled with rousing games of Operation and Battleship, a blueberry pancake "party" breakfast for Emma, two stuffed animals, and an American Girl doll, and the creation of a Lego tower that wouldn't pass architectural muster in Pisa, Cam hoisted his feet onto a recliner footrest in his mother's living room.

Positioned across from him on a cushioned settee near the fireplace, Darby sipped lemonade. Through the sliding glass door to the backyard, Cam could see Emma clapping hands with a girl close to her own age as they shouted the words to "Miss Mary Mack."

"Thanks for setting up a playdate," Cam said. "I love Emma to pieces, but we were both getting stir crazy." If Greta had, in fact, been murdered, Cam didn't expect Kacey to return home during the daytime hours. But he'd left her a note just in case.

"It's always a pleasure to have my grandchild visit," Darby said. "Now, what did Kacey say happened to the McRaes' au pair?"

Cam relayed the snippet of information Kacey passed to him during the early morning hours.

"If she fell down a flight of stairs and it wasn't an accident, how can the police be sure she didn't commit suicide?" Darby asked.

"I don't know. I'll ask Kacey."

"She was a cute one, that Greta," Darby observed.

"She certainly was." Cam reddened. "Not that I stood a chance with her had I wanted one. She was more interested in Reynold Cornell."

"That meathead? All Reynold has is a chiseled jaw and an arsenal of tired pick-up lines."

Cam arched an eyebrow.

"He didn't hit on me, silly," Darby said. "But I've seen him in action while he's tending bar. Trust me, you're the complete package, not him."

Cam shrugged. "I'm not sure I'm ready to start dating again anyway. Especially now that I'm spending more time with Emma. She must already be confused with me moving back to Rusted Bonnet."

"The girl's one smart cookie. But not dating for a while sounds very sensible." Darby paused for a moment, then said, "Reynold would certainly be strong enough to push Greta down the stairs. She couldn't have weighed more than a hundred and ten pounds."

A tremor reverberated in Cam's chest. Even if it was wild speculation, he hadn't considered putting a name or face on a real life murderer. It left a pit in his stomach.

Cam took a moment to clear his thoughts, then said, "Greta died in the middle of the night. I can't imagine the McRaes would've allowed her to invite a man into the house that late. The twins sleep down the hall from her room."

"True," Darby said. "Of course, she could have snuck him inside after the family went to bed for the night."

"How much do you know about Reynold?"

"Not much." She spun her head toward the sliding door at the sound of giggles—Emma and her friend plastered their faces against the glass. Darby waved and the pair dashed away.

"All I know about Reynold," Darby continued, "is that he started tending bar two years ago and reeks of too much Axe body spray. He didn't grow up in Rusted Bonnet and other than at the Stagger, I haven't seen him around town."

"Did you see him trying to pick up women after he started seeing Greta?"

"When did they start going out?"

Cam scratched his chin. "Greta was with the McRaes for nine months. I came home six months ago, and I think they were already an item by then. So sometime between January and March."

Darby picked pilling off of her cardigan sweater. Despite the September heat, she had dressed in layers. "I don't go to the Stagger too often. You probably frequent the place more than me. But now that I think about it, I didn't notice him chatting up anyone the last few times I was there. For all I know, he was devoted to Greta."

"Maybe, but a leopard doesn't usually change his stripes."

Darby wrinkled her brow.

"That was a bad one, sorry."

"It's not that. I just remembered, I had lunch there with a friend two weeks ago—Reynold was speaking with a man who was sitting by himself at the end of the bar. I only noticed because he looked too professional to be eating in a place like the Stagger. Tailored suit, gold watch, buffed loafers. From where I was sitting, the conversation seemed intense."

"You didn't recognize him?"

"No. He was in his early forties and had a full head of dark, wavy hair. A pinch of color in his skin. Cuban, maybe."

"Did you overhear any of their conversation?"

Darby shook her head. "The man seemed a bit out of place, but I didn't have any reason to think there was anything amiss."

"Too bad," Cam said. "I suppose that if Greta *was* pushed down the stairs, Dutch and Tatum McRae would be high on the list of suspects as well. After all, it was the middle of the night so they were probably upstairs in their bedroom."

"But why would either one of them harm their own au pair? She takes care of their children."

"Maybe they saw her mistreat Nicolas or Sophie," Cam ventured.

Darby narrowed her eyes. "Have you seen evidence of that?"

"No, I was just trying to think of a motive."

"And rather than report abuse to the police, a pair of upstanding citizens decides to commit murder in their own home? I don't think so."

Cam shrugged. "I wouldn't have thought any murder in Rusted Bonnet was probable. Maybe Chief Leftwich made a mistake."

"Perhaps. But if he had, wouldn't Kacey have come back by now?"

Cam didn't answer. He rose and ambled into the kitchen. Darby had remodeled the interior of her house several years earlier, opening up the floor plan.

"So, how was your date with the radiologist?" Cam asked as he rooted around in the refrigerator for a midafternoon snack. Two days earlier, after unloading the groceries he brought, she mentioned a man she'd met the prior weekend at a barbeque and their plans for the evening.

"It was lovely," Darby responded. "Richard and I had a late afternoon picnic, then he took me to an orchestral concert. He was a perfect gentleman and lively to boot. Too many men in my age bracket are boring old stiffs."

Cam's father had passed away fifteen years earlier—when he was a junior in high school. Only in the past few years had Darby begun to dip her toes back into the water.

"It actually turned into a double date. We ran into his daughter and her friend at the concert."

"Was that by design?"

"Honestly, I don't think so. We'd only just met. Plus, I could tell it threw him. But only for a minute.

The next thing I knew, he was trying to embarrass her to no end. But in an endearing way. Richard told me they have an ongoing game where they try to rattle each other in public."

"Did he succeed?"

"Not as well as he would've liked, I think. You could take a lesson from Cheyenne."

Cam frowned. He had been working hard to regain his confidence since returning to Rusted Bonnet. Running Peachy Kleen had proven to be a good start.

"Sorry." Darby cleared her throat.

"So how was Richard trying to embarrass her?"

Darby walked their lemonade glasses to the sink. Over the sound of running water, she said, "He told me a story about a camping trip the two of them took a couple of years back. Bare bones backpacking. No tent, just a couple of sleeping bags under the stars in a state park."

"I'm guessing she wasn't an experienced camper."

"That's an understatement. At three o'clock in the morning, Cheyenne woke up screaming—she felt something rough and moist all over her face, like getting a facial with wet sandpaper."

Cam cocked his head to the side.

"It was a bear's tongue," Darby explained. "She'd put on strawberry-flavored Chapstick before conking out for the night."

Chapter 4

"Chicken Parmesan?" Kacey asked as she walked through the front door of her bungalow at nearly ten p.m.

"You always did have a great sense of smell," Cam replied from the kitchen. "But it's eggplant." He punched pause on his tablet; a game screen shrank to an icon.

"Sounds divine. Do you have any left?"

Cam heard Kacey unholster her Glock and lock it inside the wall safe at the back of the coat closet.

"The entire tray," he said as she stepped into the kitchen. His legs dangled from a kitchen stool. "Emma had mac and cheese for dinner, and I ate a big salad. I figured you'd be hungry whenever you made it home." Emma had been asleep for close to two hours—Cam used the free time to tidy her playroom and whip together the eggplant, green salad, and garlic bread.

"Thanks a million," she said. "I'm famished. Today may have been the most exhausting day of my life." She looked down at the screen of his tablet. It had a small crack. "What happened there?" she asked, then slumped into a chair at the kitchen table.

"The computer beat me at backgammon," Cam said wryly. "But it was no match for me at boxing."

Kacey laughed and Cam rose from his seat. "Let me get you some dinner and a glass of wine. Do you want to talk about your day?"

"I'm not supposed to discuss the case with anyone but the chief," she said, "though he did ask me to interview you, seeing as how you were at the McRaes' yesterday. But first, how's Emma? Was she upset that I wasn't home when she woke up this morning?"

"She was surprised to see me instead of you, but she took it in stride. I just told her that Mommy had an important job to do today, and that you might be busy for a few more days, too. She seemed to understand." Cam set a plate heaping with food and a glass of white Bordeaux in front of Kacey. He poured a glass for himself and sat across from her. Spanish tile bordered the top of the rectangular, kitchen table.

"Thanks again for pitching in. This is the first time I can remember that both the chief and I needed to be on duty at the same time. He's usually understanding of my schedule, but Bernie won't delegate anything on this case to the junior officers so it's just the two of us. And there's more to do than I ever imagined in a murder investigation."

"So Greta *was* murdered?" Cam asked, looking at Kacey over the rim of his wine glass.

"There's no doubt in my mind."

"Was she pushed down the stairs?"

"I don't think it was that simple." Kacey slowly chewed a piece of crusty garlic bread, then said, "Cam, when you were cleaning the McRaes' home on Friday, did you vacuum the runner on the stairs?"

"I did."

"Did you notice anything out of the ordinary at the top of the steps?"

Cam thought hard. "Nothing comes to mind. But I wasn't paying any more attention than usual."

"Did you see anything out of place or was Greta acting strange in any way?"

Cam shook his head. "No and no."

"Hmm." Kacey tapped a stubby fingernail against the table.

"What is it?"

Kacey appeared to hesitate, then said, "Bernie's already made up his mind as to who he thinks the killer is, but I have a nagging feeling—a couple of things I saw today don't align with his theory. I really need to talk them through with someone."

"My mouth's a steel trap," Cam said.

Kacey's eyes softened. "You've changed, Cam," she said quietly. "For the better. Five years ago, you never would've been so helpful. With me or with Emma."

Cam took a deep breath. "I made a lot of mistakes. I'm just trying to make things right."

She reached across the table and laid her fingers on his wrist. "Keep it up," she said, then quickly retracted her hand.

Kacey speared a spinach leaf from her salad and said matter-of-factly, "Bernie thinks Dutch McRae killed Greta."

Cam's mouth squirreled into a knot. "Don't tell me he was having an affair with her. That's so cliché. Besides, he's at least fifteen years older than her."

"Fifteen years isn't *that* big of a difference." She momentarily averted her eyes.

How many older men had she dated since their divorce? Cam wondered. As far as he knew, she was currently unattached.

Kacey added, "We don't have any reason to suspect that they were sleeping with each other."

"So what makes the chief think it was Dutch?"

"First, let me tell you what we found. At the top of the staircase, there's a wall on one side and on the other, a post connected to the railing."

Cam nodded. He knew the McRae house well. The base of the stairs stood less than six feet from the home's front door. The steps rose straight up then angled sharply to the left. A carpet runner had been laid over the cherry plank steps, so only two or three inches of wood peaked out on either side. As you approached the top of the stairs, a white wooden railing stretched more than ten feet to the right, allowing a view from the upstairs hall to the home's two-story foyer. If you had just mounted the steps, to the right, the master suite stood at the end of the hall, and around a corner toward the back of the house were a bedroom and bathroom shared by the twins. To the left, a reading nook and a guest room—used by Greta, with a small attached bathroom—occupied the space.

"We noticed two interesting things on the top step," Kacey said. "On one side, in the gap of hardwood between the wall and the carpet runner, there's a small hole—just the right size for a nail. On the other side of the step, at the base of the wooden post, we found a handful of tiny fibers."

"From the carpet?"

"Our lab is checking, but I don't think so. The fibers formed a circle near the bottom of the post, maybe two inches from the base. To me, it looked like twine."

Cam put the pieces together. "So on one side of the top step someone hammers in a nail, partway at least, then wraps a length of twine around the head, stretches it across the step, and ties it off around the base of the post on the other side. A trip wire."

"That's exactly how it looks," Kacey said.

"Did you find the nail?"

"Not specifically. There are three boxes full of them inside Dutch's workbench in the garage."

"So he could've yanked out the nail and returned it to the garage before the police arrived."

"Yes. Dutch or anyone else for that matter. Each box had a handful of nails that looked as if they'd been used before, so it's not like there's a single one that's more suspicious than the rest."

"Are you testing them for fiber remnants?" Cam asked.

"We are. But even if we don't find any, that doesn't tell us much. Whoever pulled out the nail could've dropped it down a sink or through a storm grate in the street."

"Is that why Bernie's focusing on Dutch—who doesn't keep nails in the garage?"

Kacey swallowed a bite of eggplant, then wiped the corners of her mouth with a paper napkin. "This is excellent, Cam. Won't you have a piece?"

"I wish I could, but it has a breadcrumb coating and you didn't have any I can stomach." Saddled with celiac disease, Cam's body couldn't tolerate gluten.

"Sorry about that," Kacey said. "Why Dutch? Not because we found a nail hole, but because of what happened right after Greta fell. A few minutes after one thirty in the morning, both Dutch and Tatum said they heard Greta scream, then seconds later, a thud on the first floor."

"Did you interview them together?"

"No, separately. Their stories aligned. They each said it took a moment to wake up and realize that the scream had come from inside the house rather than from a dream. Dutch clicked on the bedside lamp, let his eyes adjust, then found his glasses. He grabbed a baseball bat that he keeps under the bed and told Tatum to hide in their walk-in closet. He thought there was an intruder in the house and that Greta had seen him and screamed. As Dutch opened the door to the hall, he said he saw Nicolas and Sophie come out of their bedroom at the back of the house. Dutch shuttled them into the closet with Tatum and told them all to stay put. Then he quietly closed the door to the master suite and tiptoed down the hall to the top of the steps. It was dark— Dutch said the streetlights are too far away and dim to reach through the windows at the front of the house with much effect. So, still holding the baseball bat, he felt for the wall at the top of the stairs and crept down them."

"He didn't trip over the twine strung across the top step?" Cam interrupted.

"No. When we asked, he said there was none." She munched a carrot slice from her salad.

"Maybe he was lucky enough to step over it in the dark?"

Kacey shook her head. "When Dutch reached the bottom of the stairs, he said he fell over Greta's body. He jumped up, flicked on the lights in the foyer, and saw her crumpled on the rug between the front door and the bottom step. Forgetting about an intruder, he dropped to his knees and checked her pulse. She wasn't breathing so he said he darted into the kitchen and dialed 911. They still have a landline. Then he went back upstairs and stayed in the bedroom with his wife and children until the police arrived. He didn't want any of them to see the body."

"I can understand that," Cam said.

"When he climbed the stairs, the whole foyer was lit up by the chandelier."

Cam followed Kacey's line of thought: "So Dutch would've seen the twine if it had been strung across the top step."

"Exactly, but he swore there was no trip wire, and when the chief arrived, the only evidence of a booby trap we found was the nail hole and the fibers on the post."

Cam swirled the Bordeaux in his glass. "So Dutch set the trip wire once everyone else in the house went to bed," he said after a moment. "Then, after Greta falls to her death, he secrets his wife and children away in the bedroom closet using an imagined burglar as a pretext.

That gives him time to unwind the twine, pull out the nail, and dispose of the evidence before the police or ambulance arrive."

"You could be the chief of police, Cam—that sums up Bernie's theory to a tee. Dutch is the only person who could've removed the twine, so he's the killer." Kacey rose from the table and retrieved a piece of garlic bread from the wicker basket resting on kitchen counter.

"If that's what actually happened," Cam said, "Dutch was lucky Greta went down the steps before his wife. Or one of the twins for that matter."

"Unless Tatum was the target," Kacey said flatly, then crunched into the buttery toast as she sat back down.

Cam coughed, the realization catching him by surprise. "Dutch was trying to kill Tatum?"

"I'm not sure Dutch did anything," Kacey said. "But if he did, why not her? I have no idea if Greta was the intended victim."

"I sure don't envy you. It sounds about as easy as pie in the sky."

"Or sewing buttons on ice cream," Kacey mewed.

Cam laughed. "Did either Tatum or Greta go downstairs regularly in the middle of the night?"

"Not according to Tatum—I asked. She told me that she hardly ever rose before the sun came up. And she didn't think Greta did, either. A trip wire would have been visible in the morning sunlight."

"So why did Greta get up in the middle of the night and go down the steps?" Cam asked rhetorically. But Kacey surprised him with an answer.

"Because her boyfriend sent her a text message asking her to sneak out of the house."

"Reynold?"

"The one and only," Kacey said. "I found Greta's phone. He texted at just after eleven. The message said he had a 'big score' and asked her to meet him on the street in front of the McRaes' house at one thirty in the morning."

"Did she reply?"

"She wrote him right back with, and I quote, 'About time, C U then.'"

"So do you fancy Reynold as Greta's murderer?"

"I'm not positive yet. Maybe. But it certainly keeps Dutch McRae from being a slam dunk in my book. At least by himself. We confiscated Reynold's phone. It looks like he deleted the texts, so we're having Verizon confirm that his phone was the origin of the message. When we questioned him, Reynold said Greta had gone to the Stagger for a quick after dinner drink, but swore up and down that he didn't send a single text to her all night."

"So how did he explain it?"

"He didn't. Instead, he claimed that we were making up evidence. When I pressed him, the best he could offer was that when he tends bar, he keeps his phone in a storage room locker. He doesn't like his pockets to be stuffed while he's working. Reynold said he grabs his phone and cigarettes every few hours when he takes a break, then returns them to the locker before going back on shift."

"So in theory, someone else *could* have pilfered his phone, sent the text, deleted the chain, and replaced it while Reynold was working."

"Yes, but he admitted that he keeps his locker key in his pocket. He didn't trust the kitchen staff not to steal his cigarettes."

"Too bad for him," Cam observed.

"I know. I asked him about the locker before I told him about the text message. He didn't have a chance to realize that lying about the lock would've helped him."

"Was Reynold on a break at eleven?"

"He said no. He closed down the Stagger at one in the morning and smoked his last cigarette from ten thirty to ten forty-five."

"Is there anyone who could verify that he was back behind the bar at eleven?"

"The waitress on shift did, and we found a patron who confirmed the timing, too. But we don't know that Reynold did, in fact, return his phone to his locker after the break. It could've been in his pocket. And, according to the waitress, he steps into the kitchen area all the time—to slice limes, get more ice. He could have texted Greta from there."

"Then the cook would've seen him," Cam posited.

"Food service ends at ten so the kitchen staff left well before eleven. Besides, if Reynold had the phone with him, he could've just as easily texted from a bathroom stall. Or even if he had returned the phone to his locker, he could've taken two minutes to text from the storage room."

"So as long as Verizon verifies that the text came from Reynold's phone, unless someone broke into his locker, he must have asked Greta to meet him outside of the McRaes' house at one thirty," Cam summarized. "If that prompted her to sneak down the stairs in the dark, why is Chief Leftwich still fixed on Dutch?"

"Just what I said earlier—no one else could've hidden the nail and twine before the chief arrived at the house. In his mind, either Dutch and Reynold were in on it together or Reynold's text was just a coincidence."

"That's one heck of a coincidence."

"I agree," Kacey said. "And a particularly bad one for Reynold."

"Could he have snuck inside and set up the trip wire himself after his shift ended?"

Kacey thought for a minute, chewing the last bite of her supper. "I suppose so," she said with a cautious tone. "The McRaes' house is less than a ten-minute drive from the Stagger Inn. Tatum told me that Greta went to dinner with a friend, came home, and was in her room for the night by ten o'clock. The children went to bed at eight, and she and Dutch at around ten forty-five. Dutch said he locked the front door, but he hadn't activated the alarm system in years, other than when they went away on vacation. It's possible that Greta had given Reynold a copy of her house key."

She paused, then added, "I can't see how any of this matters. After Greta tripped and fell, Reynold would've needed time to run up the stairs, pull out the nail, untie the twine, flee back down the stairs, and escape from the house before Dutch came out from the bedroom. Both he and Tatum said from the time Greta screamed to the time Dutch crept into the upstairs hall with the baseball bat was about thirty seconds."

"Did anyone hear hammering?" Cam asked.

"Not that they admitted to. And we haven't questioned the children and don't intend to unless it's absolutely necessary."

"Do they know Greta died?"

"Thankfully, no. They didn't see her body, and Tatum told them she had to move back to Germany. Apparently, Sophie was in tears, and Nicolas couldn't understand why Greta didn't say good-bye. Other than that, they're unaware of what happened."

"That's good. You said earlier, there were a couple of things that didn't jibe with the chief's theory. Was there something else, besides the text?"

"There was." Kacey rose from the table and parked her dishes in the kitchen sink. "Let me run up and check on Emma, then I'll tell you what else we found."

Chapter 5

Cam refilled his wine glass and topped off Kacey's, then meandered into the parlor, taking in the countless, framed photographs dotting shelves and end tables. Whether alone or with Kacey, a grandparent or two, or friends, Emma's lopsided smile graced every one.

He nestled into one side of a well-worn corduroy loveseat, embracing the comfortable feeling of domestic tranquility. Eating a late dinner with Kacey in her home—his home after their wedding—and discussing a case while their daughter slept above their heads felt right.

In their three years of marriage, Cam and Kacey hadn't experienced many peaceful evenings. Early on, the nights were filled with fervent lovemaking. But the frequency of those sessions dwindled quickly, replaced by bouts of shouting.

Newly married at twenty-four, Cam hadn't been ready to start a family. But Kacey was determined to begin right away. He knew they should've addressed the matter head-on before the wedding—even before getting engaged—but communication hadn't been one of Cam's strong suits. So he distanced himself from Kacey—mentally and physically. He reconnected with a group of single friends who partied hard. Graduation from college led to jobs and money, which they parlayed into trips to Las Vegas and New Orleans. And late night after late night filled with heavy drinking. The toll of his absences, morning hangovers, and terse responses to Kacey's conciliatory overtures added up quickly.

Fifteen months into their marriage, Kacey announced that she was pregnant. She begged him to settle down, to act like a mature adult. But the news infuriated him. They had been intimate only a handful of times during the previous months and Kacey promised him that she was on birth control. He accused her of lying. To this day, Cam had no idea whether she had regularly taken the pills.

His mother sided with Kacey and implored him to slow down. She feared that he would not only lose his wife but his job, too. In time, Cam lost both. A dearth of sleep and lack of focus led to a series of poor performance reviews at the packing plant. Shortly after Emma was born, recession clobbered the state and Cam was shown the door during the plant's first round of layoffs.

On top of everything else, he couldn't handle having a baby in the house, especially one saddled with colic. Rather than console his daughter, he ignored her.

Cam squeezed his eyes shut, the guilt searing his chest.

* * *

Kacey bounded down the steps and into the parlor. Her cheeks had a freshly scrubbed, reddish hue, and she had changed into Capri pants and a loose-fitting pink blouse that complemented her chocolate brown eyes.

She accepted the wine glass from Cam's outstretched hand and dropped lightly into a brown leather armchair across from him.

"Emma looks like an angel when she's sleeping," Kacey said.

"I couldn't agree more." Cam shifted in his seat. "Listen, Kacey, I've been back in Rusted Bonnet for six months now, but I haven't thanked you yet."

"For?" Kacey asked. A hint of sadness showed in her eyes.

"For allowing me back into Emma's life so willingly. You didn't have to let me spend every Sunday with her. My reappearance must have confused her tremendously, and I can't imagine it's been easy for you."

Kacey blinked away a tear. "Thank you for recognizing how difficult it's been. But I didn't think it would be fair to Emma to keep you away from her."

Cam leaned forward. He folded his hands in his lap and lowered his head. Softly, he said, "And I want to apologize, Kacey. I treated you terribly and blamed you for a having a child, who at the time, I didn't want. And now, seeing how wonderfully you've raised Emma, I'm riddled with guilt." He looked up at her. Dewdrops streamed down her cheeks. "I'm not going to ask you for forgiveness," he added. "Because I don't deserve it."

Kacey smiled and sniffed. "Just keep acting the way you have since you returned, Cam." She rose and touched a sleeve to her eyelids. "I don't want wine. I'm going to make some coffee. Would you like some?"

"Sure."

"Do you still take yours black?"

Cam nodded and breathed in deeply as she walked into the kitchen. He felt a pressure lift from his chest.

Kacey returned five minutes later and handed him a steaming mug. "There was blood on the Turkish rug at the foot of the stairs and splotches in several places on the carpeted steps," she said in a stolid voice, returning to the business at hand. The tears were gone. "The back of Greta's head was gashed open and bruised pretty badly. Most likely, she lacerated it on the way down and bled on the carpet as she fell. She ended up on the rug—it had a deep red stain from pooling."

"That'll be tough to get out," Cam observed.

"We took it down to the station as evidence, but Tatum asked me to return it when we're done. Apparently, it's from Istanbul and she wants to see if a rug cleaning place can salvage it."

"How about the carpet runner?" Cam asked.

"We photographed it and took fiber samples. I don't suppose we'll be fortunate enough to find anyone's blood other than Greta's. Tatum asked if she could clean it before the children come home—she sent Nicolas and Sophie to stay with their grandparents for a few days while we investigate. I told her to give us one more day, then on Monday she can have the carpet cleaned. I think she's planning to call you."

"No problem. Removing blood from carpet isn't as uncommon as you might think."

"Cam," Kacey said, looking at the floor. "I'm sure I'll still be working the case come Monday. Emma can stay at the extended day program until six o'clock...."

"Any time you need me, just say the word."

Kacey mouthed "thank you." She set her coffee on a coaster and began to pace. "Let me tell you what else we found. To my mind, it doesn't fit with Dutch as the murderer. Then again, it doesn't exactly resonate with Reynold either. In fact, I can't make heads or tails of it."

Cam blew cool air over the rim of his mug.

"Greta had a piece of nylon cord tied around one of her ankles," Kacey said. "That's what Bernie saw right away last night, why he was sure she didn't fall by accident."

Cam's eyes widened. "If she fell over a trip wire, why would she have a cord around her leg?"

"The chief thinks Dutch bound and gagged her first," Kacey said, her voice laden with skepticism.

"If he tied her legs together, the cord would be around both ankles, wouldn't it?"

"Perhaps, but Greta could've been tied to her bed—one ankle to each corner post. Or in a chair to its two front legs."

"Does anything else suggest she was bound?"

"The forensic techs are looking, but nylon's not the easiest thing to trace. Unlike twine, it doesn't fray easily. We didn't find nylon cord anywhere else in the house, or anything obvious that might have been used as a gag, like a bandana. Of course, the killer could have improvised with a T-shirt or underwear or taken the gag with him. But we didn't find tape remnants or any torn or rough skin near Greta's mouth—I would've expected to find something like that if she had been gagged."

"How much cord was around her ankle?"

"There was a full loop with a knot, then the cord stuck out about an inch. It looked like it had been cut."

Cam considered the ramifications. "I suppose forensics is checking all of the knives in the house."

"And scissors. If Greta freed herself, we thought we might find the cutting device in her bedroom, but I scoured it and didn't see anything with a blade."

"So walk me through exactly how the chief thinks Greta was killed," Cam said.

"Sure—mind you this is Bernie's theory, not mine." She sat in the armchair and leaned forward. "Dutch waited until about midnight, after Tatum was asleep and he figured Greta would be, too. He snuck into her bedroom, which doesn't have a lock. Before Greta had a chance to wake up and react, Dutch gagged her so she wouldn't scream and tied her up—either to the bed or desk chair."

"Tied just her ankles or her wrists, too?"

"Bernie figures it was both, but I'm not so sure. Both of her ankles showed signs of rope burn, but her wrists didn't." Kacey twisted a strand of hair with a finger. "The chief thinks that a few days ago, Dutch pounded a nail into the side of the top step between the carpet runner and the wall, then pulled it back out. That way he could set the trip wire silently on the night of the murder."

"That makes it premeditated."

Kacey beamed. "Yes. And either Dutch hadn't remembered that you and Samantha were due to clean the house on Friday or he took the calculated risk that neither of you would notice the hole."

"I certainly didn't."

"Neither did Samantha—we interviewed her earlier this evening." Kacey crossed her legs. "So according to Bernie, after tying up Greta, all Dutch had to do was push a nail into the pre-made hole then tie the twine around it on one side of the step and the post on the other. Then Dutch crawls back into bed with Tatum. Greta manages to cut herself free and tries to flee the house. Bernie thinks Dutch might have even left a knife or scissors within Greta's reach. As she tries to escape in the dark, she trips over the twine and tumbles to her death. Dutch hurries Tatum and the twins into the walk-in closet then gathers and dumps the evidence before the chief or paramedics arrive—the nail and twine, gag, pieces of nylon cord and whatever Greta used to cut it. But he didn't think to check her body, so he missed the cord tied around her ankle."

"And the eleven o'clock text from Reynold?"

"Like I said, the chief hasn't ruled him out as an accomplice," Kacey said without conviction.

Cam sipped his coffee. "There are a few things that don't make sense to me," he said. "First, we don't know why Dutch would want to kill his au pair. But let's assume that he did. There are two roads we can go down—either he worked independently or with Reynold."

Kacey nodded and encouraged him to continue.

"If Dutch was working with Reynold, then the text message would serve as the prompt for Greta to sneak out, so there'd be no need for Dutch to tie up Greta."

Kacey bobbed her head in agreement.

"On the other hand, if Dutch was working alone, we're left with an amazing coincidence that Reynold asked Greta to meet him right around the time that she freed herself. Plus, Dutch would've been taking a huge risk. After she cut herself loose, she could've called the police before rushing down the stairs to escape the house. Or texted Reynold an emergency message."

"I raised that possibility with Bernie," Kacey said.

Cam arched his eyebrows—an unspoken question mark.

"He thinks Dutch took her phone after he tied her up then returned it to her bedroom after she died. I think Bernie's straining way too hard to make the pieces fit."

"I couldn't agree more."

A smile of relief washed over Kacey's face. "Thanks. I'm not sure what I'm going to do next, but it's nice to know I'm not making too much of the discrepancies."

"Has the chief ever handled a murder investigation?"

"I don't think so. We've never had a murder in the village."

"So he's probably just as nervous about solving the case as you are," Cam said with reassurance. "Only, you're looking to make sure everything lines up perfectly and he's trying to put someone behind bars as quickly as possible. I think you should sit down with him in private and be honest about your concerns. You're a very intelligent woman. He'll listen to you."

Kacey blushed and looked away. "Thanks," she whispered. "I'll talk to him."

"Is the chief planning to arrest Dutch?"

"Not yet, Bernie has a meeting with the prosecutor first thing on Monday morning. I just wish I had an alternate theory."

Cam stretched his legs, then summoned the energy to describe the well-dressed man his mother had seen speaking with Reynold at the Stagger Inn two weeks earlier.

"It could have been anyone," Kacey commented.

"Maybe, but the Stagger doesn't get too many out-of-towners, and even fewer who are so well put together," Cam replied.

Kacey promised to keep it on her radar.

"Tomorrow's my regular day with Emma," Cam said. "I assume you'll be working—there must be a lot of red tape to jump through. But I can bring her back to you early if you'd like. I spent the whole day with her today."

"Thanks. Let me speak with Bernie. I'll give you a call in the afternoon and let you know what time I plan to finish up for the day. Can you pick her up at eight tomorrow morning?"

"Sure," Cam said with a smile.

Kacey's eyes lingered on his. "You look tired. I'm tempted to let you spend the night in the guest room, but I don't think that would be a good idea."

"Probably not." Cam rose to his feet. "But maybe tomorrow night the three of us could have dinner together?"

"Let me think about it," she said and sighed in a manner that Cam couldn't interpret.

Chapter 6
Sunday, September 20

Cam relished Sunday mornings at the playground with Emma. The day was unseasonably cool, but he built up a sweat from twenty minutes of a game she created and dubbed "ninja tag." When Emma finally jumped onto a swing, Cam trod over to a picnic table and put his head between his knees to catch his breath.

"Need some mouth to mouth?"

He looked up to see Addison Devlin standing over him. Addy—who was the younger sister of one of Cam's high school classmates—had been one of Greta's best friends and was a fellow child caretaker. Spiky red hair coupled with pale freckled skin and a tiny diamond stud in her nose would've screamed "biker chick" on most women, but she mollified the image with a heavy citrus scent and penchant for pastels.

"No," Cam grinned. "Just some air. Emma never stops."

"That's why I'm glad I have two," Addy said. "They entertain each other." She ratcheted her head toward a pair of boys mounting a climbing wall.

"I didn't think au pairs worked weekends," Cam said as Addy sat close beside him at the otherwise empty table. Despite his reputation in the village for treating Kacey so poorly, Cam's striking blue eyes and flaxen hair attracted a fair share of women.

"Technically, I'm a nanny since I'm American. But still, I don't usually watch the boys on Saturday or

Sunday." Addy looked out at her charges. "But both of the little hellions had lice last week. Even though we got rid of it, their Sunday school teacher asked that they steer clear of class this week. But heaven forbid their parents miss church, so I'm stuck with them for the morning. I suppose it's for the best as I'll need to take a few hours off for Greta's funeral." She wiped a tear that had begun to trickle down her cheek.

"I'm sorry. I know you were close," Cam said, shifting his weight away from Addy.

"Thanks," she sniffed.

"Any idea of when the funeral will be?" Cam asked,

"I'm not sure. Reynold told me the police think Greta may have been murdered." She shook her head in disbelief. "I can't believe that. I've lived in Rusted Bonnet my whole life—there's no one that sinister here."

"You spoke with Reynold?"

Addy's face colored. "He and I went out for a drink last night," she said sheepishly, then added quickly, "to honor Greta's memory."

"Did the police question him?" Cam asked, playing dumb.

Addy wrinkled her brow. "I didn't ask him. Why would they?"

"He and Greta were dating," he said casually. "They probably spent a lot of time together."

"I don't think they were too serious." She smiled coyly, then her eyes widened. "I wonder if they'll want to talk to me, too."

"Why's that?"

"Because I was at dinner with Greta on Friday night."

"You saw Greta on the night she was killed?"

"She and I grabbed a bite at the Coney Island, then stopped by the Stagger for a drink. We sat at the bar so we could bother Reynold."

"What time was that?"

Addy looked at him with curiosity. "A little before nine. Greta left at a quarter to ten to drive home. I stayed a while longer and had a second drink."

Gathering his courage, Cam asked, "Did you happen to notice if Reynold went outside for a cigarette break at around ten thirty?"

"Huh?" Addy peeped, clearly confused by the question.

"I know he's been trying to quit," Cam improvised. "I even got him started on some nicotine chewing gum."

Addy laughed. "I had no idea. He smoked half a pack last night and he and I shared a cigarette in the parking lot on Friday, just before I left the bar. I guess it was right around ten thirty."

* * *

"Bait, it sounds to me like Addy Devlin's trying to move in on Greta's man." Cam's fingers tingled from soap suds as he shouted to his goldfish over running water in the kitchen sink. Bait lived in a ten-gallon, octagonal tank on a waist-high, glass table in the dining room. The main floor of Cam's townhouse was arranged shotgun style—cut into three distinct sections from front to back: kitchen, dining room, and living room. Low wooden rails on either side of a wide aperture separated the kitchen from the dining room. On the other side, two steps stretched across the width of the narrow townhouse dividing the dining room from a sunken living room.

Cam had a similar conversation with Kacey half an hour earlier when she picked up Emma just after lunchtime. Kacey said she couldn't imagine Addy's interest in Reynold engendering enough jealousy to bump off her close friend. Cam agreed but, still, the thought lingered.

After finishing the dishes, Cam wandered into the dining room and addressed his fish directly. "It would have been nice if Kacey and Emma had agreed to go out to dinner with me tonight. Or I could have cooked here for the three of us."

Bait swam in a circle around a ceramic "No Fishing" sign.

"I know Emma has school tomorrow, but it wouldn't have been late." He sprinkled flakes into the top of the tank, and Bait beelined to them.

"I suppose acting like a nuclear family when we're not one is too much to ask. Serves me right."

Cam tapped at the side of the tank. "Are you listening to me?" Bait stopped chewing a flake, and swam to the front of the tank. He faced Cam squarely, paused, then turned back to catch a flake that had begun to sink.

"Thanks, buddy." Cam rested a hand on the top of the tank. "Kacey has a lot going on right now. I shouldn't press her while she's investigating this murder. Not to mention, I don't even know what kind of relationship I'm looking for with her."

Cam turned away then looked back. Bait had resumed circling the "No Fishing" sign.

* * *

The nerve center of Peachy Kleen evoked a case study in hypocrisy. Housed between an electric lighting refurbisher and a real estate office in a dated business park along Rusted Bonnet's commercial strip, the three-room office was not only cluttered but the floor hadn't been swept or the windows washed in weeks. It stood in the heart of the village with ample parking in back for

Peachy Kleen's three vans: Georgia, Virginia, and Montana.

The office's front door opened into the bull pen—a large communal area "decorated" with well-loved couches, a refrigerator, and an archaic television where the crew could put their feet up between jobs. A door to the left led to a storage space replete with cleaning equipment and supplies. To the right, the tiny space Cam used as an office accommodated a metal desk stuffed full of receipts, ledgers, and paper files, and topped by a vintage desktop computer, printer, and landline telephone. Years earlier, Darby had christened it the "breadbox."

Deciding to take advantage of a free Sunday afternoon, Cam was on his knees in the bull pen tinkering with a broken floor polisher. Neither handy by nature nor accustomed to other people's possessions, the polisher was one of many electric gizmos that Darby had transferred to Cam.

He heard the door crack and voices behind him.

"Mr. Cam, I didn't know you were here this afternoon." Becka Blom—a raven-haired South African—stood just inside the doorway alongside a shorter woman.

"Kacey was wrapped up at work yesterday, so I had Emma then and she has her now," Cam explained. "I was hoping to get this polisher up and running and save myself a trip to Lowe's."

"And a lot of money," Becka said. "I think those are quite expensive."

Cam nodded. "I'm not having much luck."

"Can I take a look?" the shorter woman said. "My father was pretty handy and I spent plenty of hours watching him work."

"You couldn't do any more damage than me," Cam said and stood up. He brushed dust from his jeans and introduced himself.

"I'm Missy," she said.

"My girlfriend," Becka clarified. "We're going out on a hike and I realized I left a sweater here. At least I think I did." She stepped into the storage space.

To Cam, Missy looked like a cat. Not a purring, seductive feline, but a household tabby—almond-shaped eyes, an angled jawline, and a pert nose. A horizontal-striped sweater amplified the resemblance.

A second later, Becka reemerged. "Found it." She held up a wrinkled gray cardigan.

"Just give me a minute," Missy said. "It looks like a spring came undone." She looked at Cam. "Do you have something solid and sharp I can use to latch it back in place. Like an awl or a compass?"

"A compass?" Cam asked.

"The kind you use for drawing circles."

"I have a letter opener," Cam said.

"Perfect."

* * *

"Cam, I have a flat. Would you mind putting on my spare?" Darby had rung his mobile phone shortly after Becka and Missy left Peachy Kleen, with the polisher humming like a bird.

"Where are you?" Cam asked, grabbing his jacket and heading outside. Unlike a floor polisher, a flat tire was something he was sure he could handle.

"At home. There's a whole mess of nails on the road right in front of my driveway."

Chapter 7

It looked like a load of nails had spilled from a truck. Several hundred were amassed in a mound at a corner where Darby's gravel driveway met the road, with a smattering scattered on all sides. An aluminum pail lay on its side in the nearby drainage ditch.

Cam bent at the knees to look more closely.

Chief Bernie Leftwich hunched down on one side of him while a deputy snapped photos from the other side. Darby stood next to her Chevy Cruze and its still-flat tire.

Cam had phoned Kacey as soon as Darby told him the news—he was concerned that someone dumped the missing nail on a country road to make it look like an unfortunate loss of cargo.

Kacey must have called it in to headquarters right away because the chief had arrived at Darby's farmhouse at the same time as Cam.

"What do you think?" Cam asked Bernie.

The older man stood up. Veins crisscrossed his nose like rivers on a map of the Amazon Basin.

"How did you know to call this dump into the police?" Bernie asked.

"Kacey questioned me about Greta Astor's death," Cam said. "She asked me if I noticed any nail holes at the top of the steps when I was cleaning there. Unfortunately I never looked that closely."

"How about your mother?" the chief asked. "She cleaned over there plenty of times. Maybe she's a little more diligent than you."

Cam, not appreciating the barb, strode over to Darby and quietly filled her in on the conversation he'd had with Kacey the night before.

"I never noticed any holes," Darby said. "But I hadn't cleaned the McRaes' house myself in a couple of years. Do you think the missing nail is in that pile?" she asked.

"I have no idea. Most nails look alike to me."

"Me, too," Darby said. "Except when one's sticking out of my tire."

Cam laughed. "Pop the trunk and let me put on the spare. I'll leave the nail in the flat for now—you should take it to Sears and see if they can fix it before buying a new one."

"Thanks," Darby said and pointed her key at the trunk hood.

"It seems pretty convenient that we find this pile of nails right here when we're looking for just that, a nail," Bernie said as he meandered toward the car.

"Maybe," Cam said and pulled up the trunk carpet covering the spare.

"What time did you leave the house this afternoon, Ms. Reddick?" the chief asked.

"At about two. I have dance on Sunday afternoons."

"Dance?"

"Adult tap," Darby said.

Bernie whinnied.

"What's so funny?" Darby protested. "I'm in better shape than you."

The chief grunted, then asked, "And you didn't notice the nails when you left?"

"Of course not. I wouldn't have missed them."

Cam wheeled the spare to the front drivers' side tire then retrieved the scissor jack and aligned it under the Cruze's frame.

"And you ran over the pile on your way home at around four thirty?" Bernie said, his voice sounding slightly skeptical.

"It didn't run over the pile," Darby said. "It wouldn't look like a giant ant hill if I had. I must have picked up one of the ones scattered on the road."

"I'm sure you have some ladies who can vouch for your whereabouts between two and four thirty."

"More like two fifteen and four fifteen. I had to drive there and back."

"Of course," the chief said. "And how about before that?"

"I was here doing yard work," Darby said. "And I don't know that I like where you seem to be going with this, Bernard."

Cam cranked the jack's rod in a circle and the front of the Cruze began to rise.

"I don't care if you like it or not," Bernie said with a raised voice. "I'm investigating a murder and you have a whole lot of evidence smack in your driveway."

"And since when does a murderess leave damning evidence out in the open in front of her home?" Cam said without looking up. His eyes were fixed on the flat as he cranked a tire wrench on a lug nut.

"It's a good way to throw off the police," Bernie blustered. "Milt?" he called out. "Once you're done taking photos, bag every nail and that pail and let's send them off to forensics."

Cam, who had just unscrewed the last nut, tugged off the tire and laid it beside him. He inspected it and found a single embedded nail.

"I'll need that tire as evidence, too," Bernie said to Cam. "Once you get the spare on, you might want to come on down to the station. Your mother will need a ride home after I'm done questioning her on the record."

* * *

Cam settled Darby back home less than an hour later. She had insisted on having a lawyer present and the only attorney she knew, according to his wife, would be ensconced in a hunting blind with their son until dusk.

Cam was steaming—the idea of Darby as a murderer was even more cockeyed than Dutch killing his own au pair. He wanted to make her dinner and spend the night at the farmhouse. But Darby insisted that she didn't want company, not even her son.

So Cam dropped his car at home and headed to the Stagger Inn on foot to cool his head. Twenty minutes in the crisp, late-summer air helped, but just a little.

Lacquered log rafters, red checkered vinyl barstools, and a powerful odor of stale beer—the Stagger screamed for a Food Network overhaul. Discarded peanut shells littered the floor, crunching under Cam's Brooks as he crossed from the entrance to the S-shaped bar.

He surveyed the room. It was relatively empty, even for a Sunday evening. A pair of heavyset women in baggy jeans and hooded sweatshirts held down one end of the bar. A young couple—him in cowboy boots, her in cheetah-patterned pumps—were tucked into a table at the rear of the room near an ash-filled fireplace. A two-foot stack of split poplar topped by a pair of Duraflame firestarters rested in a hearthside rack. On the inside of the bar, Reynold Cornell—sporting the look of a three-day beard—leaned on his elbows, peering down at a tattered magazine.

Cam sat at the end of the bar opposite the women. When Reynold looked up, Cam ordered a draft of Two Hearted Ale and asked for a menu.

Reynold handed him a laminated rectangle. Small squares of white paper tape with handwritten prices adorned the menu like bits of toilet paper dotting a man's chin after a bad shave. Cam studied Reynold as the chiseled man poured beer into a pint glass from a tap. A mat of black chest hair protruded from the open collar of his polo shirt. Cam noticed a bandage on one of Reynold's triceps, peeking out from under his shirt sleeve. His mind jumped—had Greta scratched him during a struggle? *If he proved Reynold was involved in the murder, maybe he could save his mother from an interrogation,* Cam thought.

Reynold set the drink on a cardboard coaster in front of him. "Anything to eat, Cam?" he asked. The two weren't close, but Cam frequented the Stagger often enough for the bartender to know him by name.

"I'll try the quesadillas. Say, what happened to your arm?"

"Flu shot," Reynold replied without emotion and disappeared into the kitchen.

Were flu shots even available in September?

Reynold returned a minute later and began wiping down the bar. Cam said, "Sorry to hear about Greta. I know you two were an item."

Anger bubbled into Reynold's eyes. He ground his teeth and mumbled something to himself. To Cam, it sounded like "I'm going to kill that bloody man with my two hands."

"What?" Cam asked.

Reynold opened his mouth, then snapped it shut. He reached a meaty hand into a plastic bowl filled with peanuts and crushed a fistful. "I wish Michigan had the death penalty," he said. "Whoever murdered Greta deserves the chair."

"Murdered?" Cam asked, feigning ignorance. "I thought she fell down the stairs at the McRae place."

Reynold opened his palm and inspected a handful of broken shells and nuts. "The police don't think it was an accident. They grilled me for hours on Saturday." He paused, then looked up at Cam. "You used to be married to the deputy, didn't you?"

Cam nodded and sipped his ale.

"She was harder on me than the chief." Reynold twisted his lips into a smile, his eyebrows slanting down toward the bridge of his nose. "Not that I minded. Your old lady is quite a looker."

That's pretty callous, Cam thought—*his girlfriend isn't even in the ground yet*. He let the comment slide by. "Why question you? Because you were dating Greta?"

"I suppose so," he replied. "Plus, she and her friend Addy were here a few hours before Greta died."

"Addy's not too bad looking herself," Cam ventured.

"She does have a ... distinctive appeal," Reynold admitted and walked to the other end of the bar where the pair of women were vigorously scratching "check, please" signs in the air.

Minutes later, Reynold set a plate of quesadillas in front of Cam with an artificial flourish and proclaimed that he was taking a cigarette break.

Cam pushed aside a snowdrift of sour cream and John Deere green guacamole. He nibbled at a wedge of quesadilla while silently counting to one hundred, then lowered himself from his barstool. A nervous curiosity coursed through his veins alongside an overwhelming impulse to assist Kacey and clear his mother's name. Cam stretched and peeked over his shoulder—the couple near the fireplace were completely engrossed with each other, her hand under his shirt like a pair of teenagers.

Cam calmly strolled around the bar and through a swinging door into a small alcove. Straight ahead he saw the kitchen, which was dominated by an immense commercial griddle, two deep-fat fryers, and a sink the size of a bathtub. A cook in a grease-stained apron and a pimpled dishwasher were speaking in rapid Spanish. Cam quickly flattened himself against a side of the alcove, out of their line of sight. On the opposite side, a heavy wooden door stood ajar. Cam took a deep breath, then shot three steps across the alcove and through the door.

Harsh fluorescent light glared onto the storage room's dull cement floor. Boxes of canned goods framed an industrial freezer along the back wall. To one side, a row of six gray metal lockers lined up as straight as a row of newly minted Army privates. On the other, a plastic bucket collected drops of water trickling down a cinder block wall along a rust-colored path. Blue and white "Hello, My Name Is" stickers decorated the lockers. Reynold's name was scrawled in blue ink on the one closest to the storage room door.

Unlike the sturdy specimens securing Javier's and Angel's belongings, the lock on Reynold's door looked as if it had been poached from an eight-year-old's diary. Cam had never learned to pick a lock, but he imagined anyone who spent ten minutes on YouTube could spring Reynold's in a matter of seconds.

Cam tiptoed back into the bar, keen to return before Reynold. He wolfed down his quesadillas, left a twenty under his unfinished pint glass, and stepped outside. Reynold was stubbing a cigarette into the sidewalk with a black-soled shoe.

Cam itched to broach the subject of the man his mother had seen with Reynold at the Stagger, but decided to avoid raising the bartender's hackles. Instead, he simply nodded at Reynold, turned up the collar on his fleece, and walked home in the twilight.

* * *

Elena Ramp balanced on her tiptoes at the top of a short stepladder. Porch light glinted off of her midriff as she stretched well-toned arms straight overhead. She swatted feverishly at a cobweb, missing by a matter of inches.

"Wouldn't a broom be more effective?" Cam teased. He placed a foot on the bottom step of his new neighbor's porch. She lowered her arms, turned, and squinted down at him.

"I suppose you're right. I came out to put in a new bulb and didn't spot the spider web until I was up here." She stepped down from the ladder and flicked auburn hair out of her pale, gray eyes.

Without another word, Cam climbed up the ladder and pulled down the web. He balled the sticky gauze in his hand and tossed it into the townhouse's front bushes.

"Thanks," Elena said. "Have you had dinner? I have plenty inside."

"I did," Cam replied, then to be polite, added "otherwise I'd take you up on it."

"How about a nightcap then? I just unpacked my pantry items, so I know I have a bottle of Cognac."

"I think I can make the time for a quick one."

The layout of Elena's townhouse mirrored Cam's, but her furnishings blazed with contemporary relish— highlighted in the kitchen by sleek mahogany cabinets with stainless steel knobs.

Elena filled two snifters with generous portions of Cognac and led Cam into the living room. A massive rug bearing a Native American-style pattern covered hardwood flooring. The motif wound its way through wall hangings, etchings, and vases around the room.

"I can see why your interior decorating skills are in high demand," Cam said. "This room is breathtaking."

Elena favored him with a broad smile. "It's Navajo. And thanks. I haven't even finished unpacking but couldn't resist getting this room in shape. You're my first guest." She raised her glass, then lowered it and sipped demurely.

Cam sat on the edge of a linen divan. Catty-corner from him, Elena snuggled into a modern wingback chair.

"Did you hear about the McRaes' au pair?" Elena asked.

Cam coughed, momentarily taken aback. Then he recalled that she was decorating their home.

"I did," Cam said. "My ex-wife is the deputy chief of police."

"Really?" Elena looked at Cam intently, then her eyes brightened. "She's a police officer, and you run a housekeeping business."

"What can I say, folks in Rusted Bonnet are just as progressive as anywhere else."

"So did you talk to your ex about Greta?" Elena asked. "I find it so interesting."

"A little," Cam said cautiously. "She asked me a few questions because I cleaned the McRae place on Friday morning. You told me you were there on Friday as well—have the police contacted you?"

"Not yet. I didn't see anything out of the ordinary. Of course, I've only been to their home a handful of times."

"Did you see Greta on Friday?" Cam asked.

Elena shook her head. "It's hard for me to visualize the potential for a space when there are children running around. I think Greta took them to play putt-putt. No, bocce ball. Something ridiculous." She moistened her lips with her tongue. "I had some ideas I wanted to run by Tatum, so I called her on Saturday afternoon. That's when she told me what happened."

"What did she say?" Cam asked with interest.

"That Greta fell down the stairs and hit her head. Apparently, the police asked Tatum and Dutch a whole lot of questions."

"They don't think Greta died by accident."

"I know. Tatum told me the police found a bit of cord tied around Greta's ankle." She paused, thinking for a moment, then said, "Of course, that doesn't necessarily rule out an accident."

Cam raised an eyebrow.

Elena cast her eyes toward the floor and said quietly, "If Greta was into some sort of ..." She looked up and asked, "Did she have a boyfriend?"

Cam nodded and sipped his Cognac.

"So she invites him over for a little role-playing fun. Afterwards, the boyfriend cuts her loose before leaving the house but forgets to untie the bit of cord around her ankle. She gets up in the middle of the night to check on the kiddos, trips over the cord, and takes a tumble down the steps."

"She wouldn't feel a nylon cord left tied around her ankle?" Cam asked dubiously.

Elena shrugged. "It was just a thought. Maybe she had a drink or two too many. Or smoked something that made her loopy."

Cam was doubtful it happened that way given Reynold's text. Besides, only an inch of cord was sticking out from the loop around Greta's ankle—that didn't seem long enough for her to trip over. But rather than raising those points, he simply said, "I suppose anything's possible."

Chapter 8
Monday, September 21

Cam strapped a dust mask over his nose and mouth to ward off pungent ammonia fumes. He had a cache of tricks to remove blood from any surface—from using vodka to meat tenderizer to dog shampoo. But for days-old blood caked onto synthetic carpet, nothing beat a mixture of liquid dish soap, ammonia, water, and elbow grease.

Chief Leftwich had given Tatum McRae clearance to have the house cleaned. She phoned Cam and asked him to rid the stairs of the blood before noon when the kids were scheduled to return home to meet an au pair that Tatum was interviewing. But when Cam arrived just after eight in the morning, it was Dutch who answered the door.

"Tatum ran over to her mother's house," he explained. Dutch's jowls, shaped liked pork chops, wobbled as he spoke. "The wretched woman's hip is acting up so Tatum has to take her to the doctor. Thanks for coming on such short notice."

Cam had only met Dutch a couple of times. He looked terrible for a forty-year-old—the man's thin hair sparsely covered a mottled scalp and his torso spouted out like a horn from narrow shoulders down to a wagon wheel waistline. The owner of a small chain of independent movie theaters by trade, Dutch had a tough-as-nails reputation about town.

"There's blood streaked in half a dozen places on the carpet," Dutch said. "Plus a few spots on the hardwood on either side of the runner, and some on the wall. I'm sure the wood and drywall will be easy enough to clean. Do the best you can on the carpet. If it doesn't come out, we can replace it, but Tatum and I figured we'd let you have a shot at it first."

Cam had nodded, and asked Dutch to give him an hour.

"Of course," Dutch replied and excused himself to the confines of his home office in the basement.

The stairs rose twelve feet from the foyer, stopped at a small landing, then angled sixty degrees to the left for another six feet before joining the second-floor hallway. White wooden railing tracked the entire left side of the staircase, and the lower section on the right. As the steps turned to the left, drywall flanked the right side underneath a railing that ran along the hallway overlooking the stairs.

Cam dispatched the blood stains on the hardwood, sensing something was amiss, but he couldn't immediately put his finger on it. In several places, the carpet looked as if it had been flattened from more than typical wear. But that could be easily explained—heavy police boots or perhaps as Greta fell, the weight of her body matted down the carpet. *What's wrong with this picture?* The thought continued to nag him.

Next, he scoured a large patch of blood from the wall where the stairs turned. The core of the spot had the circumference of a tennis ball and was centered toward the bottom of the wall, where molding met painted drywall, about five inches up from the surface of the corner landing. The location of the spot made sense to Cam—if Greta had tipped over twine and tumbled down the steps, she would have hit the wall right there as the stairs turned before her body plummeted down the twelve-foot drop to the foyer. Ferreting blood out of the creases in the Federal-style molding proved to be a difficult task that Cam finally accomplished by wielding a tissue-wrapped toothpick with surgical precision.

Now, Cam tackled the carpet. The ammonia stung his eyes, so he donned a pair of swim goggles to accompany the dust mask. He worked on the runner from the bottom step up. After nearly fifteen minutes of scrubbing a deep coppery-brown spot on the landing where the stairs turned, the incongruity smacked him— an Archimedes in the bathtub moment!

There was blood *above* the mid-staircase landing. In two distinct places on the upper section of steps, dried blood stained the carpet. If Greta tripped, fell, and cracked her head on the molding where the stairs turned, which seemed to be the obvious spot, there shouldn't have been any blood on the six-foot stretch of stairs above the landing. Unless she started to bleed *before* she fell.

Cam jabbed his ammonia-soaked rag vigorously against the carpet, his brain lurching in unison with his forearm. The only other explanation he could contrive was that Dutch, on his way back up the stairs after stumbling over Greta's body, tracked blood onto the upper steps.

* * *

Cam finished the runner and hiked down to the McRaes' basement. Berber carpet and pale yellow paint afforded an inviting feel. French doors opened into Dutch's office. The man's bald spot shone under a harsh white light as he pored over a stack of papers behind a desk. Cam stepped into the doorframe and knocked gently. Dutch ignored him for a solid minute, then looked up and flipped reading glasses onto his forehead. "All done?" he asked.

"Yes, sir," Cam said. "I was able to get it all out."

A smile spread across Dutch's face. "Good man. Your eyes look like a raccoon's."

"I wear goggles when I use ammonia," Cam explained.

Dutch nodded and bent his head back toward his papers.

Cam knew he was being dismissed, but ventured, "It must have been quite a shock to find Greta at the bottom of the stairs."

"Horrible," Dutch said and looked back up, his eyes glistening. "It's always tragic when someone dies young," he said slowly, with what appeared to be caution, then added, "I tripped right over her body. I would've turned on the lights right away but I thought there was a burglar in the house."

"Did you hear someone?"

"Just Greta's scream."

Cam pretended to think for a moment, then said, "Lucky for me you didn't get any blood on your feet, otherwise there could've been a whole lot more to clean up."

"I'm not one to panic. I took off my slippers before dialing 911 from the kitchen." Dutch puffed out his chest. "Now that I think about it, I have no idea if I got any blood on those slippers or not. Damn police bagged and took 'em away rather than just let Tatum stick them in the washing machine."

So you didn't track any blood up the stairs, Cam thought and turned away.

Chapter 9

Peanut butter-colored foundation poorly disguised the pockmarks on Tatum McRae's cheeks. She sat bolt upright in the center of Darby Reddick's camel-backed settee, spasmodically nibbling on an apple slice like a chicken pecking at feed.

Cam had driven straight to Darby's from the McRae house, intent on finding out how her questioning went that morning before jetting off to his next cleaning appointment. He and Becka Blom were slated to tackle a 1970s split-level owned by a germaphobe who once confided to Cam that she spent as much money on professional cleaning as she did on her car payment.

"Tatum and I ran into each other at the police station," Darby explained when Cam entered his mother's living room. "We decided we both needed some cheering up."

"It certainly was a nice gesture for your mother to invite me for tea," Tatum said, her eyes darting from Cam to Darby to a fruit plate on the coffee table in front of her. Her hair was as thick as a broom.

Darby sat on the edge of a recliner and pointed Cam to the stone bench stretching across the front of the hearth. Cam filled a napkin with pear and peach slices and sat.

"I didn't realize you two knew each other," he said.

Darby waved a hand. "The McRaes have been in Rusted Bonnet for almost five years. The first time I saw Tatum, she was pregnant with Nicolas and Sophie."

"Big as a house I was with those two," Tatum chipped in.

"How did it go with the chief?" Cam asked Darby.

"My lawyer was a no show," Darby said. "He dropped his boy off at school this morning and went back to his blind in the woods to meet a buddy. He called Bernie from the road."

"I don't understand grown men sitting in a tree for hours on end with guns or bows or whatever they have," Tatum said.

"My late husband hunted pheasant when Cam was little," Darby responded. "The man seemed to relish those days as much as any vacation we took. But I will say it must be better than sitting on a frozen lake watching a fishing pole in a hole."

"I'm pretty sure ice fishing is just an excuse to drink," Cam said.

"I suppose that's true," Darby agreed. "Seeing as how my need for a lawyer just sprang up and his hunting day was planned, we all agreed to an interview on Wednesday."

"At least you have a little reprieve," Cam said.

"And time to get a new tire," Darby said. "But I want to get it over with. Tatum has been telling me how pigheaded Bernie's being."

"Is that why you were at the station?" Cam asked. "For questioning?"

"Not today." She made a perturbed noise. "No, after taking my mother to the doctor this morning, I had to drop off copies of the tax forms I filled out for Greta. I can't imagine why anyone cares about those now."

"How is your mother? Dutch mentioned you were taking her when I saw him this morning."

"Oh, she's fine," Tatum scoffed. "She's an old drama queen when it comes to her health. I think she likes the attention she gets from the nurses. More importantly, how are my stairs?"

"All of the blood came out."

Tatum smiled. Coffee stained teeth clashed with her garish red lipstick. "Thank you. Now I have one more favor to ask you, Cam—can you please tell that ex-wife of yours to stop pestering me and my husband?"

Cam's head reflexively snapped back. "I'm not sure if I can do that," he managed, then added, "it is a murder investigation."

"And it seems to me that Chief Leftwich thinks my husband did it. As if! I know Kacey's just doing what she's told, but it's not exactly comfortable."

Darby rose from her chair, padded over to the settee, and sat beside Tatum. She reached out and held Tatum's hand. "I'm sure everything will be just fine."

"Oh, I'm sorry," Tatum gushed. "Look at me going on when you're as big of a suspect as he is."

Darby cleared her throat.

"Why does the chief think it was Dutch?" Cam asked with gumption.

"Because he had me and the kids stay in the closet until the police came," Tatum spluttered. "Dutch thought there was a burglar in the house for heaven's sake! So did I. After he found Greta's body, he didn't want us to see it. Stands to reason—he was protecting his family!" Tears streaked down her face. "Can you imagine what kind of psychological damage could've been inflicted on Nicolas and Sophie if they saw Greta lying dead at the bottom of the stairs?"

All three allowed silence to tick by. "I heard you're interviewing an au pair for them later today," Cam finally said.

Tatum took a deep breath. "Indeed. It'll be nice to get the house back to normal."

Darby patted Tatum's hand. "Let me get you some tea. Do you like Chinese black?"

Tatum nodded, pulled a tissue from her purse, and dried her eyes.

"I'll get you some too, Cam," Darby said and breezed into the kitchen.

Cam waited for Tatum to recover, then whispered, "Mrs. McRae, I don't mean to pry, but is there anyone you can think of that Greta didn't get along with?"

"You mean someone who would've wanted to kill her?"

Cam nodded.

A derisive smile crept across Tatum's face and her demeanor morphed from distraught wife to coconspirator. "Addison Devlin," she said in a hushed tone after a final sniffle.

"Addy?" Cam repeated. "I thought she and Greta were close."

"You know the saying, Cam, about keeping your friends close and your enemies closer. That describes their relationship perfectly."

"I had no idea. Though I think Addy may have a crush on Reynold Cornell."

Tatum blew air from puckered lips. "That's probably just a spot of petty jealousy on Addison's part. Not surprising of course—Greta was classically beautiful and Addison looks like she belongs on *Headbangers Ball*."

Cam's eyes widened. Tatum struck him as a woman who had spent more time during the early '90s taking in sermons than MTV.

She caught the change in his countenance and rebuked him. "I'm not *that* much older than you."

"Sorry," he said. "So why didn't Greta and Addy get along?" He bit into a slice of peach.

"I can't be one hundred percent positive...." She trailed off, then admitted, "But it's possible that our dear Greta may have cheated Addison's sister."

"Jasmine?"

Tatum nodded. "Mind you, I don't believe it for a minute."

Cam pictured Jasmine Devlin with her blond bangs in the shape of a Hostess fruit pie. She had been the valedictorian of his high school class—smart and determined. But she'd let herself go, intellectually speaking, since then. He'd heard that brutally demanding physics coursework at Carnegie Mellon and academic competition more fierce than any she'd experienced in Rusted Bonnet led to poor grades during her freshman year. Jasmine never recovered her aplomb. A year later, she transferred to the University of Michigan and managed to squeak out a liberal arts degree. She had settled back in Rusted Bonnet as the village librarian.

Cam felt sorry for her—so much untapped potential snuffed out prematurely. "What did Greta supposedly do to Jasmine?" he asked.

At that moment, Darby returned to the living room carrying a tray of black tea. She handed a full cup and saucer to Tatum and Cam, set the tray on the coffee table, and carefully lowered herself into the recliner, balancing a cup in her lap.

"I was just about to tell Cam about the supposed *incident* at the chess tournament," Tatum said to Darby.

"I'm surprised you didn't hear, Cam," his mother said. "The whole village seemed to be talking about it in June."

Cam shrugged. Despite providing housekeeping services to a number of homes in the town, he didn't have the same pulse of the community as his mother.

Tatum sipped her tea. "This is wonderful, thank you," she said, then turned to Cam. "Last winter, the library here in Rusted Bonnet received a very generous donation that was earmarked for technology improvements. Jasmine used the money to upgrade the online catalogue and buy four new networked computers for the study carrels."

Cam had seen the library's carrels—small, enclosed rooms, each with a sturdy desk and gooseneck lamp.

"The library had a technology festival to show off the new catalogue and computers," Tatum continued. "There was cake and punch and the Mayor's chief of staff and his daughter dressed up as Tigger and Winnie the Pooh for the toddlers to meet. Jasmine also held contests on the new computers—online puzzles for elementary schoolers, Sudoku for the teenagers, and Scrabble and chess tournaments for adults."

"I played in the Scrabble tournament," Darby said. "Got my clock cleaned by Fran Comstock—that woman is like a walking dictionary."

Tatum smiled. "Greta participated in the chess tournament. So did Jasmine—she told everyone if she won first place, she'd donate the prize money back to the library. It was only fifty dollars."

"I didn't know Greta played chess," Cam said.

"Neither did I," Tatum replied. "At first, I was surprised when I saw her name on the sign-up sheet. But I figured out why she wanted to compete. And win."

"Why's that?" Cam asked.

"The mayor gives out a higher education scholarship every year. Ten thousand dollars from some grant the village has had forever. Greta wanted to start taking nursing classes. Macomb Community College has a program for international students."

"And Greta wanted to impress the mayor by winning the chess tournament?"

"Correct. She could only be an au pair with us for another year. But she told me she wanted to stay in the States. If she was going to school, she could get a student visa."

"Did it work?" Cam asked.

Tatum looked at him in confusion.

"I mean, did the mayor give her the scholarship?" Cam clarified.

"Oh, no. He gave it to that girl whose parents died in a car wreck last year. Drunk driver." She curled her upper lip, then added, "Can't compete with a sob story like that."

Cam and Darby both looked down at their tea cups.

Tatum appeared to take no notice of their discomfort. "Besides," she said, "with the rumor swirling about Greta, Mayor Tuck was too smart to get reeled in."

"So what happened?" Cam asked.

"A few people seem to think that Greta cheated her way to victory."

"Not just a few," Darby said lightly.

"Okay, several people," Tatum admitted.

"She won the tournament?" Cam asked.

Both women nodded. Darby said, "There were sixteen contestants. In each round, the winners advanced, losers were eliminated. Everyone figured that Jasmine would sail through to the finals and play against Bennie Brenman. He's a member of the chess club in Clawson and I've heard he's quite good. Anyway, after Greta handily beat her opponents in the first two rounds, she knocked off Jasmine in the semis and then beat Bennie in the finals. According to him, she used a combination of classical tactics befitting a pro."

"Greta as a grand master," Cam mused.

"Jasmine was rankled after losing, so when Bennie told her how strategically Greta played, she decided she smelled a rat."

"Cheater, cheater, pants on fire?" Cam said.

"Better than liar, liar, pumpkin eater," Darby quipped.

Cam laughed then sipped his tea. "I can't imagine how someone cheats at chess. Did she move some pieces around when Ben got up to use the restroom?"

"No, no," Tatum chimed in. "It was computer chess. They were in carrels. The point of the event was to show off the library's new computers."

"Were the carrels closed off?"

"Yes, they have sliding doors," Tatum said

"And Greta had Garry Kasparov on speed dial?" Cam laughed.

Tatum crinkled her nose. "First of all, I don't know that she *did* cheat. She may have spent her college years in Germany in front of chess boards rather than beer pong tables for all I know. But Jasmine developed a theory, and despite writing Greta a fifty dollar check for winning the tournament, she blabbed it to anyone who cared to listen."

"It set the two women against each other," Darby said.

"And Addison took her sister's side," Tatum added, "much to Greta's chagrin."

Cam bobbed his head, waiting for more.

"Jasmine accused Greta of playing two games at once," Darby said. "One against her tournament opponent and another against a computer program." She paused to nibble on a segment of pear.

Tatum hunched forward in the settee, hands clasped between her legs. Cam noticed a bunching of fabric just above her brogues—her nylons were inside out.

"Greta opened two screens on her computer," Darby continued. "One had the tournament match. The other, Jasmine postulated, was a computerized chess game set to the highest level of difficulty. Greta would wait for her real life opponent to make a move and then make the same move against the computerized opponent. Whatever move the computer made in response, she'd use that against the person in the carrel next to hers. With the computer spitting out moves at an expert level, she was sure to win the live game."

Cam was stunned into silence. After a moment, he said, "That's ingenious."

"*If* it actually happened that way," Tatum said, still defending Greta's honor.

"Did Jasmine check Greta's browser history?" Cam asked.

"I'm sure she did," Darby said. "But Greta could've easily deleted it before stepping out of her carrel to claim the prize. The whole ordeal was quite humiliating for Jasmine. She arranged the contest to show off the library's new technology, and all anyone could talk about was whether the computers were used to cheat."

Cam finished his tea. To Tatum, he said, "You said Addy had it in for Greta. Why suspect Addy and not Jasmine herself?"

"Suspect?" Darby queried.

Tatum turned to face Darby. "If poor Greta's unfortunate death really was *murder* and not just an accident, Cam asked me who I thought might have done such an evil thing."

Darby shot Cam a questioning glance.

"I'd rather Bernie arrest anyone else if it saves you from being interrogated, mother," he said.

"And you thought of Addy Devlin?" Darby said to Tatum.

"Honestly, I did," Tatum said. "Because of the chess incident and, as Cam reminded me, everyone knows she's had her eye on Reynold Cornell." She blinked rapidly as Cam rose to his feet. "As for why I don't think it could've been Jasmine, she's just too innocent. More church mouse than lioness."

The same could be used to describe Tatum given her appearance and deportment, Cam thought. But he had yet to rule her out as a murderess.

"Any more dates lined up with the radiologist?" Cam asked Darby before turning to leave. Tatum stared at her with interest.

"Tomorrow, dear," she said with a smile. "Hopefully he'll take my mind off of those nails."

Chapter 10

Cam had arranged to meet Becka Blom in the Peachy Kleen bull pen just before two—they were slated to take Georgia to the germaphobe's home. But when he arrived minutes after the hour, Becka was nowhere in sight. Cam checked the answering machine in his office—a single message, but the best kind: a new client requesting service. He jotted down the phone number and stepped back into the bull pen to wait for Becka who, most days, was decidedly punctual. Just then, Samantha Krause strode in from the outside. Tabby Vazquez trailed her, rolling a vacuum cleaner.

"We need a man's opinion, boss," Samantha said without preamble. Her frosted hair was pulled into a dirigible-shaped bun on the crown of her head. "Kacey didn't drink when she was pregnant with Emma, did she?"

"Alcohol? No, not a drop," Cam said, sitting on the arm of a worn paisley-print sofa.

"I thought not. She's sensible, that Kacey. It's not right for a woman to partake when she's with child."

Cam sensed that Samantha was on the verge of launching into a full-blown tirade, saturated with her personal dogma. "What did you want my opinion about?" he asked.

"I'm getting to that, boss. Be patient." Samantha glowered at him—not unlike a third grade teacher reprimanding a student. "Tabby and I have a disagreement."

Tabby looked down at her shoes and reddened. Her Ojibwa mother and Puerto Rican father had raised a hardworking, but shy, daughter.

"My son took an airplane to Boston for work last week," Samantha said while Tabby pushed the vacuum into the storage room. "He had a flight home that didn't leave until nine in the evening so he had dinner at one of those grills they have in airports. All of the tables were full so he had to sit at the bar."

Cam grinned and risked a conspiratorial glance at Tabby, who had returned to the bull pen. They both knew Samantha's son, Oliver, was a borderline alcoholic. According to local gossip, he was once so hard up for a drink that he bought a plane ticket for an early morning flight with no intention of using it—the airport bar was the only place in the city that sold alcohol before noon. Whether Oliver managed to keep his weakness a secret from his teetotaler mother or Samantha just put on a strong face in public was anyone's guess.

"There was a woman sitting next to him," Samantha said. "Obviously pregnant—Oliver guessed seven or eight months along. She asked the man behind the bar for a glass of chardonnay."

Cam looked from Samantha to Tabby, who was washing her hands at the sink at the rear of the bull pen.

Tabby looked back. "The bartender refused to serve her," she said in a voice that was barely audible over the sound of running water.

"Because she was pregnant," Samantha clarified. "She was of age."

Cam nodded. An interesting dilemma.

"So what's your opinion?" Samantha asked.

"She must have fallen off the bandwagon."

Tabby snickered.

"This is isn't a matter fitting of your nonsense," Samantha scolded. "I think the bartender had every right to deny her alcohol. He was just looking out for that baby. Tabby disagrees with me. A woman's right to choose and all."

The timid Tabby shut off the water and dried her hands on a kitchen towel without speaking.

Cam thought for a moment. "My opinion is that I'm sure glad I wasn't the bartender."

"You're skirting the issue!" Samantha clamped her hands onto her substantial hips.

"You better believe it." He winked at Tabby. "Have either of you heard from Becka? She was supposed to meet me here at two o'clock—we're scheduled for the Sterns' place."

Samantha shook her head, but Tabby said, "I saw her this morning when I came to fetch Virginia."

"Becka was here?" Cam asked with incredulity. "The Stern place is the first job on her schedule today. What was she doing?"

Tabby walked toward Cam and Samantha. "She seemed flustered—running around, talking gibberish. She told me she was borrowing Montana."

"She took Montana?" He hadn't checked on the vans in the back lot.

Tabby nodded. "At nine this morning. She left her Civic—said she had a long drive and wasn't sure if her car could make it."

Cam's ears burned with frustration. He marched into the breadbox, knocked the door shut with an elbow, and dialed Becka's mobile number. No answer.

Borrowing Montana for a long drive? Cam realized that he knew very little about Becka. The twenty-four-year-old lived in a basement apartment in the village. She had been hired by his mother and started with Peachy Kleen six months before he moved back to

Rusted Bonnet. But beyond those and a few other basics, he was in the dark.

He returned to the bull pen. "Tabby, do you know Becka's girlfriend? I think her name is Missy."

"I've met her a couple of times," Tabby said. "She seems nice."

"Do you know her last name? I want to give her a call."

"It's Graves. Missy Graves."

* * *

Four hours later, after tackling the germaphobe's confines by himself, Cam found a table at the Bear Claw—a popular coffee shop and diner across the street from Peachy Kleen. A retro jukebox pumped out upbeat jazz. Dinner had been his idea—insisting to Kacey that he had vital information to relay about Greta's murder.

He had found Missy Graves' telephone number and tried to reach her. But she hadn't picked up and her voice mailbox was full. Frustrated and waiting alone in a vinyl-backed booth, Cam imagined Becka and Missy speeding off together in Montana for an unannounced vacation.

"Sorry we're late," Kacey said as she and Emma rushed inside. "With the construction in the lot, we had to park down the street."

"I know how it is," Cam replied with a smile. "I used to work in a fire hydrant factory. You couldn't park anywhere near the place."

Kacey laughed and Emma joined in, though Cam wasn't sure she knew why.

After Emma inhaled a plate of chicken tenders and steamed green beans, Kacey planted her on a stool at the breakfast bar in front of the Bear Claw's grill. Monday evenings were slow, and Emma—a regular patron—entertained herself by charming the grill cook and two waitresses.

"Now," Cam said, leveling his eyes at Kacey. "Can you please explain why my mother—our child's grandmother—is a suspect in Greta's death? The fact that she has to hire a lawyer is ridiculous."

Kacey's lips turned downward. "I know it is, Cam, and I'm sorry I wasn't at Darby's house with the chief. But I had Emma and nowhere to drop her off."

"I'm not upset about that. But can't you stand Bernie down?"

"He is my boss. But at least she's home. At first, Bernie wanted to hold her in a cell until she was questioned."

Cam managed a weak smile. "Thank you," he said quietly. "You can't imagine how frustrating it is to have someone you love suspected of murder, even if you know it's absurd."

Kacey's frown deepened. "I do know," she whispered.

Cam cringed. He had spent five years away from his wife and daughter, but Darby had never abandoned either of them. His mother made a point to spend time with Emma every week and with their constant contact, Darby and Kacey had grown closer than ever.

"Kacey, I'm sorry. That was horrible of me to say."

"It's okay." She looked down at her spinach salad.

Picking at his meatloaf, Cam passed along the information he'd gleaned since last seeing her: Reynold's lock at the Stagger looked like the prize at the bottom of a cereal box, the blood stains on the upper steps of the McRaes' carpet runner didn't square with Greta cracking her head at the turn in the staircase, and Greta running through her opponents at the chess tournament like Ina Garten at a ladies auxiliary society bake-off.

"Thanks, Cam," Kacey said when he finished. "You certainly have taken an interest in the case."

"Just keeping my ear to the grindstone," he cracked. "But as long as my mother's a suspect I can't just sit by."

"You really have to, Cam. Trust me, Darby will fall to the bottom of the chief's list soon enough. I do wish we could find a truck that lost a bucket of nails though."

"Did any from the pile have twine remnants?"

"They're still with forensics. But just eyeballing the haul before we sent the nails off, none of them looked any different than any nail I've seen. In fact, they all looked pretty new to me."

A waitress set cups of coffee on their table with an absent-minded clunk. A wave of java flowed over the top of Cam's mug and rippled across the table. "Your daughter is such a doll," she said and deftly dabbed at the stream with a napkin. Emma was engrossed in a game of checkers with the grill cook, elbows lodged on the breakfast bar, hands cupping her chin as she contemplated her next move.

"Thanks," Kacey said with a smile.

Cam grinned.

After the waitress moved off, Kacey said, "We saw Reynold's lock. I agree with you—anyone could have broken into it. Plus, I don't know if you noticed, but there's a second entrance to the kitchen, near the bathroom around the corner from the bar. The Stagger's kitchen staff finished their shift at ten o'clock, so someone pretending to use the restroom could've used that door and slipped through the kitchen into the storage room without being seen by anyone in front of the bar."

"I hadn't even thought of that," Cam said.

"As for the blood on the stairs, I noticed the inconsistency on my last visit to the house. But to be honest, I can't figure out what it means. The chief believes Greta did hit her head on the molding where the staircase turns, but rather than falling to the bottom right away, he thinks she tried to crawl back up the steps, dripping blood along the way. Then she passed out cold and fell all of the way down."

"You don't agree?"

"I suppose it's possible," Kacey scraped at a front tooth with her fingernail—a nervous tic.

"If Greta was still conscious after hitting her head, wouldn't she have cried out for help?"

"If she was physically able, I think she would have. Tatum and Dutch both said they only heard Greta scream once, seconds before they heard her body thud against the floor." She shook a packet of Splenda into her mug, then added, "There seems to be a lot of things that don't add up."

He agreed, then sipped his coffee. Cam spat it back into the cup. "Does your coffee taste like Palmolive?"

"Nope. Someone must've forgotten to rinse your mug."

He twisted his head in search of their waitress. Her thumb was busy dancing around Emma's in an apparent wrestling match as the cook eyed the checkerboard. Cam smiled and pushed his mug to the side. He didn't want anything to interrupt his daughter's enjoyment.

"What do you think about the chess tournament?" Cam asked.

"Did Jasmine or her sister kill Greta over a computer game in the village library? No way." Kacey wrinkled her lightly freckled nose. "More likely," she continued, "is that Tatum was trying to shift the focus off of her husband. She knows your mother and I speak regularly. It wouldn't surprise me if Tatum was the one who arranged for that tea with Darby—with the intention of planting Addy as a suspect in her mind."

"Thinking that the story would get back to you?"

"Exactly. And when you walked into Darby's house and started asking Tatum who she thought might be a suspect, she jumped at the chance to point a finger at Addy—because you're an even better conduit to me than your mother."

"You think Tatum's that sneaky?"

"She doesn't look the part, but I wouldn't put it past her."

"But they ran into each other at the police station."

"That may be so, but Tatum could have brought in those tax forms any time. I wonder if she heard your mother was going to be questioned and waited in her car until she saw Darby go into the station."

"So she didn't take her mother to the doctor? Both she and Dutch told me the same story."

"One that's more believable when you hear it from separate people, right?"

"You have quite a devious mind. I guess that's why you're so good at your job."

Kacey's cheeks colored. She said, "Tatum's not the only one who's trying to shift suspicion onto someone else."

"Who?" Cam asked with excitement.

"I can't believe I'm telling you five minutes after I told you to butt out."

"We're just talking," Cam said, thinking, *Kacey may have told me to back off, but I didn't agree to it.*

"Do you know Yulian Barkov?" she asked after a moment. "Russian guy, lives in a big house on the east side of the village?"

Cam squinted in confusion. "I've heard the name, but don't know him. I think Merry Maids handles his house." The national housecleaning company had a franchise in nearby Utica—its owner was one of Cam's staunchest competitors. He took a bite of meatloaf.

"Yulian's a snack foods wholesaler. We've had our eye on him for months."

"Why's that?" Cam picked up a sugar packet and rubbed it between his thumb and forefinger. He sensed Kacey's eyes bearing into him and looked up. He swallowed. "Sorry, is it the chewing?"

She nodded. "I can't help it."

Cam had almost forgotten Kacey's aversion to the sound of someone else's chewing. There was a scientific name that didn't come to his mind. "It's all right," he said.

"Do you know what black cash is?" Kacey whispered.

Cam shook his head and repeated, "Black cash?"

"It's a way to launder money," Kacey explained, "if you have a steady stream of dirty dough coming in."

"From where?" Cam asked.

"It doesn't matter." She picked up a dessert menu and scanned it as she spoke. "In most laundries, the drug trafficker or crooked politician takes the dirty money and tries to make it untraceable by running it through financial institutions and shell companies in countries with strong privacy laws. It's 'clean' when it comes out on the other end. But we don't think Yulian's doing that." Kacey sipped her coffee. "The chief and I think he's passing cash under the table to his employees. Illegals."

"In exchange for what?" Cam asked.

"For making him clean money."

He frowned. "Can you speak English, please?"

"Sorry. Yulian has a real business." Kacey set down the menu. "I've checked it out. He buys in bulk at deep discounts from major snack food manufacturers and sells smaller allotments to a slew of rinky-dink customers—convenience stores, mom-and-pop grocers, strip clubs over the bridge in Ontario."

"So if he has a real business, isn't he already making clean money?"

"Yes, but if his operation works the way I think it does, he can make a lot more with black cash." She laid her palms on the table. "Let's say Yulian has ten thousand dollars coming in every month that's linked to criminal activities. He wants to get it out of his hands, but doesn't want to lose that money, either." Kacey flipped her hands over. "He also has legitimate business. Based on public records—tax filings and the like—the chief estimates that YB Snacks has a monthly revenue of about thirty thousand dollars. From that, he pays close to fifteen grand a month for inventory, equipment, and overhead and another ten to his employees."

"Leaving him with five thousand a month in profit," Cam said.

"If he was running the business on the up-and-up, yes. But if he uses the ten thousand in dirty money to pay his employees, then he can keep another ten grand in clean money every month, tripling his profits."

"Why would his employees take dirty money?"

"They don't know it's dirty, and besides, they don't ask questions. Yulian pays them under the table so it's not taxed. That way, there aren't any records for immigration services to track. Not to stereotype, but we've seen that the illegals around here generally spend their money in very small increments. Groceries, gas, clothing, maybe a Western Union back home to El Salvador or Guadalajara—nothing's traceable back to Yulian."

"Don't Yulian's customers know they're dealing with illegal immigrants?"

"Probably not. There are plenty of legal folks around who look similar. Besides, his employees drive trucks and deliver goods to stock boys. Yulian handles the business end with the clients himself."

"So why don't you hit Yulian by nailing the employees?"

"We're working on that, but coordinating with the INS is proving to be a slow process."

"It all sounds pretty fascinating," Cam said. "What's he doing that's bringing in so much dirty money?"

"We haven't figured that out yet," Kacey admitted. "To be honest, we don't know if Yulian has a racket himself or if he's laundering money for someone else."

Cam raised an eyebrow.

"As in he buys dirty money for fifty or sixty cents on the dollar," Kacey clarified.

"I can't believe that's going on right here in Rusted Bonnet. How did you find out about him?"

"Dutch McRae," she said and waved at hand toward the waitress who was playing twenty questions with Emma.

Kacey ordered strawberry shortcake for herself and a brownie sundae for Emma. Cam declined dessert. Once the waitress was out of earshot, he said, "Dutch?"

Kacey nodded. "About three months ago, he came into the station to speak with the chief. He told Bernie that Yulian clued him into the black cash scheme one night after a bourbon-fueled poker game. Everyone else had gone home. Dutch was one of YB Snack's biggest customers at the time—Yulian supplied his movie houses with popcorn, candy, slushies. All of their refreshments."

"And Dutch turned on him?"

"He did—according to Bernie, he was worried that if Yulian got caught, he and his theaters could be dragged through the mud because he was such a big client."

"Does Yulian know Dutch ratted him out?"

"I think so," Kacey said. "We couldn't investigate in complete secrecy. So once Yulian found out we were looking at YB Snacks, he would've almost certainly linked it to his conversation with Dutch. Which is why I'm suspicious of anything the man has to say about Greta's murder."

"Yulian's been talking about Greta?" Cam's voice rose to nearly a shout.

Emma swiveled on her stool at the breakfast bar and put a finger to her lips. "Ssssh, Daddy," she said. "I'm trying to remember all of the words to 'Herman the Worm'!" Her mouth was swimming in hot fudge.

"Sorry," Cam mouthed to Emma as the waitress delivered Kacey's dessert.

"Yulian came into the police station two hours ago," Kacey said a moment later. "He told us that Dutch was infatuated with Greta. That he wanted to have an affair with her."

"Is that true?"

Kacey threw up her hands. "I have no idea." She cut the shortcake into quarters with her fork. "Yulian also said Dutch keeps a storage unit. One of those Stor-Your-Stuf places in Jasper's Cove." The small lakeside town was less than ten miles away and even sleepier than Rusted Bonnet. "According to Yulian, it's rented under a fictitious name."

"Why would Dutch do that?"

"I don't know and neither did Yulian. I'm skeptical given the source of the information, but if Dutch wanted to get rid of an incriminating length of twine, he might hide it there until things calmed down and he could burn it."

Cam looked at Kacey, his eyes twinkling. "So why are you here eating strawberry shortcake instead of searching Dutch's storage unit?"

"Because you invited me and Emma," Kacey said impishly, then added, "Plus, we have to get a magistrate to issue a search warrant. I already submitted the paperwork. With any luck, I'll go in tomorrow as soon as Emma heads off to school."

"Any chance I could go with you?" Cam asked.

Kacey shook her head vigorously. "No way. Sorry, I know I'm using you in a way."

Cam rolled his eyes playfully.

"It's one thing to have you as a sounding board, but another all together to have you running around with me while I work. It could interrupt the chain of evidence."

"Neither of us wants to see my mother in a cell."

"Which is exactly why you need to let me do my job."

He looked up at a Papier-mâché drum set hanging above the hostess stand—the artwork in the Bear Claw was certainly unique, he reflected. "Do you really think you'll find something? In the storage unit."

Kacey sighed. "It's pretty clear to me that Yulian has no love lost for Dutch, and I don't trust him one iota. But we have to follow every lead. You never know where a break will come from, or from whom." Kacey looked down at her watch. "I have to go. Emma needs to get to bed soon." She lined up the ketchup and mustard containers with the napkin dispenser and tiny box of sugar packets—Kacey never left a restaurant table unstraightened.

"No problem. Listen, one quick thing before you go. Becka Blom took off with one of my vans this morning, and I haven't been able to get in touch with her." He quickly filled her in on what little he knew.

"So Becka borrowed Montana without your permission."

"Tabby made it sound like she would've asked me, but she didn't have time to wait around. Of course, she could have just called or texted."

"I've only met Becka a few times," Kacey said. "But she strikes me as a responsible woman. Not as straight-laced as Samantha, but not impetuous either. I'm sure she has a good explanation."

"Me too," Cam said and tapped his fingers against the tabletop. "Any chance I could file a missing person report?"

Kacey laughed. "For a grown woman who left of her own volition? We don't have the resources to track down people like that. And honestly, I don't think we should. People have the right to go where they please." She paused, then added, "Now, if you wanted to report your van as stolen, that's a different story."

Cam took a deep breath. "I don't want to do that."

Chapter 11

Clusters of milky stars in the yellowing evening sky reminded Cam of Emma's favorite soup. Walking home from the Bear Claw, Cam reflected on how fortunate he was to have Emma back in his life.

After the packing plant let him go, despite her frustration with him, Darby offered Cam a position with Peachy Kleen as a housekeeper. In fact, she demanded he take it. She paired him with Tabby Vazquez, a woman now in her mid-forties with a pair of teenagers, who, unlike Samantha, kept her opinions to herself. Cam gradually reigned in his lifestyle but his relationship with Kacey had continued to sour. He resented her for "getting" the baby she wanted and failed to share in the responsibility of raising Emma. At the age twenty-six, shortly before Emma's first birthday, Kacey filed for divorce. As a final twist of the knife in her back, Cam moved out of the bungalow on Mother's Day—the first Kacey celebrated as a parent.

He spent two months flitting back and forth between his old bedroom and Harrison Fjord's basement sofa. Harrison—a friend forged from hours of shoveling snow from frozen ponds to create makeshift hockey rinks—taught eighth-grade science and had been carrying on a long-distance relationship with a woman from Minnesota. Despite his mother's and Harrison's best efforts to yank Cam up by the bootstraps, he pulled away. Deciding that his hometown had nothing left to offer him, and filled with self-righteous indignation, Cam moved sight unseen to Falls Church, Virginia.

Like an 1850s farmer lured west by stories of golden veins of earth, he reasoned that engineers would be in high demand by scores of government contractors near the nation's capital, which the media had touted as "recession-proof." But his vanilla credentials didn't stack up in a city brimming with overachievers. Four months later, his divorce was finalized and he settled for a position as a parking lot attendant.

It took Cam two years of drudgery to realize that his problems lay solely at his own feet and another three to set his priorities straight. He had failed as a husband, as a father, and as an engineer. He had sent Kacey a check every month for childcare, but given his hourly wage, it had been no more than a pittance.

* * *

Turning a corner, Cam spotted Reynold Cornell in front of the aptly named Village Laundromat—a functioning relic—one hand shoved into the pocket of his black jeans. In the other he held a cigarette like a teacher poised before the chalkboard. He was speaking with a taupe-complexioned, wavy-haired man: the well-dressed Cuban his mother had seen at the Stagger? Cam maintained a steady pace, taking note of the man's features and garb as he strode past. He was dressed in slim jeans and a forest-green barn jacket, which looked like it had spent more time on a hanger in J. Crew than on a farm.

Cam had no intention of interrupting their conversation, but he didn't want to miss an opportunity, either. He casually spun around and stepped inside the Laundromat. It was prison-cell sparse and smelled, oddly, of salt. A dozen Maytag washing machines lined one stark white wall, an equal number of dryers flanked the other. A long metal bench ran down the middle of the space atop a cheap linoleum floor. A change machine and a pair of vending machines—one for detergent, the other for drinks—sat in a back corner. Anderson Cooper's face flickered through a sea of static on a television in the opposite corner, surrounded by three empty folding chairs. An elderly woman in a wheelchair stared at the row of washing machines, her head bobbing in time to a concerto pulsing loudly through oversized earphones.

The door opened. The Cuban-looking man walked in alone, glanced at the woman in the wheelchair, then looked at him.

Cam froze, uncertain in his own skin. Realizing that he must look odd standing in the center of the Laundromat, he approached a dryer that had just finished its cycle and popped open the door. The Cuban walked toward the vending machines, his gaze still fixed on Cam.

Cam took a deep breath and started pulling clothes from the dryer. Thankfully, it was filled with men's garments, albeit sizes larger than he wore. He started to fold boxer shorts and jeans on the metal bench. From the corner of his eye, Cam saw the Cuban purchase a Pepsi and take a long drink, redirecting his eyes from Cam to the front of the Laundromat.

A minute later, Cam heard a familiar voice shout, "What in the name of Saint Peter are you doing?"

Startled, Cam hastily dropped a flannel shirt and saw Samantha Krause hovering beside him. The Cuban stared. Even the woman listening to headphones rotated in their direction.

"Sshhh!" Cam hissed. He dropped his voice to a whisper. "I can explain, but please be quiet. Play it cool."

"Play it cool?" Samantha repeated, but with a lowered voice. "I came here to wash my comforter—it won't fit in my machine at home. I figured as long as I'm here, I'll do a load of Herb's darks. I leave for ten minutes to pick up a prescription and what do I come back to? My boss folding my husband's clothes!"

Cam dropped his head into his hands. The Cuban may not have heard every word, but Samantha's body language screamed bewilderment.

He recovered after a moment and convinced Samantha to follow him outside, but away from where Reynold was smoking. Cam quickly explained that he was investigating Greta's death to clear his mother's name and was interested in the Cuban man drinking Pepsi.

"Is he the killer?" Samantha asked excitedly.

"I don't know," Cam said. "In fact, I don't know anything about him, except neither my mother nor I recognize him and he seems to be spending a lot of time with Reynold Cornell."

Samantha tapped a foot against the pavement. Her black Mary Janes were dulled from wear. "Well, I don't recognize him, either. And I know everyone in the village. Follow me." Without waiting for Cam to respond, she marched back into the Laundromat and approached the man with the confidence of a Jenny Craig dropout attacking an Old Country Buffet. Cam followed, but stopped at the pile of Herb Krause's clothes resting on the metal bench. The woman in the wheelchair had gone back to studying the washing machines.

"Do you have clothes in here?" Samantha asked the man directly.

He smiled broadly and replied with a faint accent, "No, ma'am."

She crossed her arms over her chest. "So, what are you doing here?"

"Just waiting for a friend. Are you the owner of this…" he looked around the bleak Laundromat, "fine establishment?"

"No, but he's a neighbor of mine. Who are you waiting for?"

"Just a friend," the man said smugly, as if Samantha Krause was a child who could be placated with a teaspoon of honey.

Samantha made a *ggrrmph* sound. She pointed to a sign. "See that? It says no loitering."

"I'm not," he replied casually and held up his Pepsi. "I bought this pop, and now I'm drinking it."

Samantha apparently didn't have a response, so she turned heel on the Cuban and strode back to Cam. "Right fishy, he is," she whispered. "Let's take our time folding these and see what he's up to."

Cam began to roll a pair of socks. The tension in the Laundromat was thick enough to slice and serve with a side of string beans. Samantha didn't appear to notice—she asked Cam if he'd heard from Becka Blom.

"I haven't," he said.

The Cuban picked up a remote control and flipped television channels until he found one without static—a home and garden network.

Minutes later, Reynold Cornell strolled into the Laundromat. He nodded at Cam and proceeded past him. The Cuban tilted his head toward Cam and Samantha, then he and Reynold exchanged a few quiet words and walked straight past and out the front door.

* * *

Leaving Samantha with her suppositions at the Laundromat, Cam took a detour past Becka Blom's living quarters—the basement apartment of a historic Victorian. The red-, green-, and white-colored home featured a striking array of dormers, gables, and turrets. Cam stepped onto the portico and rang the bell.

A gray-haired man sporting an Einstein-inspired mustache and a knit sweater fraying at the cuffs opened the door.

"Good evening, sir," Cam said. "Is Ms. Blom home?"

"I wouldn't know for certain," the man said convivially. "She has a separate entrance around the back. But I haven't seen her car all day."

"It's at my office." Cam explained that Becka worked for his cleaning company and hadn't been seen since early in the morning.

"That doesn't sound like Becka. Come on inside. Let me get my wife and see if she's spoken with her."

Cam followed him into a formal living room decorated in a French provincial style. While the man went off to find his wife, Cam looked down at his sweatshirt and jeans, feeling out of place.

"Please sit down," a woman's voice commanded with the authority of a general.

The mustachioed man immediately sat on a sofa.

"I wasn't talking to you, Reg," she said sternly and extended her hand toward a high-backed chair. Cam sat as directed.

She introduced herself as Diane Archambault. Pronounced Dee-Ahn, she was as put together as her husband was disheveled. "Reg tells me that Ms. Blom works for you. Is that correct?"

Cam nodded. The mistress of the house stood over him, her sapphire blue eyes piercing his.

"I heard her car back out of the drive at seven thirty this morning," Diane said crisply. "I assumed she was going to work. Did she arrive?"

Cam told her she had, then ran off in one of his cleaning vans and hadn't returned any of his messages.

"That certainly is worrisome." Diane took a step back. "The girl came to the United States four years ago," she offered. "Just she and her father. He was a shipbuilder from South Africa."

"Why did they move to Rusted Bonnet?" Cam asked.

"I don't know," Diane said. "Ms. Blom's father passed away two years ago. That's when she moved in here." She paused, then added, "I thought she worked for a woman."

"That was my mother," Cam explained. "I took over when she retired."

Diane folded her hands and sat on the edge of the sofa next to her husband. Her fingernails were flawlessly manicured.

Suddenly a *clank* came from directly below the living room floor. Cam's eyes shot open wide and he jumped to his feet.

"Sit back down," Diane ordered sharply. "I don't have her locked up in the basement. The girl has a cat, always knocking about down there."

A disturbing thought flashed into Cam's head. Becka was twenty-four, almost the same age as Greta. *Was this mismatched couple sitting in front of him murdering young women in the village?*

But Reg Archambault mitigated his fears by asking, "Should we call the police?"

"My ex-wife is the deputy chief here in Rusted Bonnet," Cam said. "I spoke with her earlier this evening. She told me that the police don't spend time looking for adults who leave under their own power."

"Too bad," Reg said. "Why don't you try that friend of hers?"

"Missy?" Cam asked. "I've tried."

Reg stifled a sneeze. "Sorry, darn moustache hair is always getting up in there."

Diane shook her head with apparent disgust. "That's the only one who comes around now and again." She stood and motioned for Cam to rise and take his leave. At the door, Diane added, "I won't say that Ms. Blom is like a daughter to me, because we don't have that kind of relationship. But I certainly hope she hasn't run off. She's a good tenant and a proper young lady."

Cam returned home, then laid awake all night, envisioning Becka Blom tied to a chair in the Archambaults' basement.

* * *

Tuesday, September 22

Fall leaves blanketed the communal spaces framing the garden-style apartment complex where Missy Graves lived. At eight o'clock on Tuesday morning, Cam knocked on her door. Missy didn't answer. He knocked a second time, harder.

The door cracked open. Bleary eyes stared at him.

"Missy?" Cam asked.

The door widened. "Cam, right?"

He nodded. "Is Becka here?"

"No," she said softly and sniffed. "She's not returning my calls or texts."

"Mine either. Can I come in?" Cam asked. Missy had traded in the horizontal-striped sweater from two days earlier for one with vertical stripes.

Missy led him inside to a studio apartment. It was clean but sparse. Two Barcelona-style chairs faced a television that was mounted on a side wall between a pair of bookshelves. A small kitchen and a square table covered in puzzle pieces took up the opposite side. At the back of the room a permanent ladder led to a lofted sleeping area.

Missy sat at the table near the kitchen and Cam followed suit. "She took one of my cleaning vans yesterday morning," he said.

"What?" Missy shouted. "She took a van? Where's her car?"

"Parked behind Peachy Kleen. According to Tabby—one of my other housekeepers—Becka said she had a long drive ahead of her."

"Tabby saw her leave?" Missy's voice sounded confused.

"She did."

Missy closed her eyes and inhaled deeply. "So she wasn't abducted. Thank goodness."

"It doesn't look that way." Cam inspected the puzzle at the table in front of him—a mélange of vegetables. One thousand pieces, according to the box. It looked as if Missy had finished nearly half. "I met Reg and Diane Archambault last night," he said. "I went to their house to see if either had seen Becka."

"I stopped by during the afternoon, but no one was home. I have a key to the basement so I peeked inside, but Becka wasn't there."

"Did anything seem amiss?"

Missy shook her head. "I'm sorry, I didn't offer you anything to drink."

"I'm fine," Cam said.

"This makes no sense. We've been together for nearly a year. On Sunday, right after we saw you, we hiked the Pitchman trail. She never said a word about any sort of trip. And it's not like her not to respond to my messages."

"How about Facebook or Twitter? Has she posted anything?"

"She doesn't use it. Her father drilled into her that social media was the root of modern day evil."

"That seems a little extreme," Cam said.

"Old world views, I guess. He raised her by himself so I'm sure he was a little overprotective, too."

"What happened to Becka's mother?"

"She died of dengue fever, a common enough occurrence in Kenya from what Becka says."

"My mother told me Becka was from South Africa," Cam said.

"She was born in Mombasa, so she's Kenyan by birth. But after her mother passed away, her dad took a job in Knysna. That's in South Africa right near where the Atlantic and Indian oceans meet. He was a welder."

"Shipbuilding is what I heard," Cam said.

"That's right, welding ships."

"So what prompted the move to the US?"

"I'm not positive. He died before Becka and I met, but I'm pretty sure he was working for a repair shop that serviced boats navigating the Great Lakes."

"You don't happen to have a set of keys to her Civic, do you?" Cam asked.

Missy shook her head. "Do you think there might be something inside that could tell us where she's gone?"

"I have no idea. You said you looked in her apartment. Did you search it?"

"No." Missy locked the tab of one puzzle piece into the blank of another—a radish's roots. "I just fed her cat."

Cam mentally checked a box—Becka did own a cat. "Maybe we should take a look," he said.

Missy couldn't take off of work on such short notice, so Cam made plans to meet her outside of the Archambault's house that evening.

* * *

Cam knocked on his new neighbor's door.

Elena answered in a toffee–colored slip that fell to her knees, a glass of an opaque liquid the color of raw beef in hand. "Morning," she said and sipped from the glass.

"What's that?" he asked, his stomach churning.

"A cactus pear smoothie."

"Why's it that color?"

"That's natural. Don't ever cut one open if you're squeamish," she said. "It looks like a human heart." She smiled, then added, "Want one?"

"I'll pass. Are you busy today?"

"Not if you want to jet off to Paris. On your dime, of course."

"Of course. But I had somewhere even better in mind. Grand Rapids."

Chapter 12

Tucked between Grand Rapids Community College and a children's museum, the stone and glass library commanded attention with its quiet grandeur. The trip from eastern Michigan to the western side of the state had taken Cam and Elena almost two and a half hours. Cam couldn't just sit on his feet with his mother slated to be questioned the following morning and Elena had expressed curiosity in the case so he had invited her for company.

During the trek, at her insistence, he recounted his days of drudgery in Falls Church and she described Cincinnati and Lucerne, the latter sounding much more appealing. Moated castles and a monastery that made fine cheeses would've bested any city the Midwest had to offer, he thought.

Cam had found a website listing the librarians' conference Jasmine supposedly attended on the night Greta died. The conference committee's chair was the head librarian in the Grand Rapids edifice. A block of rooms for the event had been booked at a nearby Marriot.

"Let's hope Miss Jessie Lynne Reeves is working today," Cam said as he and Elena mounted a formidable staircase to the library's front double doors.

"Do you want me to go in with you?" Elena asked. "I was happy to take a drive with you because, well, I like you. And I'm interested in the case and all but I'm not going say I'm with the police. Or lie about anything for that matter."

"I definitely want you to come in." Cam pushed open the doors. Arcs and arches swept his eyes up toward six floors, all visible thanks to a massive open foyer. "We probably should have spent part of the drive discussing what we were going to say," he said. "I suppose we just opt for the truth."

"Well, there's the circulation desk," Elena said and pointed to the center of the foyer. She tottered beside him on ankle strap heels.

After waiting for two other patrons to be helped, Cam and Elena approached a slender man behind the desk. "Is Ms. Reeves in today," Cam asked.

"Most certainly, most certainly," the man said, then added, apparently for good measure, "she most certainly is." He didn't move.

"And where might we find her?" Cam asked.

Elena, who was standing half a step behind him, poked a finger into his lower back. Cam struggled to keep a straight face.

"Ah," the man said as if the concept was ingenious. "She's in France."

"France?" Elena said. "I thought you said she was here."

The man pressed his top teeth down onto his lower lip. "No, no, third floor near the restroom. Shame it is."

Elena stepped to Cam's side and said, "A shame? I'm completely lost. Is Ms. Reeves in France or next to the third floor bathroom?"

"Restroom, ma'am," he said. "We call it a restroom not a bathroom. Restroom's what it is."

"So she's not in France?" she asked.

"No, she is, ma'am. We relocated him. Anatole France won a Nobel Prize in Literature. Shame to put his work next to the restroom. It's just not right."

* * *

"Lordy," Elena said as they mounted a circular staircase. "That guy is nuts."

"Let's hope the head librarian has her head screwed on a little straighter," Cam said.

Jessie Lynne Reeves didn't look a day over thirty to Cam. A part in her bangs three fingers wide made her hair resemble an inverted letter U. They found her hunched over a rolling book cart near the women's room.

"The guy at the circulation desk doesn't appreciate Mr. France's new environs," Cam said by way of greeting, then added, "Are you Ms. Reeves?"

She straightened up and faced them. "I am and I can't go around listening to the likes of him. He'd put all of the dead authors front and center. He figures people would stop, peruse, and select a work from a literary genius." She stuck a forefinger in the air. "But instead I'd get an earful from dozens of patrons who have to schlep up five flights to find the latest in vampire erotica."

"We're definitely not in the market for anything vampish," Cam said. "Actually, we just want talk with you."

"Philanthropists I hope?" she said. "If so, I can give you the grand tour. Anatole here can wait another century for someone to read his prose."

"Sorry, we're not donors," Cam said. "We have a few questions about the conference you just had."

"I didn't figure you to be here to write the library a check, but you never can be too sure. Plenty of folks give their children, or even their grandkids, some say when it comes to the charity-picking game." She ran a hand along the spines of a series of hardcover books on the cart. "We had a solid turn out at the conference. It's all about the keynote speaker. A good one draws even the most reserved librarians."

"Like a moth to the woodwork."

"I don't know what that's supposed to mean," Jessie said. She shot a quick breath of air up toward her bangs and the part spread even wider then settled back in its original place. "So what about the conference has you interested?"

"We were wondering if you knew all of the attendees. Actually just a librarian named Jasmine Devlin."

"From Rusted Bonnet. Sure, I've known Jasmine for years. Is that where you're from, Rusted Bonnet?"

Cam thought he felt Elena's breath on the back of his neck, but when he turned his head in her direction, he saw that she was facing away from him, seeming to peer at the books on a nearby shelf. *Avoiding participation in whatever I'm going to say,* Cam thought.

He wanted to tell this woman the truth, but he didn't want her to clam up. And he definitely didn't want word to get back to Jasmine that he went all of the way to Grand Rapids to find out if she murdered a woman over an argument about online chess.

"No, we're local," Cam fibbed. "Jasmine's my sister. I'm wondering if you might know where she was on Friday night. She called and told me she was in town for this conference. We were supposed to meet up for a drink. I waited at the Lumber Baron for an hour but she didn't show up and I haven't been able to get hold of her."

"That's most unfortunate. There was a dinner after the last session on Friday night. I imagine she was going to meet you afterwards."

"Yes, it was on the later side."

Jessie slapped a palm on the cart of France's best literature. "Jasmine was sitting at the table next to mine. The only reason I remember is because she left just before the keynote speaker started. I figured she had to slip out to the ladies' room, but she didn't return. After the speech, I was speaking with a colleague from Milford who had been sitting at her table. She told me Jasmine was having stomach pains."

"Was she at breakfast the next morning?" Cam asked.

"Oh, yes. I asked her if she was all right. She said she found some of that pink bismuth at the mini mart next to the hotel and it calmed her stomach down, but by that time she was snug under her blankets and didn't want to venture back to the restaurant."

"The hotel was the Marriot downtown, right?"

"That's right. Say, why didn't she stay with you?"

* * *

"She skipped out of dinner," Cam said as they drove toward the Marriot.

"Which would've given her plenty of time to drive to Rusted Bonnet for a spot of murder and be back before breakfast," Elena added, completing his thought.

The "Minny Mart," emblazoned with a poor woman's cartoon mouse, occupied a street corner adjacent to the Marriot. Air freshening trees hanging from the ceiling failed to ward off an overpowering scent of burnt grease.

Cam and Elena approached a bespectacled counterman in short sleeves. Deep wrinkles lined his forearms. Other than the three of them, the market was empty.

Cam's eyes shot to a roller grill to one side of the counter—hot dogs and other sausage-shaped meats turned at a snail's pace. He looked at the counter man. "Is there any chance you were working on Friday night?" he asked.

The man scratched behind one ear. "Sure I was."

"We were wondering about a woman who might have come in. A librarian."

The man laughed. "They was in and out of here for days. Flock 'a hens them."

Cam described Jasmine, down to her blond bangs.

"They all looked alike to me," the counterman said. "Not a looker in the bunch."

"She might have bought some pink bismuth," Elena tried.

The man's eyes widened. "There was one. You said Friday night, right?"

Cam nodded.

"I remember. On account of what she bought."

Did the Minny Mart sell nails? Cam thought. He shot a glance at Elena. She looked like she was holding her breath.

"What's that?" Cam asked.

"Well, the pink bismuth you mentioned. And a bag of Fritos. But she also bought a greeting card. Only, the kind you give to someone at a funeral."

"A sympathy card?" Elena asked.

"That's it. I carry plenty of birthday and anniversary cards, but that sympathy card's the only one of them I had and it's been gathering dust for 'least a year. I wrote the owner here a note telling him we're now plum 'outta funeral cards."

* * *

"A murderer buys a sympathy card hours before offing someone?" Cam asked rhetorically. He and Elena were on the road back to Rusted Bonnet.

"It must be a coincidence," Elena said. She pulled off a thin scarf that had been tied around her neck and tossed it onto her handbag in the back seat.

"I wonder if anyone else in the village died recently."

"That would explain it. But the card could be for almost anyone—a relative, a family friend from Ft. Lauderdale, you name it."

"What if Jasmine knew her sister was going to kill Greta?" Cam asked. On the trip in, he had explained to Elena not only the chess incident, but also that Jasmine's sister seemed to have a crush on Reynold.

Elena swallowed a bite of the chicken salad on rye they had picked up from a deli on their way out of Grand Rapids—it looked only slightly more appetizing than the Minny Mart's tube steaks. "So Addison tells her sister that she's going to kill Greta," she said, "and Jasmine decides to pick up a card for Dutch and Tatum while she's out?"

"I don't know," Cam said. "It's all so strange. Speaking of strange, who buys Fritos when they have a stomach ache?"

"Do you think she actually had one?" Elena asked. She kicked off the flats she had changed into.

Cam tapped his fingers on the steering wheel. He had scarfed down a pair of bananas for lunch and had a Granny Smith in the console. "Who knows."

"Well, if she was in the market anyway, she might have been picking up a snack for the next day's drive. As for the sympathy card, she could've just been in the habit of looking at cards in case she needed them down the road."

"I know my mother will pick up extra cards sometimes, but only when she's perusing them for someone's birthday or a special occasion and sees more than one she likes. And the Minny Mart is a far cry from Papyrus."

"Too true. So unless someone she knows recently died, it seems strange. And if she didn't actually have a stomach ache?"

Cam stomped the brakes as a Pathfinder cut him off. He resisted the urge to swear. "Then Jasmine went to some length to make it seem as if she did. Not only did she tell her tablemates she had a stomach ache, but she actually purchased the pink drink. Why? To have it in her purse the next morning as evidence of the illness?"

"You think she whipped it out and showed her fellow librarians over eggs and toast?"

"I have no idea. She could've been more subtle and left her handbag unzipped on a chair with the bottle at the top."

"So then the question becomes why the ruse?" Elena asked. "To murder Greta would be one reason, but there must be others. Maybe a tete-a-tete sans clothing with a fellow librarian?"

"A married one?"

"Either married or they just didn't want their colleagues to know."

"And they decided a bed full of Fritos was better to flounce around in than rose petals?"

"I didn't say it was the best idea," Elena said.

"And, of course, whisper passages of sympathy in their dirtiest voices."

She laughed, then added, "though romping about with a partner in Fritos sounds pretty fun."

Chapter 13

At eight-fifteen, Cam met Missy on the street in front of the Archambaults' house. "Any word from Becka?" he asked.

"Actually, yes," Missy said, "two hours ago she texted me."

Cam jerked his head back. "That's great! Where is she?"

"I don't know; it was a two word text. 'I'm okay.'"

"Well, that's good news."

"Is it?" Missy asked. Her voice trembled. "It sounds to me like something a kidnapper would write if he got hold of her phone."

"Tabby saw her drive off," Cam reminded her.

"I know, I know. I'm just scared." She wrapped her arms around her shoulders.

"So am I," Cam admitted. "Come on, I want to have a look inside her apartment. Should we tell the Archambaults we're here?"

"Let's not," Missy said. "They might prefer we not go inside. I have a key so let's just be quiet."

* * *

They crept down the external, back steps to a basement entrance. Missy unlocked the door and flipped on an overhead light. A flash of fur scurried out of the room.

Becka's apartment was cheerily decorated—bright pastel pillows embellished the living room sofa, small glass frogs and lizards crowded glass end and coffee tables.

Missy gave Cam a quick tour—at the back of the living room was an eat-in kitchen, and to one side a bedroom, bathroom, and small den.

"What do you want to do?" Missy asked. "Look through her drawers?"

"I think so," Cam said. "I hate invading her privacy, but I'm as concerned as you are."

"I think she'd understand. Why don't you let me do the bedroom?"

"That makes sense," Cam agreed. "I'll start with the den."

Becka's den was no more than an eight-by-eight windowless square consisting of a desk, swivel chair, and a handful of framed photos on the wall—one of Becka and Missy smiling in front of a hot air balloon's basket and two of a man who looked to be in his sixties. Probably her late father, Cam surmised.

He pulled open the desk's top drawer—it was filled with neatly organized stationary, stamps, and paper clips. Printer paper stuffed the bottom drawer. What did he expect to find—cryptic messages contrived of capital letters cut from magazines?

"Cam, have a look," Missy said from behind him ten minutes into his search. "I found something. If it means what I think it means…." She trailed off.

He turned to see her standing in the doorframe with a beaten up cardboard box cradled in her arms.

She carried it into the living room and he followed. "This box and two others were stacked in a corner of her closet," Missy said and set it on the floor. "I asked Becka about them once. She told me that when her father died and she moved out of the house they had been sharing, she took her father's clothes and tools to Goodwill but kept a few of his boxes. Becka said she knew there were a few ship blueprints inside, but she hadn't had the heart to dig through them—looking at his things made her sad that he was gone."

"Is he the man in the pictures in the den?"

"Yes, Gakuru. I guess having photos of him was different than picking through physical items."

"But she held onto the boxes," Cam said and sat cross-legged on the carpet beside the cardboard cube.

"I'm sure she figured at some point she'd want to look through them and keep some things as mementos."

"What's inside?"

Missy sat on the side of the box opposite from Cam and pulled open the flaps. "The other two were full of blueprints, welding magazines, and plaques—commemorating the completion of newly built ships."

"That's pretty cool," Cam said. "To be part of creating something from nothing."

"This box has some of those things, too, but look at the articles on top. They were inside a manila envelope."

Cam picked up photocopies of two clippings from a Kenyan newspaper—*The Mombasa Times*.

"They're not in Kenyan," he said.

Missy smiled ruefully. "I don't think that's a language. They speak English there. In South Africa, too."

"Of course," Cam said, feeling embarrassed. He skimmed the articles. The first referred to the kidnapping of a three-year-old named Afya Njoroges—taken from her mother Malika while they were sleeping in their home in Mombasa. The second story—a follow-up—added that the child's father, who lived less than a mile away, had disappeared at the same time. The father's boss was quoted, stating that 'Gak' Njoroges, an experienced metalworker, just stopped coming to work one day.

Cam set the articles back inside the box. "Is Gak short for Gakuru?" he asked.

"I imagine," Missy said. Tears began to well in her eyes. "Becka mostly just called him 'Dad.'"

"But wasn't his last name Blom, like Becka's?"

She lifted a wooden plaque from the box. Upside down to Cam, he read its engraving: "Africana II, With Supreme Appreciation to Mr. Gakuru Blom, Skilled Welder."

"So it's a different Gak," Cam concluded. "Njoroges, not Blom. Besides the girl's name was Afya."

"Then why would her father have it in his things?" Missy asked.

"There could be any number of reasons," Cam said.

"Like what?"

"I don't know. Maybe it was a coworker?"

"I doubt it. Becka told me she doesn't remember Kenya at all. And she could only recount fleeting images of her mother."

"Who died of dengue fever," Cam said.

"He must have told her that." She sniffed. "She told me she had a delightful childhood. That her father doted on her."

Cam quivered. "But instead you think he kidnapped his own daughter, took her to South Africa, and changed both of their names?"

"From Njoroges to Blom. And hers from Afya to Nombecko." Tears streamed down Missy's face. "The dates line up. Look at the year on this newspaper. She handed the first article limply to Cam. "Three years after Becka was born. She never had the chance to know her own mother."

Cam swallowed hard.

Missy nodded. "All of those happy childhood memories with her father just run over and stomped into the dirt."

"So where did Becka go?" Cam asked. "Her father died, so she wasn't running away from him."

"I don't know," Missy sniffed. "To Mombasa to find her mother?"

No, Cam thought, *she wouldn't have taken Montana if she was going to the airport*. But instead he said, "If Becka came to the same conclusion as you did, what would her next step be?"

Missy looked at Cam with eyes laced in red. "I would have thought she would have called me."

Chapter 14
Wednesday, September 23

The following morning, Cam returned to the McRae house. Tatum had decided to hold a small remembrance gathering on Friday evening for Greta. The police had sullied the house over the weekend, she said, and asked him to cleanse it thoroughly, despite his scouring blood from the carpet runner the previous morning.

Cam had paired Samantha and Tabby to tackle four homes over the course of the day, while he took on the McRae residence solo. Tatum let Cam inside. "I'm heading out for a while," she said. "I have to take the twins to their gymnastics class. And I might do a bit of shopping afterward."

"No problem," Cam said. "How did the interview for the au pair go?"

"Wonderfully. She starts next Monday. Dutch is on the road for work so I had to take some leave." Tatum edited copy for the *Oakland Press*, a countywide newspaper. She excused herself, and Cam lugged a bucket filled with supplies down to the basement.

After cleaning the bathroom and vacuuming the Berber carpet, Cam turned to Dutch's office and a thought struck him. He had unfettered access, not only to the scene of Greta's murder, but to her bedroom and the office of one of the prime suspects.

As soon as he heard a door slam, Cam tiptoed up the steps and, through a front window, spied Tatum McRae backing her Audi out of the driveway.

Cam hurried back down, taking two stairs at a time, and quickly searched Dutch's office. He felt far less anxiety about searching the McRaes' house than Becka's rooms. Though he had resigned himself to the fact that his mother would be questioned by the police in a matter of hours.

Dutch's desk drawers were locked. Cam flipped through the books on the shelves lining the walls of the office, then dropped to his knees and inspected the underside of the desk and chair. Nothing. Discouraged, he finished cleaning the office and remainder of the basement.

Skipping the main floor, Cam toted his supplies straight up to Greta's room. He hunted in vain until pulling off the lid of a large plastic bin that formed a makeshift stand for a small television set. It was crammed full of well-worn stuffed animals. Picking through them, an inconsistency struck Cam. All of the animals were familiar to him—Beanie Babies, Looney Tunes characters, Alvin and the Chipmunks. Every one, an American-branded toy. Not a single plush in the bin looked German or even European. *Had Greta confiscated them from Nicolas and Sophie as a punishment?* No, they looked too old. Cam sat on the carpet, leaned back against the frame of Greta's bed, and appraised each animal closely in turn.

When he squeezed a Nerf football-sized Pepé Le Pew skunk, he felt something stiff. Cam flipped the toy over and located a small zipper buried under a fold of black-and-white felt. He slipped out of the bedroom and listened at the railing overlooking the staircase—it looked steeper and more sinister ever since Greta died. Silence: Tatum hadn't returned with the children. He returned to Greta's room and shut the door.

Cam unzipped the back of Pepé Le Pew, pushed two fingers deep into cheap, gray batting, and promptly scratched his forefinger. He stifled a curse and pulled out a miniature spiral notepad. Batting fluttered to the carpet. One end of the wire spiral spun out from a tight coil—the source of the scratch.

With the exception of two pages near the middle, the notebook was blank. One page held a list of six names—all men's. Cam recognized every one: a laundry list of Rusted Bonnet's losers and hard cases. It included two ex-cons, a trucker who was rumored to supplement his hauls with backpacks full of opioids, a junkie who pilfered copper piping, and a thirty-something-year-old cosplayer who lived in his parents' basement. Each name was struck through with pink ink, with the exception of the final one, marked by a large pink asterisk: Reynold Cornell.

The other page had a single name and address: T. L. Crutchfield. 23217 Woodland Ave., Cleveland, OH.

Cam spent another minute rooting around the skunk's plushy bowels, but there was nothing else to be found. He zipped up the toy, tossed it back in the bin and sat on the edge of Greta's bed.

Greta Astor had been looking for a man, Cam decided. A village deadbeat. Though as a bartender, Reynold was positively thriving compared to the others on the list. *What had Greta been looking for from the lowest of the low?* Cam's brain reverberated like the hum of a fly ricocheting in a back porch bug zapper.

The address wasn't as puzzling as the list of names. Greta had been an au pair in Cleveland before moving to Rusted Bonnet. Most likely, for the Crutchfield family. *But why secret the address inside a stuffed animal?*

* * *

A skittish knock sounded at the front door. Cam looked up—he was bent in half, wiping down the

McRaes' eat-in kitchen table. The sound came again—a cat's scratch.

He opened the front door to Addy Devlin chewing a fingernail. "Cam?" she said in surprise. "I was looking for Mrs. McRae. Is she home?"

"She's out with the kids, though I expect she'll be back soon."

"Can I wait inside?"

"I don't see why not," Cam said. "I'm just finishing up. Tatum's planning to have a little party in Greta's honor on Friday night."

"I know," Addy said, stepping inside. She was dressed in a boat-necked high-low tee and black skinny jeans. "Tatum called me." She followed Cam toward the kitchen.

"Did you come over to help her prepare?" Cam started to pack up his gear. Determined to meet T. L. Crutchfield, he hoped to make the two hundred mile trip in three hours. He'd phone his mother on the way to ask her about the police interview.

"No," Addy said and resumed biting her nails. "I suppose I should offer, though. I came by to see if Mrs. McRae would let me have Greta's shoes."

Cam looked up. "Her shoes?"

"Greta had great taste and we both wear size sevens." Addy set a large handbag on a kitchen chair, rummaged through it, and pulled out a folded Nordstrom shopping bag. "I think I can fit most of them in here," she said by way of explanation.

It sounded plausible, Cam thought, then his cynical side bullied into the picture. *Was Addy Devlin fabricating an excuse to purloin the stuffed skunk from Greta's bedroom? Did she know about the notepad?*

"I'm not sure what Tatum and Dutch are planning to do with Greta's things," Cam said. "Though I can't imagine her parents will want to pay to ship them to

Germany." He wondered if they would fly in to claim Greta's body once it was released by the police or if it would be loaded into the cargo space of a plane by its lonesome.

His mind shifted to the sympathy card Jasmine had purchased. "Say Addy," he said, trying to sound casual, "all of this talk about death has made me feel really sad about my father. He died when I was sixteen."

"I remember Jasmine telling me," she said.

"Have you lost any close family members?"

"Just an uncle a couple of years ago. And three of my grandparents."

"Recently?"

"No, years ago. I can hardly remember them anymore."

"How about any friends?"

She scrunched her nose. "Well, just Greta. She was pretty much my best friend."

Tatum McRae returned home minutes later and Cam excused himself. As he stepped onto the porch, he heard Tatum agree to let Addy pick through Greta's shoes and the rest of her clothing.

Chapter 15

Twenty-three lettuce-wrapped fast food hamburgers—bun-less and gluten-free. Cam tracked the number of burgers he'd eaten since the beginning of the year on the backside of an Office Depot coupon that he kept in the center console. His Chevy Malibu was pushing six digits on the odometer. At a Wendy's halfway to Cleveland, Cam considered phoning Kacey. He was eager to find out if she'd unearthed anything of interest from Dutch's storage unit. Plus, he longed to tell her what he found in Greta's stuffed animal and about Jasmine excusing herself from dinner in Grand Rapids on the night Greta was killed. But against his better judgment, he didn't call—afraid that she'd ban him from poking around in Cleveland. He promised himself that he'd touch base as soon as he found out as much as he could from his day trip.

He had knocked on Elena's door before leaving to see if she was up for another mini-adventure, but she hadn't answered. Cam figured she must be working— something he really should have been doing himself. But his mother trumped business any day.

He tossed the burger wrapper and dialed her number.

"Hi, Cam," Darby answered after the second ring.

"How did it go with Bernie?" he asked. "Did Kacey interview you, too?"

"They were both there, but nothing much happened," she said. "Craig instructed me not to say anything for now. He's only just returned from his hunting trip and is catching up on his other cases. He said he didn't know enough yet about Greta's murder and until he bones up on the facts, he told me to stay quiet."

Cam slammed a fist gently onto the window above the trash can. "That seems pointless. Why even go in today?"

"Because Bernie insisted."

"Doesn't pleading the fifth make you look guilty?"

"I'm not sure if that's what I did exactly," Darby said. "But Craig told him the only reason he didn't want me answering is that he hasn't had time to prepare himself, or me."

"And how long will that take?"

"I don't know for sure. The chief gave him some documents and I'm meeting Craig tomorrow for a prep session."

* * *

At two thirty in the afternoon, Cam hit the city limits, and ten minutes later, he closed in on the Woodland Avenue address wrung from Pepé Le Pew. The navigation app led him to the Central neighborhood, a derelict wasteland bordering an enormous cemetery and the public housing capital of Cleveland. Rows of boxy brown brick apartment buildings corralled by rusted chain-link fences edged the streets. A group of teens, caps pulled low over their eyes, shuffled along a sidewalk. A senior citizen in torn clothing pushed an empty white-washed wheelbarrow down the opposite side. Cam counted at least half a dozen police cars slowly cruising the streets. Despite their presence, he felt unsafe.

He parked in front of the Woodland Cemetery and fixed a yellow club-style lock on the steering wheel. Huge slabs of Gothic-designed stones lay on the ground just inside the cemetery's entrance. Cam read a flyer taped to the sidewalk: "Listed on the National Register of Historic Places. We Need Your Help to Reconstruct the Historic Gatehouse."

Rather than enter, he crossed the empty street and turned left, passing a series of tattered row houses and a steel shipping container with grimy mattresses strewn about the floor—doorless living quarters. Two blocks west, Cam hit 23217 Woodland Avenue: definitely not the elaborate home of a family requiring the services of a German au pair. Not even a home. The address matched an empty dirt lot marked by a three-foot-high metal post with "23217" painted in white.

Cam trod slowly onto the lot, careful to avoid broken glass, animal waste, and heaps of refuse. If it was intended as a public green space in the midst of urban development, the city maintenance department had failed miserably.

He canvassed sun-hardened ground in rows, squashing countless cigarette butts and small patchwork tufts of grass and weeds. Looking for anything that appeared out of sorts, he discounted a long, clear rod with a bowl the size of a jawbreaker on one end.

A small gathering congregated near a metal post, watching Cam. He tried to ignore them, focusing on the grounds. Midway across the lot, toward the back, he noticed an anomaly—freshly dug dirt. He backed up and considered the plot of earth, three feet long and two feet across. *Too small for a grave*, he thought, then gagged: *unless it's a baby.*

Cam sank to his knees and began to dig furiously, his fingers scraping hard against gravel and stones. A few inches down he hit red clay. He heaved clumpfuls over his shoulder. The crowd of onlookers cheered. Three minutes later, Cam sliced his index finger on a shard of glass. *Shit.* He winced and jammed the dirty finger into his mouth to stanch the flow of blood. With his other hand, Cam tugged off a sneaker, slipped it up to his wrist, and kept digging. He found more glass, lots more—broken shards and, even deeper down, entire bottles and jars.

Sitting back on the ground, Cam wiped dirt from his mouth and pressed his tender finger to his side. As his sweatshirt soaked up the last drops of blood, he racked his brain to remember the last time he'd received a tetanus shot.

Cam stood, brushed himself off, and finished traversing the empty lot. He found nothing further of interest. *So why was this place so important that Greta Astor kept its address hidden? And where did her first host family live? Could the reason she left Cleveland be tied to her death?*

Cam inspected his finger. He didn't need stitches, just antibiotics and a bandage. He trudged back to the front of the lot. The crowd had dispersed save for an elderly black man holding a tin of dip tobacco near the address post. He wore a peaked brown canvas cap and suspenders over a short-sleeve, collared shirt.

"Find what you were looking for?" he asked as Cam approached.

"No, I didn't," Cam said.

"What exactly *were* you looking for, if I may ask?"

"To be honest, I'm not sure. I just thought I'd find something here."

The man rubbed his chin. "Hmm. You're a ways from home, aren't you?"

"I am. Have you lived here long?" Cam asked, gingerly placing his hands in his pockets. His finger throbbed.

"Only my whole life." The man squeezed a pinch of dip from his tin and wedged it under his lower lip.

"Do you know a T. L. Crutchfield?"

The man shook his head, "no."

"How about Greta Astor? She's an au pair from Germany."

The man laughed and spat to one side. "I can assure you no one with a name like Greta Astor would set foot in this neighborhood. And the closest thing to an *o-pair* we have in Central is Bonnie Mitchell. Herself struts around with a stroller, borrows babies to run..." He grunted. "You a cop?"

Cam shook his head. "I suppose Greta would stick out like a sore throat. Did you know there's all sorts of glass buried under there?" He jerked his chin in the direction of the lot. "At least in the area where I was digging."

The man spat again. "Stands to reason. I imagine it takes a long time for glass to decompose. Used to be a dump, this place was. County filled it over some ten years ago."

"A dump? As in a landfill?"

"I suppose you could say that. Not so big as a county fill, but folks started leaving trash here fifteen odd years ago. So the county made it legit, dug a big hole. Didn't take but five years to fill the thing up. County covered it over. Now we take our trash over to a place off of Seventy-Ninth."

"You don't have a waste disposal truck?"

The man snorted. "Folks 'round here can't afford that. So who's this Greta?"

"Good-looking blonde in her twenties. She was the au pair for a family who live an hour north of Detroit. Before that, she was with a family in Cleveland."

"And she gave you this address?"

Cam nodded, not that Greta had exactly given him the location.

"Well, she sent you for a ride, friend."

"That's for sure," Cam said and started to walk toward his car.

"So why were you digging?" the man said to his back.

Cam turned. "I'm not sure. There was a square of ground that looked like it had recently been turned over. I wanted to see what was down there."

"Must have been Hannibal, the neighborhood mongrel. He's buries stuff back there every now and again, then digs it up a few days later."

* * *

After patronizing the Cleveland Clinic to get his finger dressed by an expert, Cam booked into a Hampton Inn near Shaker Heights. He showered and changed into stone-colored chinos and a slim-fit checked button-down from Vineyard Vines. On the recommendation of the hotel's desk clerk, he ventured by foot into a hole-in-the-wall Italian bistro.

Diners at the Venetian crammed into twelve tables along one side of a narrow galley-shaped dining room under the watchful eye of an eight-foot-tall frescoed gondolier. Cam was seated at the very back, near the kitchen, where he could hear the dishwasher's every clink mixed with intermittent bursts of what sounded like authentic Italian. The hotel clerk had not recommended this place for its quiet ambience, but for its gnocchi. Cam passed on the potato pasta, instead splurging on monkfish with lime-zested artichokes and capers, and real gelato for dessert, which the waiter assured him was gluten-free.

Cam spent the meal wishing he could bounce his thoughts off of Kacey. Or at the very least, Bait. *Why would Greta Astor write down the address of a long-vacant lot in her hidden notepad, and what did it have to do with T. L. Crutchfield and Reynold Cornell?* Cam knew who the other men on Greta's list were—two he had met in person and the others he knew by sight. If he spoke with Kacey about them, might they be able to shake something loose? But he wasn't ready to leave Cleveland. Not until he found T. L. Crutchfield.

On a street corner near the restaurant, a young man wearing a bandana on his head and a T-shirt that said "Life" handed him a lemon. Cam smiled, dropped the fruit and a crumpled dollar bill into the man's open guitar case, and walked on.

Back at the hotel, he booted up his laptop, connected to the free Wi-Fi, and searched the Cleveland white pages for T. L. Crutchfield. No matches for T. L., but a T. Crutchfield lived in Hudson, twenty miles south of Shaker Heights. Cam checked his watch—7:40 p.m.

He made it to T. Crutchfield's neighborhood by a quarter after eight. Half-acre lots edged a well-lit street lined by sidewalks and magnolia trees. Autumn wreaths, store-bought scarecrows, and an Adirondack-style bench bedecked the porch of the Tudor matching the Crutchfield address. A basketball hoop hung above the garage. *Now* this place, Cam thought, *screamed au pair*. And the inside lights were on.

Cam left his car at the curb and tracked a stone path to the front porch. He closed his eyes, counted to ten, and lightly rapped a brass knocker.

Moments later, a woman graced by a daffodil-yellow dressing gown opened the door. Glossy dark hair framed her face, complementing latte-colored skin.

"May I help you," she asked cautiously. From the upstairs, Cam heard boys shouting and bathtub water splashing.

"Yes, ma'am," Cam said amiably, trying not to appear threatening. "I'm looking for information on a Ms. Greta Astor from Germany. I understand she was your au pair."

The woman took a step back. "I'm sorry, sir," she said. "You're mistaken. We've never had an au pair."

Cam couldn't tell whether she was telling him the truth. "Is this the Crutchfield house?"

"It is," she said softly.

"Leslie, who is it?" came a voice from the top of the stairs.

The woman said more firmly to Cam, "Perhaps it would be better if you spoke with my husband." She turned and shouted up the stairs, "Tom? Please come down here for a minute."

A ruddy-faced man with close-cropped russet hair bounded down the steps. The woman whispered something to him, then excused herself and disappeared up the stairs.

"You're looking for an au pair?" Tom Crutchfield asked.

"Yes, sir. A Ms. Greta Astor. I was led to believe that she was an au pair for you before moving to a village north of Detroit."

"I'm sorry, but you've been misinformed," he said calmly. "Isn't it a bit late to be knocking on doors?"

"It is," Cam said and dropped his voice. "And I apologize. It's just that Greta's been murdered, and I'm trying to find out some things about her past."

Tom's face hardened. "Murdered? And you're coming to my house? I think you'd better leave and not come back." He started to shut the door.

"What's your middle name?" Cam blurted out. "Does it start with an L?" The door slammed squarely in his face.

* * *

Cam lay awake in his hotel bed. Tom Crutchfield's demeanor had soured when he found out that Greta had been killed. *Was he concealing something, or did he just want to distance himself from a murder investigation?*

After a fistful of sleepless hours, Cam rubbed his eyes and reactivated his computer. He spent forty minutes searching for information on Thomas Crutchfield of Hudson, Ohio. He gleaned only two snippets of data on the man: he practiced cardiology and he belonged to the Southport Golf and Tennis Club.

Before crawling back into bed, Cam checked his phone—he'd turned it off before dinner—and found a message from Missy: "I haven't found Becka yet, but she is most definitely Afya. And her mother is alive! At least she was a year ago."

* * *

Thursday, September 24

Soaring oaks lined the drive of the Southport Golf and Tennis Club. Dew-specked ivy climbed the walls of a mammoth clubhouse. Cam counted five cobblestone chimneys, all heartily puffing smoke at nine o'clock in the morning.

Dark wood paneling and black-and-white photographs of hunt scenes covered the walls of the entrance. Straight ahead, a large room with brown leather club chairs encircled a magnificent stone fireplace. To his left, interior mullioned windows festooned a pro shop. To the right stood a reservations desk.

"Can I help you?" a man no older than Cam asked him from behind the desk, then added "sir," with a perfunctory air. The clerk's Windsor knot pressed so tightly against his Adam's apple that Cam gagged reflexively. In sneakers, jeans, and a zip-up fleece, he was severely underdressed—an amateur's mistake.

"I'm looking for T. L. Crutchfield," Cam said nervously.

"If you mean Dr. Crutchfield, he's not here this morning, and I've never heard anyone call him T. L."

He pushed wire-rimmed glasses up the bridge of his nose. "Perhaps I could help you with something?"

"I'd like to speak to some of the other members about Dr. Crutchfield," Cam blustered. "Can you direct me to the locker room?"

The clerk shook his head curtly. "The men's *lounge* is not open to the *public*." His voice dripped with disdain. "You have to be accompanied by a member."

"The restaurant then, please," Cam tried.

The desk attendant sneered. "I'm sorry. No one is permitted to dine at Southport unless he or she is the registered guest of a member. Perhaps you can show yourself out, sir."

Cam huffed in frustration, swiveled, and hoofed back outside. He stood in front of the clubhouse and blew hot air into his hands. A chill blemished the morning air despite a strong sun and cloudless sky overhead.

An indigo-blue Jaguar XJ curled around the clubhouse's circular drive. A valet sprang forward from a nearby weatherproof hut. Cam stood to the side as the valet opened the car doors for an elderly couple dressed in jogging suits. They slung tennis racket cases over their shoulders in unison and entered the club. The valet carefully drove the Jaguar to a parking spot a few spaces from Cam's plebian Malibu.

Less than two minutes later, the valet returned. "Is that your Chevy?" he asked. Shaggy blond hair crowded his face.

Cam nodded.

The valet took in his sneakers and jeans, grinning. "Not a guest here, are you?"

"No, I'm looking for information on one of the members. The guy at the front desk wasn't exactly obliging."

The valet laughed. "No surprise. He takes himself *way* too seriously. But still, you can't park there."

"I promise I'll move it," Cam said. "But maybe you can help me. Do you know Thomas Crutchfield?"

"Sure. Charcoal Lincoln MKX. Awful tipper. What's his story?"

"Does he ever come here with his kids?"

"Not too often. Every couple of months for brunch."

"Have you ever seen them with an au pair or a nanny?"

The valet shook his head, reminding Cam of an English setter shaking out wet fur. "Not that I can remember. Just his wife—good looking for her age."

"Have you heard of a woman named Greta Astor?"

Another head shake.

"How about Reynold Cornell?"

"Sorry, man. What's this all about?"

"An au pair named Greta got herself into some trouble up in Michigan. I thought she had a connection to Dr. Crutchfield. But it's possible that I have the wrong guy. How long have you been at the club?"

"A little less than a year," he said and stubbed a toe against the drive. "You really do need to move your car."

"Sure," Cam said with disappointment. "Is there anyone else who works outside? Maybe someone who's been here longer than you?"

"Plenty of people, but most of them aren't going to speak with you if you're not a guest." He pushed a wisp of stray hair behind his ear. "Tell you what. Take your car around back to the service lot. Then try Ray Mickland near the first tee. He's in charge of golf carts and caddies."

"Thanks," Cam said and handed the valet a ten dollar bill.

Cam parked in the service lot between a pair of freshly waxed F150s and walked briskly toward the caddy stand.

A tall elderly black man hefted golf bags into carts for a waiting foursome. As soon as the golfers sped off to the first tee, Cam approached the man.

He introduced himself and asked, "Are you Ray?"

A nod, "yes."

"The valet said you might be able to help me," Cam said.

Ray leaned back against a canopy-topped cart and cracked a smile, showing a full set of impeccable teeth. "Depends on what you need, young man."

"I'm looking for information on a woman who may have worked for the Crutchfield family."

"Doc Crutchfield?"

Cam nodded. "Do you know if he and his wife had an au pair for their children? Greta Astor." He described her.

"I've never seen this Greta woman. As far as I know, the missus takes care of the kids herself."

"Is Dr. Crutchfield a good guy?" Cam asked.

Ray looked askance at Cam. "What exactly are you trying to accomplish here?"

Cam took a deep breath, then admitted that Greta had been murdered at a home in Michigan. "She had a diary with the address of an empty lot downtown and an entry for T. L. Crutchfield."

Ray's eyes widened. "Are you a police officer?"

"No, but my ex-wife is. She's working the case."

"So what does that have to do with you?" Ray's question cut Cam to the bone. *What exactly was he doing?*

"It's a small town, and she can't track everything down," he replied unconvincingly.

Ray closed his eyes and touched his fingertips together in front of his mouth, as if in prayer. After a moment's silence, he said, "T. L. Crutchfield?"

"Yes."

"Doc Crutchfield's initials are T. W.—Thomas William."

Cam's spirits sank. "I'm sorry for disturbing you," he said and started to turn.

"Wait," Ray said, his eyes still closed. "T. L. was his father, God rest his soul."

Cam took a step closer to Ray. "His father?"

Ray lifted his lids. "Best caddy I ever saw. He could pick the right club with two hands tied behind his back in the middle of a hurricane. He and I caddied here together not long after this course opened. Getting on close to sixty years ago." He paused to reflect. "T. L. moved on. Became a pharmacist. I stuck right here, been overseeing the carts and caddies for almost thirty years now."

"How did T. L. die?" Cam asked.

"His obituary said stroke. Maybe two years ago or so. Pity I wasn't able to go to the funeral—had to work. Suppose I could've just asked for the morning off. But I pay my respects any time I'm passing through Central."

Cam breathed in sharply. "He's buried in Central?"

"Right beside his parents in the Woodland Cemetery."

Chapter 16

Victorian mausoleums, Egyptian obelisks, and crack-ridden statues of angels littered the grounds of the Woodland Cemetery. Cam plodded methodically through the overgrown grass, examining each gravestone in turn. He passed an African American couple in trench coats hunched over a weather-beaten marker, the woman's face buried in her hands.

Fifteen minutes into his search, near a thicket of hackberry trees, he spotted a granite headstone bearing the name, T. L. Crutchfield. To the marker's left were stones for a pair of Crutchfields who had each died more than thirty years before T. L., presumably his parents.

Cam spun around slowly. Dead air. He crouched on the balls of his feet and searched the space around the Crutchfield graves. Nothing stood out. He rose, stretched his back, and surveyed the area. Vibrant green moss covered a nearby hackberry's trunk and exposed roots—bringing pesto-covered fusilli to mind. Cam crept to the elderly tree and inspected the ground between the roots. Around the back of the hackberry, he spotted a clump of grass—it looked like a chunk of earth pressed back into a fairway divot.

Cam heard a rustling sound and jerked his head up— just a squirrel in the tree's branches. He planted his knees on either side of the conspicuous mound and pulled it out. The dirt beneath was loose. Cam dug carefully with one hand, the finger on his other still smarting from the prior day's excavation.

Six inches down, his fingernails scraped a hard surface. Cam looked back over his shoulder. Still alone. He wrenched his fingers deep into the ground, found the edge of a container and uprooted a small galvanized lockbox. Using his fleece, Cam wiped caked soil from the box's surface. It had no markings but was secured by a Master brand combination lock. Cam gently shook the box. A single object slid back and forth across the base. Something light.

Cam sat and rested his back against the hackberry, staring at the lock. He didn't know Greta's birthday or any other dates that might have been significant to her. He thought for a moment then pulled out his phone. He located the McRaes' landline number. Seven digits—too many for a standard three-number combination lock. Besides, Greta surely had a mobile phone of her own. The McRaes' street address? Cam shook his head. Chances were high that Greta hid the box before she even moved to Michigan.

Cam buried his head in his hands. A minute later, he smiled, then set to work on the combination lock.

He tried 2-32-17, then 23-21-7, and finally—with 23-2-17—the lock sprang open. 23217 Woodland Avenue—just down the street. Greta must have seen the address painted on the post in front of the vacant lot and used the numbers to set the combination.

Cam eagerly popped the lid. A small black velvet drawstring pouch lay inside. He gently tugged it open.

* * *

"They must be worth a couple hundred thousand dollars," Cam said. "At least." He was ensconced back at the Hampton Inn, tucked in bed under the comforter with his phone pressed to his ear.

"You S.O.B. I can't believe you're digging around on your own," Kacey growled from the other end of the line. "Do you want Bernie to throw you in jail? And get me fired."

"I'm sorry," Cam mumbled into the phone.

"That's hollow succor, my friend."

"The chief wouldn't really fire you, would he? We're not married anymore."

"No, but he thinks I can control you. Apparently that's not the case." She paused then said, "But what you found is incredible. How many are there?"

"Twenty-six—I counted." Cam couldn't keep the nervous excitement out of his voice. "And they're not small by any account. Most of them are at least three or four times the size of the one I gave you." The velvet pouch was secured inside a zipped pocket of his overnight bag—he didn't know where else to put a trove of loose diamonds.

Cam had raced back to the hotel after replacing the divot under the hackberry tree. He immediately called Kacey and described his treasure hunt—from finding the notepad in Greta's stuffed animal, to tracking down T. L. Crutchfield, to locating a hidden cache of diamonds.

"I'm coming down to Cleveland right now," Kacey said. "I'll see if your mother can pick up Emma from school and watch her tonight. Thank goodness she's not behind bars. Don't move a muscle until I get there. We'll take the diamonds over to the sheriff's office and go from there."

"Thanks Kacey. I won't even let housekeeping into the room."

She chuckled. "Your big chance to have someone else clean for you and you can't take advantage of it."

Cam laughed, thankful that Kacey had softened her tone. "So what do you think it means?"

"I have no idea. But it definitely throws any theories I had about Greta's murder into a tailspin."

* * *

Three hours later, Kacey tapped on Cam's hotel room door. He pressed an eye to the peephole and could see his ex-wife holding up one of Emma's reusable lunch bags.

"I figured you'd be hungry," Kacey said as she stepped inside and lowered herself into the room's desk chair.

"Thanks, I'm famished." Cam bit into salami and tomato on gluten-free "rye-less" rye. "They don't have room service. And I was too paranoid to even venture down the hall to the vending machine." He retrieved the velvet pouch from his bag and handed it to Kacey.

"I'm really sorry," he said.

She smiled. "Maybe sorry for getting me in hot water with Bernie, but not for finding these." She looked inside and whistled. "That's a motive for murder if I ever saw one." Kacey reached a slender hand inside the pouch and let the diamonds run through her fingers. "I wonder if the local sheriff will know anything about them. I called the station on my way down." She looked at her watch. "He's free to meet us at four o'clock. Just enough time for you to finish your sandwich."

Cam sat on the edge of the bed and took another bite. "The chief was upset?"

"Beyond belief. But thankfully for me, just at you. I think your interest goes beyond your mother. You like investigating"

"It's definitely more exciting than vacuuming carpet. What did you find in Dutch's storage locker?"

"Cam, I've spent the past three hours convincing myself not to strangle you. You're done on this case."

"I'm in too deep," he said. "Besides, you can't argue with my results."

Kacey rolled her eyes playfully. "The unit was packed pretty full, mostly outdated movie theater equipment. Just what you'd expect from someone who owns a chain of cinemas. We found several bankers boxes, too, stuffed with financial papers and a handful of zip drives. The papers looked related to his business, but I'm no CPA. The chief thinks Dutch might be playing fast and loose with the IRS, which would account for having the unit under a fake name."

"What's on the zip drives?"

"I'm not sure. Back-up of the financial print-outs if I had to guess. We couldn't confiscate any of that. Our warrant was limited to anything obviously related to Greta's death."

"Well, how can you tell whether the drives are related without looking at them? Or having an accountant review the financial papers?"

"I had the same question. We put it to the county prosecutor's office but haven't heard back yet. What's interesting is what we found inside an envelope tucked under an old movie projector."

"What?" Cam asked, wiping his mouth with a sleeve.

"Love letters. Actually, more like lust letters. From Dutch to Greta."

"Exactly what Yulian said, right?"

"Correct." Kacey rolled her head in a circle. "Sorry, I had a kink in my neck from the drive," she explained. "There weren't any letters penned by Greta, just Dutch. Three of them. My question is, if he wrote the letters, why were they in *his* storage unit?"

"Maybe he never sent them. He wanted to make a move on her but was too chicken. What did they say?"

"I don't remember the exact words, and the chief took them as evidence. But the general gist was the same. At least in the first two. She was the most beautiful woman he'd ever seen. He wanted to tear her clothes off. That sort of thing."

Cam smiled. He'd had similar thoughts about Greta.

Kacey read his mind. "It's one thing to think it, Cam, but another to put pen to paper with graphic detail."

Cam smirked.

"But I'm not convinced that Dutch wrote the letters," Kacey said.

Cam swallowed the last bite of his sandwich. "Too convenient?"

"Exactly. Yulian Barkov, who I suspect has it out for Dutch, points us to a storage unit. Low and behold, ten minutes into searching the unit, we find a motive for Dutch to kill Greta."

"Because he wanted her in the biblical sense?"

"And Greta spurned him. At least according to the third letter. Dutch made a move on her, and she rebuffed him."

"So if you don't think Dutch wrote the letters, who did?" Cam asked. He rose to his feet and pulled a windbreaker over his head. "Yulian himself?"

"That would be my guess." Kacey knotted the drawstrings of the velvet pouch and zipped it into her shoulder bag. "The key the Stor-Your-Stuf manager gave us didn't work, and the sliding door to Dutch's unit was dented. I think one of Yulian's goons broke off the lock with a sledgehammer, planted the letters, and put on a new lock."

"It definitely sounds suspicious," Cam admitted. "Unless Dutch dented the door himself to throw your focus off of him."

"He didn't know *we* knew about the storage unit. Besides, if he knew we were coming, why not just destroy the letters rather than create a ruse?"

"True," Cam conceded. "Were the letters handwritten?"

"Fat chance," Kacey said and walked out of the hotel room. "They were printed from a computer."

* * *

"So how does Reynold Cornell fit in?" Cam asked as he and Kacey drove to the sheriff's office in Kacey's cruiser.

"Does he have to?"

"His name had an asterisk next to it in Greta's notepad. Everything else in the pad is related to the diamonds—T. L. Crutchfield's name and the combination to Greta's lockbox."

"Maybe she was just scouting for a boyfriend and happened to use the same notepad." Kacey grinned.

"No way," Cam said. "Those other guys were nowhere near Greta's league."

"True." Cam had turned over the notepad, and she knew the other men on the list. "Reynold may not be the sharpest knife in the shed, but he could've helped her steal the diamonds," Cam ventured.

"Assuming they were stolen." Kacey turned into a parking spot.

The Cuyahoga County Sheriff's Office stood as a monument to white stucco. State and county flags flapped in a gentle breeze atop steel poles.

Kacey led Cam through a glass door. She strode with confidence to a front desk covered in scattered papers where a harried-looking woman barked into a telephone receiver.

She hung up moments later and snapped a terse, "How may I help you?"

"I'm Kacey Gingerfield with the police in Rusted Bonnet, Michigan." Cam winced—she had wholly dropped Reddick from her name. Kacey flipped open a wallet to show the woman her identification. "We have an appointment to see the sheriff."

The woman behind the desk brightened. "Yes, Ms. Gingerfield. Sheriff Lackey is expecting you. Unfortunately, he was just called out a few minutes ago. Some sort of emergency. He suggested you wait in his office and peruse this file while you wait." She handed Kacey an inch-thick manila folder, then led them through a warren of hallways and cubicles to a back office filled with cut-rate furniture. The woman pointed to a pair of wooden chairs in front of the sheriff's rough-hewn desk, then departed, leaving the door cracked.

As soon as they were alone, Kacey flipped open the folder and quickly rifled through it. She plucked out a case file for herself and handed Cam a printout of an article from the *Cleveland Plain Dealer*.

Cam's eyes gravitated to the date, almost exactly eighteen months earlier. He read:

> Bungled   Robbery   at   Ginsberg
> *Jewelers—A Stomach Ache for the Ages*
>
> An armed robbery of a jewelry store at upscale Beachwood Place mall was foiled yesterday afternoon when a store clerk tackled the alleged culprit before she could escape with diamonds worth $250,000.
>
> Police arrested Erin Mack of the 600 block of Iberian Avenue in connection with the armed robbery. She is accused of entering Ginsberg Jewelers at 2:15 p.m., holding a hunting knife to the neck of a clerk, and demanding the manager open the safe. The manager, Jahi Shalabi, triggered a silent alarm before handing over a gem purse filled with twenty-six loose diamonds.

"Once I opened the safe, she pushed Trisha (the store's sales clerk) away, quickly poured the diamonds into a latex glove, and began running toward the door," Shalabi said of the assailant. "Trisha tackled her. She was so brave. We managed to keep the robber on the floor until the police arrived a couple of minutes later, but before they showed up, the crazy woman swallowed the diamonds. I couldn't believe it."

After arresting Mack, police had x-rays taken of her digestive track to look for the missing diamonds. "They're in there for sure," said Rosie Topaz, spokeswoman for the Cuyahoga County's sheriff's department. "We checked the film, and it's plain as day."

"The diamonds should pass through Mack's system within twenty-four to seventy-two hours," Topaz said.

No customers were present during the attempted robbery, which was taped by the store's security camera. This is the first time this store has faced an armed robbery, Shalabi said.

Twenty-six diamonds, Cam thought, *the exact same number as in the velvet pouch.* He handed the article to Kacey.

She scanned it, then said, "The case report has the same basic information. The thief's name is Erin Marie Mack. Five foot five, one hundred and twenty-eight pounds, brown and brown."

Cam leaned back in his chair. "So Greta was a jewel thief who changed her name from Erin Mack?"

Kacey shook her head. "Hair and eye color can be changed. So can weight for that matter. But Greta was taller than five-five, wasn't she?"

"I thought so. More like five-seven. At least. And I saw her around the house a lot without shoes, so it's not like she was wearing lifts. Could the police have screwed up her measurement?"

"I doubt it," Kacey said. "Besides, the report says that the police recovered the diamonds from the Ginsberg theft."

"Right." He frowned. "But that's quite a coincidence. Twenty-six diamonds in a botched jewelry shop robbery and another twenty-six hidden by Greta before she's murdered." Cam put a hand to his temple. He could feel a headache coming on.

"We obviously don't have all of the facts," Kacey said. "And we don't know for certain that Greta was the one who planted those diamonds under the hackberry tree. She may have had the keys to the castle stuffed into that plush skunk, but it doesn't mean she hid the treasure chest."

Chapter 17

"Sorry I'm late." The gravely voice came from behind. Cam turned to see a stout man with the face of an English bulldog—wrinkled but cute in a grandfatherly way—and nickel-sized earlobes. The sheriff introduced himself, first to Kacey, then Cam.

"Would you like some coffee?" he asked, wedging himself behind the desk.

"No thank you," Kacey said. She reached into her shoulder bag and removed the black velvet pouch. "This is what Cam dug up this morning in the Woodland Cemetery. It was in a galvanized lockbox. Twenty-six diamonds."

Lackey eyed the pouch but didn't extend his hand. "Do you have the box?" he asked Cam.

"No, sir. I reburied it where I found it." He described the location of the hackberry tree near T. L. Crutchfield's headstone, then at Lackey's request, recounted the steps he'd taken to find it.

When he finished, the sheriff said, "We'll retrieve the lockbox and run it for prints, though I suspect the only ones we'll find are yours and those from the au pair." He directed his attention to Kacey. "Thank you for e-mailing me the murder file. I had a chance to skim through it a couple of hours ago."

Lackey wrinkled his brow. To Cam, he said, "When we're done here, I'll need to take your fingerprints, Mr. Reddick. You should have given Deputy Gingerfield the notepad straight away." He gave her a fatherly smile, then engineered a stern expression for Cam. "Or at least brought it to my office instead." He sighed and added, "But we are where we are."

To Kacey, he said, "May I see the diamonds, please?"

She handed Sheriff Lackey the pouch. He loosened the drawstring and peered inside. A smile widened across his face. "I sure hope they're real this time."

A wave of nervous confusion coursed through Cam. "What do you mean?" he asked.

Lackey pinched a diamond and scrutinized it. "I wish I could tell the difference between the genuine article and cubic zirconia. That's what we recovered from Erin Mack."

"Ginsberg Jewelers was peddling fake diamonds?" Cam asked with incredulity.

"I don't think so," Kacey said quietly. "I'll bet these are the real stones from the robbery."

"Me too," Lackey agreed.

Cam grunted in frustration.

"So I assume there's more information than I read in the file," Kacey said.

Lackey nodded. "The only report in there was the initial one. There's a follow-up you can review, but I wanted to speak with you first."

"I can appreciate that," Kacey said. "So what are we missing?"

"Just what you're thinking. The gems we recovered were phonies. We kept that out of the papers." He clasped his fingers together. "We held Ms. Mack at a medical facility for thirty-six hours—until we recovered the latex glove through regular bodily functioning. The prosecutor wanted to have the stones appraised before we returned them to Ginsberg's. He figured their value could help sway the jury."

"And they weren't real?" Cam asked.

"No, sir. Cubic zirconia, every one of them. The whole kitty was worth less than two thousand bucks."

"So what happened to Ms. Mack?" Kacey asked. She gripped her jeans at the knees.

"The prosecutor backed off," Lackey said. "Despite the video footage and eyewitness accounts from the manager and sales clerk, he knew any sentence would be small without the real goods. Plus, Mack drew a decent public defender, and they played it smart. She kept her mouth firmly shut. In the end, Mack pled guilty to a weapons charge and served just under a year in the pen." He flipped through a thin file folder he'd brought into the office and stopped at a page toward the back. "She got out six months ago and was given five years of parole. Looks like she met with her probation officer the first three times as required but has missed all her monthly appointments since then. No longer resides at her last known address." Lackey put his hands in the air. "I'm sure she skipped town. Decided to move on with her life."

"Did you try to track her down?" Cam asked.

"Her name and photo are on a few lists, but our resources are limited. Any chance you've seen her?" He slid a mug shot across the desk.

Feathered brown hair—a cut straight out of the early '80s—framed Erin Mack's round face. Her eyes looked vaguely familiar to Cam, but he couldn't place her. *Had he met her when he was living in Falls Church, maybe at a house party in the District?*

"I haven't," Kacey said and, seeing Cam shake his head 'no,' passed the photo back to the sheriff. "So let's assume the diamonds Cam recovered are real. What do you think happened in that jewelry store?" She cracked her knuckles.

Lackey ground his teeth. "It has to be insurance fraud. The store manager—Jahi Shalabi—was almost too helpful. Within five minutes of questioning, he claimed the attempted robbery was no big deal—even if the thief had gotten away, the diamonds were insured."

"Shalabi," Kacey said. "What nationality is that?"

"Egyptian. At the time, he'd been the manager of the store for five years, and he's still there. I checked this afternoon after you called."

"As the manager, he'd know exactly when a new batch of loose diamonds was coming to the store," Kacey said.

"He signed for them," Lackey said. "The delivery came in the night before the attempted robbery. According to Shalabi, Ginsberg's keeps new shipments in its wall safe for a couple of days while the diamonds are verified and catalogued—the four Cs: color, cut, clarity, and carat weight. After the diamonds' vitals are plugged into the store's database, a few get set on display under glass, and the rest are secured in a vault."

"The vault is in the store?"

"Yes, at the rear. The safe is embedded in a wall in the showroom. There are a few hundred diamonds in the vault at any given time. Plus another thirty or forty in glass showroom cases. The safe is only used when shipments come in. At least according to Shalabi. He and Ginsberg himself were the only people who could open the safe or the vault on their own."

"Hundreds of diamonds in the vault, but Mack goes for the safe with twenty-six. Why?" Cam asked.

"It was much quicker to get into for one thing," Lackey said.

"Plus, Mack might not have known about the vault," Kacey said. "She could've just screamed 'Give me all the diamonds in the safe' and Shalabi did just that— went straight to the wall safe rather than the vault."

"Maybe," Lackey replied, "but my guess is that both Shalabi and Erin Mack knew exactly what they were doing—"

"Let me see if I follow you," Cam interrupted. "The manager gets a shipment of twenty-six loose diamonds the night before the robbery. He puts them in the safe temporarily, so they can be catalogued. Meanwhile, he has an equal number of cubic zirconia stones, say from eBay or Sears. That night or the next morning before the store opens, he switches the stones and hides the real ones. The plan is for his partner, Erin Mack, to steal the fake ones. Then Shalabi can file a claim with Ginsberg's insurance company. Ginsberg's not out of pocket anything because insurance covers the loss."

"Meanwhile, Shalabi has a quarter million in real diamonds," Lackey said. "Which he could easily sell on a secondary market."

Cam's mind sprang to Yulian Barkov and the cash he was laundering.

"But the sales clerk foiled the plan," Lackey added. "Shalabi triggered the silent alarm. He had to, otherwise it would cast suspicion on him. The alarm system was connected to the local police rather than mall security at Beachwood Place, so that gave Mack a few minutes to operate. But when the clerk tackled her, Shalabi had to act accordingly. He couldn't wrench the girl off of Mack and let her escape. There'd be no way to explain that. So he grabbed the knife from Mack's waistband and held it over her until the police arrived."

"But she managed to swallow a glove full of cubic zirconia?" Cam asked.

Sheriff Lackey shook his head. "Crazy that was. Or maybe not—my guys never searched the jewelry store. Why would we? We thought we knew exactly where the stolen goods were—in Erin Mack's digestive system."

"Did you hear about the boy who swallowed a roll of dimes?" Cam asked.

Kacey rolled her eyes.

"He was taken to the hospital," Cam said. "When his grandmother phoned to ask how he was doing, the nurse said, 'No change yet.'"

Lackey chortled.

Kacey tapped a thumb against her knee. "What about the sales clerk? Any chance she was the insider rather than Shalabi? Or anyone else who worked there?"

"The girl who tackled her assailant? I don't think so," the sheriff said. "Besides, my deputies spoke with her and all of the other employees on Ginsberg's payroll. The owner, too. The clerk was in an expected state of shock, the owner appropriately angry, and the employees who weren't at work that afternoon had nothing to offer other than relief that no one held a knife to their throats. Not to mention, supposedly no one other than Shalabi and the owner had the code to the safe."

"And what did Shalabi have to say for himself?" Kacey asked.

"Like I said before, he was very *helpful*. The first time we interviewed him—one of my deputies, that is—was before we found out the stolen diamonds were fake. He corroborated the story the sales clerk gave us, and it all aligned with what we saw on the store's security camera. But after we found out Ms. Mack had swallowed cubic zirconia, we put on more pressure. That time, I spoke with him myself. I hadn't been too involved in the case until then." Lackey grunted. "Shalabi kept his cool—he didn't even ask for a lawyer, claiming he had done nothing wrong. Without any evidence, we couldn't arrest him. To be honest, it's mainly my gut telling me that he's involved."

* * *

"What do you think?" Cam asked Kacey over dinner at a country-style all-you-can-eat seventy miles south of Rusted Bonnet.

"I think buffets are gross." Kacey gulped down a forkful of scalloped potatoes. "Why did we come here?"

"It was either here or the Waffle House. Besides, there's a gas station next door and I need to fill my tank."

"I suppose it's no worse than fast food. I can't figure out why Greta had the stash. If Jahi Shalabi pilfered them, why give them to Greta?"

"Maybe Greta stole the diamonds from him. So he killed her."

Kacey sipped ice water. "Maybe. I'd like to speak with Shalabi myself, to get my own impression of him."

"So why are we at a feed trough two hours outside of Cleveland instead of at Ginsberg's?"

"Police etiquette. First, the sheriff needs to verify whether the diamonds you found are real. If they are, I imagine he'll want to question Shalabi himself. The robbery is his crime."

"But the murder is yours!" Cam nearly shouted. He clapped a hand over his mouth, though the din from the buffet line had drowned out his voice.

"Yes, Greta is my concern," Kacey said softly. "When I get back to Rusted Bonnet, I'll talk with Bernie. He'll want to give the sheriff a call and see if one of us can have a go with Shalabi after he does. Or maybe together."

Cam nodded.

"What are your thoughts, now that we know there's a good chance these diamonds are involved with her death?" Kacey asked.

"I'm still keen on Reynold Cornell. He's linked to the murder through his phone and to the diamonds from the notebook. But I can't seem to sandwich him into a plausible story. Yulian Barkov, on the other hand, seems to fit nicely."

Kacey shook her head gently. "He may have dirty money flowing through his operation, but that's a steady stream. I can't see how Yulian would get a monthly allotment of black cash from a single heist, especially if the diamonds were buried in the ground."

Cam pondered the conundrum while he picked at the Greek salad and grilled catfish on his plate. "Maybe Greta bought the diamonds from Yulian. And he's paying his employees in small increments with the proceeds."

"An au pair had over two hundred thousand dollars to spend on diamonds? And then buries them in the ground? That doesn't sound too likely."

* * *

At ten, Cam and Kacey pulled their cars into the Rusted Bonnet police station lot—Kacey had asked Cam to file an official report immediately. Two cups of decaf coffee and two hours later they emerged.

"I'm exhausted," Kacey said as she shut the front door behind them. Light from a single lamp post cut through sky the color of pitch.

"Kacey," Cam whispered and grabbed her elbow.

She turned toward him. "What are you doing?"

"Look," he murmured. Three men leaned against Kacey's cruiser no more than fifty feet from them.

Kacey shook her arm free of Cam's grasp and touched her hip. *Feeling for her Glock,* Cam thought. "The small one in the middle is Yulian," she said quietly.

"Should we call someone?"

"If there's trouble, call 911 and ask for a police dispatcher. The deputy on call tonight lives less than five minutes away." She stepped toward the men. Cam followed. The lugs on either side of Yulian wore olive green jackets and camo-print cargo pants.

At ten feet away, Kacey stopped. "Mr. Barkov, could you and your companions kindly not lean on my vehicle?"

Yulian straightened up and the men on either side of him followed suit. The goons each stood at least six foot four with white and off-white complexions, respectively. "My apologies deputy chief," Yulian said. "I know it's a little late for a visit." Dark hair circled his scalp in the shape of a horseshoe.

"Do you have another statement to make?" Kacey asked. She didn't introduce Cam. He stood a pace behind her to one side and tried in vain to look menacing.

"Nothing formal," Yulian said.

"How about your friends. Have they broken any locks lately?"

"I don't know what you're talking about," he said. "But I did want to introduce you to them. My colleagues here are getting a little tired of you paying so much attention to my business." All three men glared at Kacey.

She put her hand to her hip. "Is that some kind of threat, Mr. Barkov?"

Cam slowly slid a hand into his pocket, reaching for his phone.

"Not at all, deputy chief. They're simply looking out for my well-being." Yulian directed his attention to Cam. "I suggest you take your hand out of your pocket, sir. Because I don't know what you're reaching for and I'd prefer my men not to have to reach into their pockets."

Cam slowly retracted his hand. "I was just getting my phone," he said.

"No need to call anyone. We're leaving now."

Chapter 18
Friday, September 25

"Thanks for meeting with me," Cam said after they ordered breakfast. He was not only exhausted, but shaken after the prior night's run in with Yulian.

"No, thank you," Missy replied in a jittery voice. "I can't fathom trying to find Becka by myself." Today, she wore a navy blue dress peppered with miniature jack-o-lanterns, but the ensemble did nothing to assuage her feline veneer.

"I just want to know she's all right," Cam said and rubbed his eyes. He was also starting to worry about Peachy Kleen. Without Becka and Montana, he was down to two employees and two trucks. Plus, he'd been spending more time running around the Midwest than focusing on work.

"So do I. That's why I called the Kenyan newspaper."

"You got through?"

"Yes. Those clippings we found were twenty-one years old so I couldn't track down anyone who worked there when the stories were written. But one of the editors put me in touch with a helpful woman who works at Mombasa police headquarters. She was able to locate a paper file for a Malika Njoroges." Missy paused while a waitress set juice before her and coffee in front of Cam. "There wasn't much more about the kidnapping than what was in the newspaper, except that Becka's father had been officially named as a suspect in light of his disappearance. But the file had a telephone number and an address for Malika."

"Were they still good?" Cam asked with eagerness.

"The person who answered at that number had never heard of Malika. I imagine numbers get recycled in Kenya just as they do here. So I did a bit of Internet fishing and found a directory that was able to match the Mombasa address from the police file to a current phone number. I spoke with a woman who had only lived in the home for the past year. She didn't know Malika but said that one of her neighbors had been in the area for over forty years and was a fount of information. So I was able to get her number.

"The neighbor knew all about Malika and her plight. She had been inconsolable after Becka, I mean Afya, disappeared—crying for days and nights on end. According to the neighbor, Malika pressed the authorities as much as she could and the Mombasa police went through their routine channels but never took the search outside of Kenya. Malika didn't have many other options. She didn't have the money to hire a private investigator and couldn't afford to travel, not that she knew where to look. She didn't know any relatives or friends Gakuru had outside of Kenya."

"What about the ones who were local?" Cam asked.

"They clammed up. Malika told the neighbor that as soon as Afya went missing, Gakuru's family went from being as sweet as pie to stone cold."

"Are you calling her Becka or Afya now?" Cam asked.

Missy let loose a spate of tears. "I don't know what to call her anymore!"

Cam let her sob for a minute.

The waitress brought blueberry pancakes for Missy, and a spinach omelet and grapefruit half for Cam. "Are you okay, dear?" she asked Missy.

Missy nodded.

Cam waited for her to recover, then asked, "Did Malika contact the shipyard?" He speared his grapefruit with a spoon and was rewarded with a spray to the cheek.

"She did. Unfortunately, they didn't know anything about the disappearance. Gakuru's boss was upset to have lost a good worker. He gave her a list of other shipyards in southeast Africa—with names, addresses, and phone numbers. Malika called them all, but no one knew of a Gakuru Njoroges. He must have already changed his name to Blom."

"It sounds like she hit a dead end." Cam leaned forward and his chest dipped into his plate of food. He jerked his head back and cursed as he looked at the grease stain on his button down. He swiped at it with a napkin.

Missy didn't appear to notice. "I imagine she did. The neighbor said she prayed every day, put up posters around town, and every year renewed her appeal to the police. Nothing worked. Then, a little less than five years ago, a retired couple moved into their village— Emmanuel and Miriam Botha. A gift from God." Missy raised her eyes. "They were active in Malika's church."

"The neighbor told you all of this?" Cam asked.

"Yes. Apparently they were close." Missy slurped orange juice though a straw. "One evening, while they were cleaning up after a potluck, Miriam asked Malika if she had any children. Malika told her about Afya. Miriam listened intently, then called in her husband who was outside smoking cigars with some other men from the church. After Malika repeated her story, the Bothas exchanged a knowing look. At least that's what Malika told the neighbor."

"They knew who Gakuru was?" Cam asked, rubbing the stain on his shirt between his thumb and forefinger.

"Yes. And it wasn't by happenstance that the Bothas were at Malika's church."

Cam squinted at Missy.

"Let me explain," she said. "Emmanuel taught high school level geography in Knysna. That's the city in South Africa where Becka grew up. She had been one of his students, and he knew that she lived with her father. Of course, having a single parent wasn't atypical. Emmanuel was a grandfatherly sort of figure and Becka took to him. One day after class, she confided to him that she'd been having dreams about her dead mother. She couldn't picture her but had cast a South African actress's face in the role. Emmanuel probed a little, but Becka didn't remember much, just that one day she was a toddler living with her mother in Mombasa and the next day her father whisked her off to South Africa because the dengue fever bug had bitten. Emmanuel asked about a funeral, but Becka couldn't remember one. She figured her father had wanted to save her from the pain of seeing her mother's lifeless body at such a young age. And that's why they never visited any family in Kenya—to save her from emotional distress, although her father's parents and brother visited them in Knysna a handful of times."

"So his family knew where they were."

"Most certainly. Emmanuel thought something sounded off-kilter. A psychological counselor came to the school once a week, and Emmanuel asked Becka to see him, under the pretext of interpreting her dreams. The counselor wasn't able to glean any more information, so Emmanuel took it upon himself to find Becka's father and meet him casually. At a local bar. He bought Gakuru a couple of drinks and tried to suss out his story. Unfortunately, Becka's father wasn't an open book. When asked about his late wife in Kenya, he simply replied that she had died of dengue fever.

Emmanuel didn't push it—he was only a few years from retirement and had other students with pressing educational problems. Besides, Becka was a smart and well-liked girl. At the time, he thought it best to leave things be."

"Until he went to Mombasa?"

Missy smiled and sipped her juice. "Emmanuel retired three years later, a year after Becka graduated. Retirement meant Emmanuel had more time on his hands. Time to think. Time for guilt to set in."

"Guilt?"

"Because he had a suspicion that something wasn't quite right about Becka and her father, but he hadn't followed it to the end of the rope. Emmanuel and his wife, Miriam, had talked about traveling in retirement, and Mombasa is a vibrant, coastal city. It has more cultural and entertainment options than Knysna. Plus, Emmanuel wanted to see if he could set his conscience straight. Hearing the story, Miriam agreed, so they leased an apartment for a year to see if Mombasa would suit them long-term."

Missy paused to take several bites of a pancake. Cam waited patiently.

She said, "Shortly after they moved, Emmanuel went to several shipyards asking about a man named Gakuru Blom. The name didn't ring a bell of course, because Becka's father had gone by his real name in Kenya—Njoroges, not Blom. But Becka's uncle worked at one of the shipyards. He probably caught wind of Emmanuel and tipped Becka's father off that a schoolteacher from Knysna was sniffing around. Malika's old neighbor figured that as soon as Gakuru heard from his brother, he started applying for positions in the States. Emmanuel also tried the police station without avail—again, because he didn't know to connect Gakuru and Becka with the name Njoroges.

"A week later, Miriam contacted a local shelter and was directed to a support group for women who were struggling with the loss of a child. Most of the group's members had an infant who passed away, but there were a handful whose children had vanished. When Miriam mentioned a shipyard worker named Gakuru to the group's director, the other woman burst into tears of joy. She told Miriam about Malika Njoroges, who had heavily depended on the group a decade earlier. And the director knew which church Malika frequented. The two women agreed that Miriam should befriend Malika and see if the man Emmanuel knew of in Knysna was her former husband and if Becka Blom was, in fact, Afya. So Miriam and Emmanuel joined Malika's church."

"And after the potluck, they told her Gakuru and Becka were in South Africa?"

Missy nodded. "They sat Malika down and explained that they had been looking for her. Emmanuel asked if Gakuru had any distinctive physical characteristics—in the bar in Knysna years earlier, he had noticed a long scar on one of his forearms. Of course, Emmanuel didn't know whether the scarring happened before or after moving to Knysna. But Malika mentioned it right away—from a shipyard accident when Gakuru was nineteen. At hearing the confirmation, Miriam wrapped Malika into a bear hug and whispered into her ear—we're taking you to South Africa to see your baby."

Missy launched into a fresh fit of tears and Cam began to cry as well.

After a minute, they both wiped their eyes. "It took Malika a little time before she could afford to make the trip down to Knysna. She had to save money and build up leave days from her job. Emmanuel and Miriam offered to loan her money, or even pay for her trip, but according to her neighbor, Malika refused. She'd grown so self-dependent that she wouldn't take charity of any kind from anyone. Of course, that was a huge mistake—by the time she made the three thousand mile trip to Knysna, accompanied by her new friends, Becka and her father were gone. The shipbuilder in Knysna knew Gakuru went to the United States with his daughter, but didn't know where they'd landed. So Malika returned to Mombasa, deflated but not defeated. She spent the next three years saving money to come to the States."

"Is she here now? In the US?" Cam asked.

"I sure hope so," Missy said. "The neighbor said Malika chose New York because of its size and landed a housecleaning job to stay afloat while she searched. From Emmanuel, Malika knew that Gakuru had changed her daughter's name from Afya Njoroges to Nombecko Blom, and she prayed that it hadn't been changed again. That, of course, hadn't happened— Becka didn't know her name had been swapped in the first place so her father couldn't very well ask her to change it when she was twenty years old."

"Housecleaning," Cam said to himself and smiled.

"That was the last the neighbor heard from her. Just about a year ago."

"Have you heard again from Becka?" Cam asked.

Missy shook her head. "I texted her yesterday and told her that you and I found the articles and that we knew what happened. I begged her to call me."

"No response?"

"None."

Chapter 19

At six o'clock in the evening, Tatum and Dutch had opened their home to those wishing to honor Greta's memory, which in practice amounted to lighting a small votive candle on the dining room table, then stuffing oneself full of pastries and cake. Cam refused to drink Coors Light or Lynchburg Lemonade from a stocked cooler—it struck him as insensitive.

A handful of Greta's au pair friends attended, as did his new neighbor Elena. He nodded hellos and wandered into the kitchen. With one hand clutching a beer and the other firmly planted on Addy Devlin's waist, Reynold Cornell held court with Dutch, Tatum, and Jasmine. *All of my suspects in a neat, little circle,* Cam thought, *save for Yulian Barkov.* Bernie Leftwich and Kacey huddled in a far corner, the chief glaring at Dutch.

Cam longed to devour a slice of carrot cake, but it was sure to be filled with gluten. Instead, he opted for a tumbler of Vernors and took a step toward Kacey. She shifted her eyes to one side, clearly trying to signal something. Bernie pushed himself away from the kitchen counter.

"A nice affair, chief," Cam remarked.

"I suppose," Bernie growled. He moved in close to Cam. "Listen, son. I don't know what you think you're doing running around Cleveland like Barney Fife reincarnate. You're lucky I don't put you in the lock-up. You're not a policeman." The chief bared his teeth.

His breath smelled like gas station peanuts. "Hell, you're not even married to Kacey anymore."

"What do you expect?" Cam shot back. "My mother is a suspect just because a bucket of nails fell out of a truck near her house."

"None of us has any idea how those nails got there and you know it. I'm just doing my job as the chief of police."

"And I'm just doing my job as a son," Cam retorted and quickly retreated from the kitchen.

He took a deep breath then spotted Elena in the dining room.

"Fancy seeing you here," Cam said and clinked his tumbler to hers, which was filled with a clear liquid. A skin-tight, silver sweater hugged her torso.

"Tatum invited me," she said. "I think she wanted to fill the room." She sipped her drink, then said, "I hear you did a bit of sleuthing without me."

Cam swallowed hard. "I knocked on your door to see if you wanted to come. Besides, not being home saved you—Chief Leftwich just tore into me. What did you hear?"

"Just that you and your ex-wife were running around Cleveland, and that it had something to do with Greta's murder. But the chief wouldn't give me any specifics— I asked."

Cam set his Vernors on the dining room table. "You spoke with Bernie?"

Elena nodded. "He finally got around to interviewing me this afternoon. I was here on the day Greta died, remember?" She looked around the room. "We were supposed to meet a few days ago, but he rescheduled. I got the sense he was just going through the motions with me."

"Did you tell him about Jasmine?"

"I felt I had to. He was annoyed that we stuck our noses in his business, but he didn't put much stock in it. He thinks Jasmine's too prim."

"And my mother's not?"

"I guess not, but he obviously knows who he's going after."

"Still Dutch?" Cam asked quietly.

Elena nodded. "He told me he was ready to arrest him yesterday when your ex called him about whatever it was you were doing in Cleveland."

Cam chuckled. "I suppose I opened a huge can of Pandora's box."

Elena smiled sweetly. "So what did you find out?" she asked quietly and tilted her head toward him.

He briefly considered whether he could use Elena as a sounding board, but after the chief's latest rebuke, decided against it. "I don't think it's for me to say. It's in the hands of the Cleveland police."

Elena made a pouty face. She took a long sip from her tumbler, then asked, "Who's that woman with the red hair?" She surreptitiously pointed at Addy through the opening between the dining room and kitchen.

"That's Addison, Addy—Jasmine's sister."

"Hmm, Ms. Pink Bismuth's sibling." Elena tapped a fingernail against her glass. "She's a nanny, right?"

"And was one of Greta's closest friends. You haven't met her?"

"Not really, but I overheard something interesting that she said to Tatum on Wednesday morning."

Elena must have arrived at the McRae house while Addy was picking through Greta's clothes, Cam thought. "What did you hear?"

"I came over to walk Tatum through fabric samples," Elena said. "Addison was upstairs in Greta's room. A few minutes after I arrived, she came down with armfuls of clothing and a bag filled with shoes.

Tatum met her at the foot of the stairs, near the door. I was sitting in the living room, but could hear them well enough."

Cam picked up his Vernors.

"She asked Tatum for Greta's job," Elena said.

Cam brought the drink to his lips.

"She told Tatum that as an American she wasn't restricted on how long she could stay with a family like an au pair is. She went on and on about stability. Tatum asked about the family she was currently working for. Addison sounded pretty dispassionate—the boys she's watching now are animals and the parents, a couple of religious zealots. She said she's uncomfortable with them."

"So she's in the market for another family?"

"It certainly sounded like it."

Cam thought through the ramifications. He couldn't imagine anyone committing murder for a job. Especially one that was by no means guaranteed. In fact, he knew that Tatum had already hired a replacement for Greta, and it wasn't Addy.

"What did Tatum say?" Cam asked.

"She told Addison that she'd have to think about it."

Cam just nodded. Most likely, Tatum hadn't wanted to hurt Addy's feelings.

Elena excused herself to refill her tumbler as the group in the kitchen broke up. Cam sidled toward Addy, who left Reynold to warm herself by the fireplace in the family room.

"How are you holding up?" Cam asked. To his left, he noticed Jasmine and Tatum approach the other side of the room. In a full-length flowered caftan and pince-nez glasses, Jasmine reminded Cam of a schoolmarm.

"The gin helps," Addy said, holding up her glass. "Though I don't know what the point is of this little shindig. Greta deserves a proper funeral."

"Is there one scheduled?"

"Not that I'm aware of. Tatum told me a few minutes ago that the police are ready to release Greta's body, but they can't locate her parents."

An alarm bell sounded in Cam's mind, but he wasn't sure what to make of it. "What happens if the police can't find them?"

"I suppose the county will bury her. They can't just leave her body in the morgue." Addy cringed as she spoke.

"Did you find some shoes that fit when you were here the other day?" Cam asked neutrally.

"Yes," she said with a hint of envy. "Greta had so many nice things." Tonight, Addy had gone in for retro glam—pinned with a rhinestone comb, extensions lengthened her normally spiky red hair. The dress cinching her waist befitted a Parisian café more than a suburban McMansion. But Cam had to admit, she looked fetching. The polar opposite of her sister.

"The McRaes must have paid her well," Cam proffered.

"Perhaps. But au pairs don't usually make much money. They get room, board, and the biggest attraction, of course, is the chance to live in America. I wouldn't be surprised if Greta came from money. She just never talked about it."

"Do you make more than au pairs?"

"Yes, but live-in nannies provide more continuity for a family and are better equipped to help with homework and things like that." She paused, then added in a low voice, "Has Tatum said anything to you about replacing Greta?"

"She hasn't," Cam fibbed, feigning mild bewilderment. "Are you leaving your current job?"

Addy nibbled on her lower lip. It was painted blood red. "Maybe. The McRae children are so well behaved."

Cam was about to respond when Kacey stepped across the family room to join them. Addy said a brusque hello, touched Cam on the arm—for a hair longer than socially acceptable, then shuffled off.

"Sorry," Kacey said to Cam. "I didn't mean to break up your conversation."

"Is she upset with you?"

"Most of the folks in this house are. Probably because I've questioned almost everyone. No one seems to understand that I'm just doing my job. They take it personally."

"I suppose it's hard not to." Cam proceeded to tell Kacey that Addy Devlin was interested in Greta's job with the McRaes.

She pursed her lips. "That's a pretty weak motive."

"It is," Cam agreed. "But she's also after Greta's old boyfriend."

"From the way she touched *your* arm just now, I'm not so sure Reynold's the man she wants."

Was there a hint of jealousy in Kacey's voice?

Addy had moved into the dining room and Cam could see her sharing a moment with Reynold. "No, I think she prefers Reynold," Cam said. "Could she be trying to replicate Greta's entire life?"

"Kill her to become her? I suppose it's a possibility. How are you holding up after our little run in with Yulian and his thugs?"

"Me?" Cam asked. "I'm okay, though I have to admit it was pretty nerve racking. How are you?"

"I had a gun, remember?"

"I suppose. But still, you must have been nervous."

"A little," Kacey said then hardened her expression. "I heard you and Elena took a trip to Grand Rapids. Are you keeping secrets from me now, Cam?"

"Sorry," he said. "You were already so upset in Cleveland. I didn't want to make it worse."

She sighed. "Well, I heard Jasmine bought a sympathy card just before Greta died, so I asked her flat out if someone near and dear to her passed away. She was surprised at the question, and said no one she was close to, but told me that the father of one of her librarian friends had a heart attack and died a couple of weeks ago."

"So she picked up a sympathy card to give the friend during the breakfast on the final morning of the conference?"

"That's her story."

"It certainly sounds plausible." Cam shifted gears. "I saw Bernie looking daggers at Dutch."

"He had me working on an arrest warrant when you called me from Cleveland yesterday. The notes we found in the storage unit were the icing on his cake, even though I'm not putting much stock in them. The diamonds complicate matters, of course."

"So has Bernie backed off of my mother?"

"Not entirely. He wasn't happy that her lawyer stalled. We're all meeting tomorrow morning. I promise, I'll make it as easy on her as possible."

"Thanks. How about Reynold—have you asked him about the notepad?" Cam asked quietly.

Kacey shook her head vigorously. "We're keeping the notepad tight to the vest. But we are planning to bring him back in for more questioning tomorrow—he's up right after Darby."

Bernie Leftwich waved to Kacey from across the room, then put his thumb and pinky to his ear and mouth in a "call me" gesture. His eyes shifted and bore into Cam's.

Kacey said, "I should get going, too. Emma's with your mother. I mean that nefarious suspect."

* * *

Cam walked Kacey to the front door. As soon as he closed it behind her, he sensed a presence at the top of the stairs. He turned and looked up. Wearing racecar "feet" pajamas, Nicolas McRae slowly trod down the steps, dragging a patchwork quilt behind him.

The revelation smacked Cam in the face like a stiff winter gale. As soon as he saw the four-year-old, he knew exactly how Greta Astor died. Not why or at who's hand, but the method. He thrust his head out the door but Kacey was already gone.

Cam tendered condolences to Tatum and hastened away from the McRae home. He needed time and space to think.

* * *

Twenty minutes later, Cam hunkered down at his kitchen table with a legal pad, ballpoint, and a large coffee and box of sour cream-glazed Timbits from Tim Hortons.

Nicolas McRae's quilt. Yellow and red and green squares of fabric rubbing against the steps, across and down, across and down. Cam popped a doughnut hole into his mouth and held it there, letting the Timbit's sticky sweet icing melt onto his tongue before chewing. Greta Astor hadn't tripped and fallen down the stairs— she had been dragged. By her feet.

The flattened carpet, blood on the steps above the mid-staircase landing, the patch on the molding where the stairs turned. If Greta had been bludgeoned to death *before* being dragged down the stairs, the pieces fit.

Scalding hot coffee sloshed between his gums as Cam pictured the scene. *Reynold Cornell sends a text message to Greta at eleven o'clock at night—he has a "big score" lined up. She sneaks down the McRaes' steps at one thirty to meet him. But Greta doesn't trip over a length of twine stretched across the top step of the staircase. There is no trip wire. Instead, she leaves the house without a scratch and steps down from the front porch and onto the driveway, twisting her head from one side to the other—looking for Reynold. Her final breaths. A blunt instrument unceremoniously bashes Greta on the back of the head—a single fatal blow.* Had the police checked for blood in the driveway or had the killer wiped away any evidence outside the house?

Cam's lips twisted as the vision intensified. *The killer scoops up Greta's lifeless body and silently carries her inside and up the stairs. On a previous visit, he had hammered in, then pulled out, a nail to leave a hole—no way to do that in the middle of the night without waking the family. He pulls a length of twine from his pocket and rubs it around the rail to leave traces of fiber, then ties nylon cords around Greta's ankles. The killer briskly but gently hops down the steps holding the opposite ends of the cord lengths. He sets a knife next to his feet on the Turkish rug and yanks the cords taut. Greta's lifeless body hurtles down the steps, dragging against the carpet, blood from the gash on the back of her skull marring the steps as it bounces off of them. Her head hits the wall at the turn on the stairs, leaving a tennis ball-sized stain. As Greta's body crashes down against the rug, the killer lets out a feminine shriek. Knowing he has only a matter of seconds from the first thump, he swiftly cuts the nylon from Greta's legs—accidentally leaving a loop around one ankle in his haste—and slips out the front door just before Dutch emerges from the master bedroom, baseball bat in hand.*

Chapter 20

"What do you think, Bait?" Cam's goldfish bobbed up and down. He'd just called Kacey, and she conceded that his theory on the method of Greta's death made sense.

"Chief Leftwich wants Kacey to nail down a relationship between Jahi Shalabi and Dutch," Cam said. He took a long drink from a can of Fanta Zero. "But neither one of us thinks she'll find one. If there's a link between Shalabi and Rusted Bonnet, my money's still on Reynold. Or maybe Yulian." He bent down and peered into the tank at eye level. Bait rewarded him by darting from the back of the tank to the front and back again.

"And there has to be a connection with Erin Mack." He grunted. "We know who the players are, but we have no idea what game they were playing. And I don't know anything about Erin or Jahi." Cam crunched his toes.

He patted the top of Bait's tank and lowered himself into a chair at the kitchen table in front of his laptop. A search for Erin Mack yielded hundreds of hits—the name was too common to find anything concrete. Coupling it with Shalabi's name resulted in links to the same article he'd read in Sheriff Lackey's office. But a straight search of Jahi Shalabi pinpointed the man: the thirty-three-year-old, originally from Port Said on the banks of the Mediterranean, now lived in Cleveland. And he was the drummer in a band.

A schedule of gigs splashed across John Candy Crush's bare bones website in electric green. On Saturday night, they were playing at a bar near Bowling Green's campus. The university was less than two hours away.

* * *

Saturday, September 26

"How was the interview?" Cam asked his mother over an afternoon glass of Prosecco and plates of crackers with brie in her kitchen.

"Easy," Darby replied. "Craig prepared me well. He basically told me to tell the truth and not hold back."

"Was there anything to keep quiet about?" Cam sipped bubbles.

"Not a thing. I just walked Bernie and Kacey through exactly what happened. Kacey must have calmed him down ahead of time, because he never raised his voice."

"So what happens now?"

"As far as I know, nothing. The police picked up all of the nails and took them away. I doubt I'll get my tire back, but I've already had a new one put on. As far as I'm concerned, I'm done."

"Did the chief say you're no longer a suspect?"

"No, but he didn't tell me not to leave the country or anything like that. Not that I'm going anywhere."

Cam set his flute on the granite countertop. "Are you okay? It doesn't sound too awful."

Darby smiled and sipped Prosecco. "I'm completely fine."

A few minutes later, Cam carted their empty plates to the kitchen sink. Turning on the faucet, he asked, "So what's happening with you and the radiologist?"

"I went out with Richard again last night," Darby said loudly over the sound of running water. "He took me to the Chop House in Rochester. He said he wanted to take my mind off of today's interview."

"Nice," Cam said over his shoulder. "And?"

"We had an interesting time," she said without inflection.

"Interesting?"

"Well, he's a lovely man, and I enjoy his company, but he has a bit of baggage."

Cam turned toward his mother. "He's divorced?"

"Well, yes. But that's not it. Most men I see are divorced. Comes with the territory at my age—too young to be widowers and lifelong bachelors don't interest me."

"So what's the baggage?"

"He has a lot of emotional guilt."

Cam winced. "I can relate to that."

"I know," Darby said gently. "Richard's situation is different, though it did ultimately lead to the end of his marriage. He wanted to clue me in before we became too attached, which was very considerate. He didn't want to spring something like this on me after months of dating."

"What in the world happened?"

Darby climbed onto a kitchen stool and sipped her Prosecco. "Cheyenne isn't Richard's only child. He and his ex-wife had a son as well. Deacon was three years younger than Cheyenne."

"Was?"

"Yes, he died. Richard accidentally hit him with his car."

"My gosh," Cam said. "Did he back over him?"

Darby shook her head. "They weren't even at their own house." She laced a finger around the rim of her glass. "It was a Sunday afternoon and Deacon was on a playdate at a friend's house. He was five years old at the time. Richard had run to the grocery store and was rushing home—there was a football game coming on that he wanted to watch. As it happens, his path from the store home took him by the house where Deacon and his friend were playing—in the driveway near an intersection. When Richard turned the corner, he said he was going too fast. He didn't want to miss the kickoff. All he saw was a blur in the road before impact."

"Deacon."

Darby nodded. "He ran out into the street after a remote control car. Died on impact."

"Wow. I can't even imagine how awful Richard must've felt."

"It tore him apart." Darby looked past Cam, out the kitchen window. "Richard wasn't prosecuted, but he told me that he thinks about the accident every single day. Like a bald man who carries a comb in his pocket—he can't let it go. His wife left him eighteen months later—he'd become a shell of his former self. Now he says he tries to cover up his pain by being outwardly gregarious."

Cam walked around the counter and wrapped his arms around his mother's shoulders from behind. "I think it says a lot about his character that he was so candid with you."

"Me, too." Darby clutched one of Cam's forearms with her hand. "I'm going to keep seeing him. He doesn't deserve to suffer forever for a single mistake."

* * *

Jasper's Club K in Bowling Green was dive-bar kitsch exemplified. Neon signs over the bar proudly displayed—in eye-numbing glory—the offerings of Pabst Blue Ribbon, Budweiser, and Molson Canadian. Five dollar live-band cover fees had Cam and Elena in the door at nine thirty. John Candy Crush was scheduled to take the stage at ten, followed by Laura Palmer Lives, a speed metal band.

Cam spent the late afternoon teaming with both Samantha and Tabby to knock out two jobs—after alerting them to what Missy had discovered about Becka—then cleaned himself up, escorted Elena to his Malibu, and rocketed down I-75 to Ohio.

"Thanks for inviting me to tag along again," Elena said when they arrived. "First a library and now a college bar, you do take me to the nicest places."

Cam grinned and climbed onto an empty stool at the end of the bar. He ordered seltzer for Elena and a Jack and ginger for himself. Elena stood behind him. "I sat the whole trip," she explained.

"Even though the chief's no longer hot after my mother, I think I'm so invested in this case that I just want to keep pushing."

"I can appreciate that," Elena said. "Plus, I'm sure some part of you wants to help your ex. You don't seem at each other's throats like so many people after they part ways."

"We're definitely not," Cam said as the bartender brought their drinks. "I wish we had this good of a relationship while we were married."

A man in a camel-colored sweater rounded a corner and lowered himself onto a stool two spots down from Cam—probably the only patron older than he was.

"Do you know anything about the opening band?" Cam asked him.

The man twisted his neck toward Cam without shifting his shoulders, then looked up at Elena. She wore a Smashing Pumpkins T-shirt, jeans, and hipster glasses.

Patches of gray poked through the man's dark brown sideburns. "Not much," he said. "They sent me a demo tape and a few videos."

The bartender set a pint of Guinness in front of the man. "Are you the owner here?" Cam asked.

The older man nodded. "For the past fifteen years. Manager before that. Are you grad students or are you some sort of agent?"

Cam hesitated. He hadn't contrived a plausible explanation for his presence in the college town. "I suppose I do stand out like a green thumb," he said.

"I think that's sore thumb, son."

Cam smiled. "I'm a manager from Detroit," he improvised. "Though I brought a date tonight." He flicked his eyes toward Elena who smiled. "I have a solid band that's sparked some interest with a couple of smaller labels. Problem is, they need a better drummer. I heard the kid with the opening act is first class, so I thought I'd check him out." He sipped his drink. The ginger ale was flat. "If you don't mind, don't let him know I'm here until I hear him play."

"No problem." The older man wiped foam from his upper lip. Nicotine stained his fingernails and the veins in his cheeks flared under neon light. "Which labels?"

Cam slumped his shoulders. He might be in a dive bar, but the owner hired live bands. Chances were he knew a decent amount about the local music scene. Cam spat out a pair of fabricated names.

"Hmm," the man said and picked up his Guinness. "If you'll excuse me, I have to go check the stage. Enjoy the show."

Cam sipped his cocktail in silence. *Had the owner believed him?*

Elena slid onto the stool beside him. "You're not very good at this," she whispered.

"I know," Cam said.

She pecked his cheek. "Com' on date, It's five minutes to ten, let's go see if the band's any good."

They meandered into the adjoining room. A small clutch of students gathered at the front of a trapezoid-shaped platform. Others continued to shoot pool and drink in clusters. Cam and Elena stood toward the back, his hands shoved into his jeans pockets. She pulled out a hair tie and let her locks fall in front of her face, then lightly wrapped an arm around his waist. "To make it look legit," she said.

John Candy Crush swaggered onto the platform minutes later—four men dressed in black denim, Chuck Taylor high-tops, and faded Ed Hardy T-shirts. The man seated behind a five-piece Yahama drum set had caramel-colored skin and a mop of gelled black hair that dangled down to his shoulders.

The band broke into a fast-paced rockabilly number. *Not bad*, Cam thought to himself and leaned back against the wall to enjoy the show. During the band's third song, Elena joined a group dancing near the stage. Cam was glad to have her as company, and had to remind himself more than once that he wasn't in the best frame of mind to start dating.

"Come join in," Elena said, returning after the song ended. The lead singer chugged water from a plastic bottle before waving a finger in the air to start the next piece.

"I can't," Cam said. "I don't think that's something a talent manager would do. Besides, I'm a terrible dancer."

"Suit yourself," Elena shouted and pushed back to the front of the room.

Near the end of the set, after Elena had rejoined him, Cam said, "I'm going to find the owner again. Would you mind staying here?" He thought it would seem more realistic to have a conversation with Shalabi on his own.

"Not at all," Elena replied. "I'll watch the next band. Though I need a break from dancing—I can't keep up with this crowd."

Cam headed into the bar area and ordered a gluten-free beer, surveying the room for the owner. He spotted the man engaged in an animated argument with a stocky man in a hooded sweatshirt jockeying a keg dolly.

When Shalabi's band finished its set, the owner made his way to Cam's side. "What did you think?" he asked.

"Not bad at all," he replied coolly. "They're a little more up-tempo than what I'm looking for, but I'd like to see the drummer play with the rest of my band. Would you introduce me to him?"

"Sure. Just let me get the headliner squared away. You can wait in my office."

The tight environs of the office reminded Cam of his own—a five-by-five-foot square partitioned off from the kitchen by a folding screen embellished with Japanese cherry blossoms. Cam sat in the space's only chair beside a folding table cluttered with receipts and a calculator the size of a bathroom scale.

Five minutes later, Jahi Shalabi entered. His barrel chest protruded from a tightly tucked T-shirt. Cam rolled back in the chair to allow Shalabi room to stand.

Cam breathed in deeply, willing his confidence to mount. "Nice set," he said and introduced himself using his real name.

"Thanks." Shalabi held a bottle of Budweiser in one hand and took a long pull from it. "We're from Cleveland so it was a bit of a hike to get here, but worth it now that I'm talking to you. Who are you with, again?"

Cam crossed one leg over the other. "I manage a number of bands in the Detroit area. One of the groups is stoner rock, but we're moving closer to mainstream—need to satisfy the producers and labels I have lined up."

"Labels, plural?" Shalabi sputtered.

"Small, but legitimate," Cam said vaguely. "The band needs a new drummer. Are you interested in seeing how you gel with them?"

"You better believe it," Shalabi said with excitement. "When and where?"

"How's Wednesday afternoon in Detroit?"

"I'll be there. I just need to speak with the owner of the place where I work. It's a two-and-a-half-hour haul from Cleveland to Detroit."

"I'll be honest," Cam said and laid out open palms. "The owner of this place told me where you guys are from and the distance concerns me. I'm lining up shows at some decent-sized venues across the Midwest in the spring, but the other band members all live north of Detroit. That's where they practice. And our recording studio is in Detroit. Is your job flexible?"

The drummer's eye twitched. "If this is my shot, I'll do whatever it takes. I manage a jewelry store so I can arrange the staff's schedule however I need. Plus, I have Ginsberg wrapped around my little finger."

"Ginsberg?" Cam asked.

"He's the owner."

"Ginsberg Jewelers? That's a high-end spot in Beachwood Place, right?" Cam tried to impart a casual tone to his voice.

"You know Ginsberg's?" Shalabi leaned against the folding screen, then had to catch it from falling. He resumed an uncomfortable straight-up position.

"My ex-wife was living in Cleveland when we got engaged," Cam lied. "I looked for rings at a few places, including Ginsberg's. I didn't buy anything from there but remember it was a nice place. How long have you been there?"

"About six years."

"I didn't think I recognized you," Cam said. "I was there almost eight years ago. I don't think I could work around so much nice jewelry without being tempted to snatch a piece or two," Cam ventured with a laugh.

Shalabi didn't flinch. Instead he steered the conversation back to music. "Tell me more about this band in Detroit."

Cam crafted a plausible yarn, then tried another approach to gauge Shalabi's reaction. "The band has a really strong nucleus. Lead guitarist is a guy named Reynold Cornell."

No effect.

"Yulian Barkov plays bass," Cam continued. Shalabi blinked impassively. He tried again, "Lead vocals is a woman. Greta Astor."

Shalabi's eyes darted out of focus for a moment.

Name recognition. Bull's-eye. "You know Greta Astor?" he queried.

Jahi Shalabi slammed his beer down on the table. It rattled. "What the hell is going on here?" he shouted. Shalabi leaned forward, pressing his face close to Cam's.

"What's your relationship with Greta Astor?" Cam blurted out with as much bravado as he could muster.

Shalabi bore down on him, his nose inches from Cam's. "I only recognize that name because a sheriff from Cleveland threw it in my face this morning!"

Cam crouched back in his chair like a snail curling into its shell.

"Who are you?" Shalabi demanded and balled his hands into fists.

Cam could smell the alcohol on his breath. "No, no one," he stammered.

"Out with it!"

Lacking a plausible explanation, he cried out, "Greta was my sister. I'm trying to find out who killed her."

Jahi Shalabi's face contorted into a sneer, but he took a step backward and relaxed his hands. "So she *was* killed," he said quietly.

"Sheriff Lackey didn't tell you?" Cam asked in disbelief.

The Egyptian man shook his head. "He danced around it. He brought me into the station this morning and grilled me on my relationship with a woman named Erin Mack—she robbed the store a while back."

"I know." Cam straightened up.

"How's that?" Shalabi asked with genuine interest, then added, "And come to think of it, how the hell do you know about me?" He plucked the Bud from the folding table and drank.

"It's a long story, but the gist of it is that Greta used to live in Cleveland and after she was killed, the police recovered a pouch of diamonds." Cam left out his role in the discovery.

Shalabi's eyes widened. "The ones from my store? They need to be returned to Mr. Ginsberg. He'll have to notify the insurance company."

"Sheriff Lackey has them," Cam explained. "I'm sure he'll contact the store owner as soon as he verifies they're real."

Shalabi shook his head with frustration. "This doesn't make sense. Where did this Greta girl get the diamonds? I know the ones Erin Mack took weren't real, because I followed her court case. What a mess— the police were on my ass for weeks. And old man Ginsberg had a heck of a time getting his insurance company to pay out."

"Did they?" Cam asked.

"Eventually. I swear there was only one set of diamonds in that safe and Erin Mack stole them. Then the crazy bitch swallowed them. I told the sheriff and some female detective who was on the phone this morning. Same as I explained to the cops at the time."

Kacey, Cam thought.

Shalabi continued, "If Erin Mack stole phony rocks, the person the police should be looking at is the guy who delivered them. I can't understand why they keep coming after me instead of him."

"Who do you get diamonds from?"

"There's a middle man, more than one actually," Shalabi said with animation and finished his beer. "They come in from overseas originally, Botswana I think. Then they get funneled through New York to be cut and polished before going out to the wholesalers. There are some big outfits that cut and polish in Tel Aviv and Johannesburg, too, but the wholesaler Ginsberg buys from uses a place in Manhattan. It's the wholesaler the sheriff should be looking at, well … their delivery man in Ohio. He *must* have been the one who swapped the real diamonds for cubic zirconia."

"You didn't check the stones when they came into the shop?"

Shalabi shook his head. "Not right away. I got complacent, and I admitted as much to Mr. Ginsberg and the police. Ginsberg's has used the same wholesaler for just about forever. R&R—Roth and Rimmel out of Allentown. We never had any problems with them, so I took it for granted that the stones were the real deal when they came in the door." He cast his eyes down, then added, "I never would have sold them. I would've figured it out when I verified their classifications for our database."

"So you think the wholesaler delivered fakes."

"There's no doubt in my mind."

"So why the delivery man?" Cam asked. "Why not someone at R&R who had handled the diamonds before handing them off to be delivered? Or why not someone with the cutting and polishing place in New York?"

"It couldn't be the outfit in New York," Shalabi said matter-of-factly. "The wholesaler inspects them thoroughly before they hand over any money."

"Unless the person doing the buying is *complacent*," Cam jabbed.

Shalabi grinned. "I doubt it. And R&R runs a tight ship. Ginsberg told me there are cameras everywhere with a guard in a control booth watching every move— like at a Las Vegas casino. Makes sense with so many diamonds moving though there. So my money's on the delivery guy."

"Did the sheriff's office check him out?"

"Sheriff Lackey told me he did way back when, after Erin Mack shat out cubic zirconia." He laughed. "Pardon my French. Ginsberg's insurance company went even further—they have an investigation unit. I heard they looked into everyone at R&R. According to Mr. Ginsberg, they didn't find a thing. Which is why that S.O.B. Lackey keeps coming back to me. But let me tell you, if your sister got killed over these diamonds and you're out for blood, the guy you want is Ray Brewer. He was the delivery man."

"Did he drive an armored car?"

Shalabi shook his head and combed his fingers through his hair. "That's only for major shipments coming in from overseas. Or Hollywood. Ray had a Prius and a bulletproof briefcase. He tried to get me to call him Q-Tip." Shalabi laughed. "The guy was a tool."

"Did you ever talk about the heist with him?" Cam asked.

"Nope. Never had the chance, even if I wanted to. That was the last delivery Ray made. To Ginsberg's at least."

"What happened?"

"I have no idea. I don't know if R&R fired him or just took Ginsberg's off of his route after the investigation. Heck, the guy might have caught a flight to the Cayman Islands for all I know."

"So you have no idea where I can find Ray Brewer?"

"Sorry, I don't."

"Can you at least describe him for me?"

"Short, white guy. Five-five, always wore sneakers. Maybe forty years old, curly brown hair. A real loser."

"Thanks." Cam extended his hand. "This all helps me a whole lot."

Shalabi shook Cam's hand. "Hey, no problem. You don't happen to be a real band manager, too?"

Chapter 21
Sunday, September 27

"A penny for your thoughts, Mother?" Cam had just finished reciting the details of his exploits with Jahi Shalabi. He set a chocolate chip Belgian waffle down in front of Darby at her kitchen table and poured the remaining batter into the iron.

"To be honest," Darby said, "I think you need to cool your jets, at least a little. You could impede Kacey's investigation by talking to suspects."

Cam's eyes fixed on the yellowish-brown ooze creeping down the waffle maker's stainless steel edging. "Kacey said the same thing," he said, looking up after a moment. "I know she appreciates bouncing ideas off of me, but she was upset that I met Jahi Shalabi. I told her on my way home last night."

"I'm not surprised." Darby smiled at her son. "Will she look for Ray Brewer? And does he go by Mr. Q or Mr. Tip?" She grinned.

"Lackey told Kacey he didn't think checking Ray out again was worth the effort. I tried to find him online after I got home but struck out."

"You want to know what I think you should do?"

"Quit while I'm behind?"

"Yes."

"I can't. You might not be on top of the chief's suspect list, but Barkov threatened Kacey and if he's guilty I want him behind bars where he can't touch her."

Darby sprang to her feet. "He threatened Kacey?"

"And me." Cam described the run-in.

"Why didn't you tell me yesterday?"

"I was too focused on your interview with Kacey and the chief."

"And Kacey never said a word about Barkov," Darby said quietly. "I suppose she couldn't have then and there at the interview."

"Did you have a real idea about what I should do?" Cam asked.

Darby sat back down. "If you insist on staying involved, I think you need to focus on the diamonds themselves."

"How so? Kacey told me that the sheriff down in Cleveland confirmed the ones I found were the real deal."

"That's a good start. I imagine the insurance company can be made whole now."

Cam nodded and stretched his back muscles.

"What I'd suggest," Darby continued, "is tracing the path of the diamonds. How did they get to Greta and what did she plan to do with them?"

Cam took a deep breath. "That's great in theory, but how do I go about it?"

"My money's on Yulian Barkov."

Cam smiled at his mother. "Because he threatened us?"

Darby touched her tongue to her upper lip, licking away a bead of syrup. "It's not just that. Kacey said he has a steady stream of dirty money passing through his business. My guess is he got his hands on the diamonds and sold them." Her eyes twinkled. "He could've pawned the stones at a discount and now he's laundering money through his snack foods business at a rate of ten thousand a month."

Cam pried open the waffle iron and pricked at his breakfast with a fork. Perfectly spongy. "Let's play that out." He set the waffle on a plate and sat across from Darby. "Assume for the moment that Ray Brewer and Yulian are in on it together. Brewer steals the diamonds, swapping them out for counterfeits, and passes along the real stones to Yulian. He shops the diamonds to a pawn shop, maybe here in Michigan to put some distance between the robbery and the sale. Yulian collects a truckload of dirty money, gives a cut to Ray—who promptly disappears—then launders the rest of it in monthly increments through his business. That all makes sense." Cam closed his eyes. "But Sheriff Lackey and Ginsburg's insurers couldn't find a thing on Brewer. And how does Greta end up with the diamonds? Did she buy them?" He answered his own question. "Probably not, otherwise she wouldn't need to hide them."

"Maybe she stole them from the pawn shop," Darby ventured.

Cam couldn't picture pretty little Greta holding up a hardcore pawnbroker with a handgun, but for the sake of argument said, "If she stole a sack of diamonds, I imagine Kacey would've seen a burglary report."

Darby shrugged.

"And why would Greta bury the diamonds in Cleveland—why not somewhere closer to Rusted Bonnet?" Cam asked.

"She did live there, Cam," Darby said. "Maybe she knew that area would be safe."

Cam laughed. "If there's one thing the Central neighborhood is not, it's safe. And I'm starting to wonder whether Greta even lived in Cleveland. All I have is her word for it."

"Well, I'm sure the agency Tatum used to find Greta verified her past employment."

"I suppose," he admitted, then perked up. "That's how I can find the family Greta used to work for—I can contact the agency."

"It's certainly worth a try," Darby agreed.

Cam poured maple syrup over his waffle, rivulets splaying like tentacles. "There's one other thing that's been gnawing at me. And it doesn't mesh with Jahi Shalabi's theory that Ray Brewer was the thief. Let's say Brewer switches cubic zirconia for the real gems prior to delivery. The very next day Erin Mack just happens to rob Ginsberg's? Two separate thieves making a play for the same stones on back-to-back days? It doesn't smell right."

Darby smiled. "You're good at this, Cam. Now that you put it that way, it doesn't make sense to me, either."

* * *

The yellow pages listed more pawnbrokers within a forty-mile radius of Detroit than Starbucks—134 to be exact. After finishing a midmorning job for Peachy Kleen, Cam started with the shops closest to Rusted Bonnet and worked his way south toward Detroit.

The owners of the first three spots Cam visited all refused to divulge any information about their customers. Each claimed to be an ardent supporter of the police's efforts to crack down on theft, but insisted that customer privacy trumped the curiosity of a well-intentioned citizen. The addresses of the fourth and fifth pawnbrokers matched a condemned building and a nail salon touting its grand opening, respectively.

At two o'clock, Cam ventured into Grady's Pawn in Madison Heights. Jabs of stale cigar smoke scuffled with the murmur of buzzing flies for Cam's sensory attention. A gray-skinned man flipped through a stamp album on a metal desk near the front door under a comically large security camera. A younger man leaned against a stack of audio equipment forming a pylon on one side of the counter at the center of the shop.

The young man introduced himself as "Lucky." His Fresh Prince high-tops matched the shop's dated décor. "Need to sell your wedding ring for cash?" he asked.

Cam shook his head. "I'm not a seller, but I am looking for jewelry."

A toothy smile crossed Lucky's lips. "Best selection anywhere's right here." He pointed toward a display case to his left.

Cam didn't turn his head. Instead, he said, "Do you do business with Yulian Barkov?"

Lucky's grin disappeared, and he cinched his lips together.

"Did I strike a nerve?" Cam asked.

"You could say that," he said through clenched teeth.

"Is he a regular?"

"Not lately, man. He doesn't mess with us anymore."

"Why's that?" Cam cracked his knuckles.

"You a cop?" Lucky asked.

Cam shook his head. "Just a guy trying to find out if Yulian sold any diamonds."

The counterman drew a pack of cigarettes out from under the counter and rapped it against his palm. "Never seen Yulian with diamonds. Gold coins is what he's after. And the man be buying, not selling."

"But you don't sell to him now?"

"Nope. The boss put him on the naughty list some six months ago."

"Why's that?" Cam asked. The man flipping stamp album pages stopped to listen.

"Boss says his money's dirty. Only a matter of time before the cops start asking questions."

Cam's muscles tensed in anticipation. "Dirty?" he repeated with an air of indifference.

Lucky slid a cigarette from the pack and rolled it between his thumb and middle finger, waiting. Can took the hint, pulled a twenty dollar bill from his wallet, and pushed it across the counter.

Like a living statue on a beachfront boardwalk, Lucky sprang into action as soon as the bill hit his hand. "Grady—he's the owner of this joint—found out good 'ol Yulian was buying gold coins from us, then going to the Cash-for-Gold place on Eleven Mile to sell them."

"Now how did Grady find that out?" The stamp collector chimed in. "Barkov ain't so bad—I gave him directions one day and the man bought me an 1857 one-center. That baby's worth thirty bucks."

"Mind yo' own damn business," Lucky snapped at the older man. "No one cares about yo' stamps." Then he smiled. "I'm surprised you can hear us all the way over there, deaf as you are."

"I'm not as old as you are rude, son," the man shot back.

Lucky waived a hand at him, then turned his attention back to Cam. "Grady and Johnny Chiu at the Cash-for-Gold place are friendly-like. They got to talking one day over some beers. Johnny told him he had a Russian guy—a regular seller—who brought him a fat stack of Maple Leafs."

"Those are gold coins from Canada," The older man chimed in.

Lucky ignored him and said, "Grady sold Yulian a heap that very morning. So the two of them compared notes, then checked their books. Eight times in eight months, your man Yulian bought gold here at Grady's then turned around and sold it to Johnny. Same day every time. No reason to do that 'cept taking out some laundry and getting himself some fresh bills. Clean as a virgin's honeypot."

Cam smothered a laugh. "So Grady cut him off?"

"You better believe it, friend. Next time Yulian came in I told him his bills wasn't no good here anymore."

"And what happened to the money he paid the shop from the other purchases?"

Lucky snapped his fingers. "Gone. This here's a cash business. Comes in, goes out. Besides, we sold him good gold. Why should Grady get the short end of the stick?"

"But he does make a profit."

"A little surcharge, sure. Same with Johnny no doubt. It's only right—have to earn a living. But for Yulian, I expect eighty percent of clean money's better than a hundred percent of the dirty stuff."

"So you told Yulian to get lost. Didn't want to wreck your reputation."

"Man, I don't need anybody else wreckin' it. I can do that on my own." He smiled, teeth gleaming. "You sure you're not a cop and just forgot? You sure sound like one."

Cam laid a second twenty on the counter. "I'm not, but I know one pretty well. Police up in Rusted Bonnet have been looking at Yulian Barkov for laundering. I suspect they'll want to hear what you and Mr. Grady have to say."

"Mr. Jones," Lucky said, then answered Cam's quizzical look. "Grady Jones."

* * *

Cam spent the next five hours slogging in and out of seventeen more pawn shops north of Detroit. Just before 7:45 in the evening, he hit pay dirt.

Chapter 22

"Becka found her mother," Missy blurted through the telephone. Cam had just arrived home when his mobile rang.

Cam rubbed each of his eyes in turn with a knuckle, then pulled a dining room chair in front of Bait's tank. "That's amazing!" he said into the phone and stepped toward the kitchen. "Is she back?"

"She's on her way now. With Malika in tow. Becka found her in Queens." Cam could sense the relief in her voice.

"Why did it take her so long to get back to you?" Cam asked.

"She said she didn't want me to worry about her," Missy said. "But really, I think she just wanted to go it alone."

"How did she find her?"

"The easy way. You and I are dummies."

"How so?" Cam pulled a Founders All Day IPA from the refrigerator. IPAs were Cam's sole concession to gluten—worth the discomfort it would cause his stomach later. He uncapped it and sat in the dining room to watch Bait swim laps.

"Social media."

Cam groaned. "Of course. Which must have been why her father told her it was the devil."

"Exactly. As soon as she moved to the States, Malika started her search by calling on shipbuilders in San Diego and Norfolk."

"I think Bath, Maine, has a big shipyard, too," Cam said.

"True. I suppose Gakuru came to Rusted Bonnet because he took whatever job he could find—as long as the company was willing to sponsor his visa."

"I'm surprised Becka moved here with him."

"I'm not. She told me she'd always wanted to visit the US, so when her father decided to move, she came along. She had no other family in South Africa and, to her, America sounded glamorous."

Cam drank from his bottle of beer. "Rusted Bonnet and glamorous don't usually go hand-in-hand."

"Ain't that the truth," Missy said. "But not only did Malika call the shipyards, she got herself onto social media. From Emmanuel, she knew Afya Njoroges was going by the name of Nombecko Blom."

"But she wasn't on Facebook or Twitter or Instagram."

"Not until a few days ago. Becka told me that as soon as she read the articles and put two-and-two together, she created accounts on five different social media sites. There aren't many women with the name Malika Njoroges. She popped up just like that! Becka sent her a message, and she replied less than six hours later. After a tearful reunion over the phone, Becka took off for New York."

"In my truck," Cam said with a laugh. "I gladly would've lent it to her."

"She knows that," Missy said. "But she said she was on an emotional roller coaster and didn't want to break down in front of you. Or me for that matter. Her car isn't trustworthy enough to drive the seven hundred miles to New York. Neither's mine. She could've rented a car or even flown, but as soon as she found out where her mother lived, she wanted to get on the road as soon as possible. She told me she'll pay you for wear and tear of course."

Cam shook his head. "That won't be necessary." He paused, then asked, "Do you suppose she'll move to Queens or ask Malika to come here? Or even move to Mombasa?"

"I certainly hope they decide to live here," Missy said, sounding wistful. "But as long as they're together, that's all that matters."

Chapter 23

"I have major news on the investigation," Kacey said, her backside bouncing in a staccato rhythm on the edge of Cam's leather sectional. She had just tucked Emma into the twin bed in Cam's guest room, which was slowly morphing into a space of the girl's own.

Cam handed her a mug of hot chocolate, made with milk, real cocoa powder, and sugar. "So do I," he said, blanching apologetically as he sat on an opposite corner. "You first." He hoped to delay the inevitable rebuffing.

Kacey raised her eyes toward the ceiling, then smiled sweetly. "I know who put the nail hole in the floorboard at the top of the steps."

Cam choked, hot chocolate flying from his mouth. "You know who killed Greta?" he shouted, then he wiped the front of his shirt with a sleeve.

"Shush." Kacey set her mug on a napkin on the glass coffee table and rubbed her hands together. "I have no idea who killed her," she said with a drip of disappointment.

"But surely whoever put that hole there did it," Cam protested. "Who was it?"

"Greta."

"No way," Cam uttered with disbelief. "Whoever said they saw her do it must be lying."

"Find the liar and you've found your killer?" Kacey asked.

"Exactly! The final nail in the tire. Who told you it was Greta?"

Kacey smiled meekly. "Nicolas McRae. He's four."

"One of the twins?" Cam whimpered, feeling deflated. "I didn't think you were going to question them."

"I didn't, per se. And the boy still doesn't know Greta was murdered," Kacey assured him. "At the chief's insistence, I went back to question Dutch. We were talking in his kitchen—I asked him flat out if he made the nail hole at the top of the stairs. Before he could answer, I heard a small voice say, 'I saw someone hammer the stair.' I turned and saw Nicolas standing in the passage from the dining room to the kitchen. He must have just wandered in.

"Dutch asked him who he saw. Nicolas said, 'Miss Greta, Daddy, before she moved away forever.' As soon as he said it, my heart sank. I asked if he remembered when she had hammered the stair. Nicolas didn't have a precise recollection, just 'a long time ago.' 'Since Christmas?' I asked. He thought it was after Christmas, closer to his mother's birthday. That's in April."

"Greta put a nail hole in the floor five months before she was killed?"

"It appears so." Kacey crossed her legs. Yellow light from a pair of wall sconces reflected off of her toned calves. "I suppose it helps in a way."

"How in the world does that help?" Cam gasped. "Greta set up a trip wire to kill herself?"

"No, silly," Kacey replied. "It helps cement *your* theory about how Greta died. If Greta was killed outside the McRaes' house and carried back inside, then the killer didn't need to string twine across the top of the staircase."

Cam sighed. "The killer was lucky enough to have Greta hammer in a nail hole exactly where he needed it, months ahead of time?"

"I don't think it was luck at all," Kacey said. "I think the murderer spotted the hole and it gave him the idea to concoct a ruse to throw us off—the evidence would point squarely to someone who had an opportunity to set up a trip wire."

"Dutch as the fall guy?"

Kacey nodded.

"I can't believe I never noticed the hole. I must've vacuumed that stair runner half a dozen times since April. Samantha did, too."

"It's not something most people notice. And even if you did, why would it stand out—homes have all sorts of minute building flaws."

"You said before the murderer is a 'him.' Do you think it was a man?"

"Not necessarily. Greta weighed very little. A woman could have carried her up the steps almost as easily as a man."

Cam sipped his hot chocolate, savoring the taste of froth against his upper lip with the tip of his tongue. "Any chance Dutch is pulling a fast one—told Nicolas to say he saw Greta hammer in that hole?"

Kacey stood. "I hadn't thought of that." She started to pace about the room. "Dutch's idea about why Greta might have hammered into the top step seemed so plausible."

"What did he say?"

Kacey plopped back down and picked up her mug. "That she must have done it when she removed the baby gate in April. Apparently, they used to have a swinging door at the top of the steps so the twins wouldn't fall down the stairs. Like the one we had when Emma was born. Neither Dutch nor Tatum had gotten around to taking it down once Nicolas and Sophie were old enough to manage the steps on their own. I imagine Greta got sick of opening it anytime she went up or down the stairs. According to Dutch, the bottom of the gate used to rub along the top step. He and I took a close look, and on one side of the carpet runner—the side with the hole—there are two nails driven into the step, flush with the wood. So we figured that when Greta took down the baby gate, she realized the board was loose and nailed it down herself."

"But then why was there an *empty* hole?"

"If she hammers like I do, I'm surprised there's only one!" Kacey laughed. "I bend a nail or two for every one I get to go in straight. Greta probably bent a nail halfway down, so she pulled it out."

Cam stood and cracked open a window. The early autumn air gently chilled his cheeks.

"So if the nail hole is a dead end, does this mean my mother is officially off of the suspect list?"

"She is in my book, not that she was ever on it. But yes, even Bernie admits that Darby is pretty much in the clear."

"Thank goodness."

"Now, tell me what your news is, Cam," Kacey said, then added with an exaggerated simper, "You do realize I'm getting a little tired of scolding you, don't you?"

"I know," Cam acquiesced. "I can't help myself. I think I'm as engrossed in this investigation as you are."

"Except it's my job."

Cam tried his most winning smile.

"Not working," Kacey said but allowed a giggle to creep in. "It is exciting, isn't it?" she said. "I've never felt so invigorated about my job. But the chief is not happy with you."

"I suppose I'll have to burn that bridge when I come to it. Can't you just tell him you found out everything that I did? I'm not looking for credit."

"I can't do that." Her face appeared rich with regret. "Okay, what have you been up to since you were hanging out in college bars?"

"It was just one." He hunched forward and conveyed the substance of his conversation with Lucky. "Not that it necessarily has a bearing on Greta's death," he added in summation.

"Maybe, maybe not, but it's really good information. And that's not even your big news, is it?"

Cam shook his head. "You can read me like the back of my book."

"You're on a roll," Kacey groaned. "Don't keep me waiting."

"Reynold Cornell," Cam said. "He *was* involved with the diamonds."

Kacey's eyes popped open. Full moons. "You know that for sure?"

Cam grinned. "After I left Grady's, I trolled another dozen and a half pawn shops. The last one I tried was Lasky Park Pawn in Hamtramck. I spoke with the owner, a Polish guy named Dave Bielak. He didn't know Yulian, but when I asked whether he'd heard anything about a cache of twenty-six loose diamonds, the man's eyes lit up."

"He'd seen them?"

"I don't think so. At first he clammed up—he seemed nervous. But I suspect his better judgment ruled the day. He said he hadn't done anything wrong so he figured it was better to talk to me rather than be accused of hiding something."

"What did he know?" Kacey set down her cocoa and rubbed the thighs of her dark jeans.

"About three weeks ago, a man fitting Reynold's description went into Lasky Park Pawn and started asking Bielak questions about his interest in diamonds. Of course, he was interested, he said—he dealt in all kinds of jewelry. But Bielak's no dummy. Most stones come through his shop set in rings or necklaces, so he's wary of loose gems, especially in large quantities. Reynold didn't come right out and say he had twenty-six diamonds, but according to Bielak, he said enough to trigger his internal alarm."

"That was a mistake," Kacey said. "Reynold should have sold them off piecemeal, taken them one at a time to separate pawn shops."

"Bielak said thanks but no thanks, especially since Reynold didn't even have the diamonds on him. But Reynold pushed hard—he was anxious to find a buyer. Or at least someone who knew how to fence them properly. So for a hundred dollars, Bielak gave him a name. A guy who deals in channels that may not be *completely pristine*. Those were his words."

"Anyone we know?"

"I think so." Cam reminded her about the Cuban his mother had seen at the Stagger. "Based on the physical description Bielak gave me, I think he's our man. Mateo Olivia. Dark wavy hair, early forties, piercing eyes—black as night. I saw him at the Laundromat with Reynold a while back."

"Any idea where he lives?"

"Bielak didn't know, but he's pretty sure it's somewhere in the Detroit metro area. He gave me Mateo's mobile number, the same one he gave to Reynold." Cam hopped over to the coat closet in the front hall, rooted around in the pockets of his windbreaker, and came back with a slip of paper. He handed it to Kacey.

"Thanks, Cam. You'll have to come down to the station to make a statement. This information is genuinely helpful. The chief won't like the source, but I know he appreciates the results as much as I do. And the next time you have a hunch, please call me first. Not afterward."

Cam begrudgingly nodded. "Okay."

"I'll talk to the pawn shop guy, then bring Reynold in for questioning and track down this Mateo Olivia. I just hope my interrogation skills are up to snuff. I haven't had much experience outside of small-time crooks. To be honest, I don't think Bernie has either."

"He does seem a little green behind the ears."

Kacey rolled her eyes.

"You'll do wonderfully, I'm sure," Cam said. After a moment's thought, he added, "I just remembered something Reynold said to me in the Stagger. I was in there shortly after Greta died. When I offered my condolences, Reynold said something like, 'I'm going to kill that bloody man.' I asked him who he was talking about, but I think he fudged his answer, said 'whoever killed Greta.' I had the feeling he had someone in particular in mind."

"Mateo?"

"That would be my guess."

"Hmm." Kacey tapped a slender forefinger against her chin. "Reynold takes Dave Bielak's advice and hooks up with Mateo. The Cuban listens to the story, tells Reynold he's 'in.'"

"Then Mateo knocks off Greta, which is why Reynold said he'd 'bloody' kill him," Cam interjected. "But before Mateo can get to the diamonds, I find them first."

"Possibly, but that assumes Reynold told Mateo where the diamonds were buried. We don't even know if Reynold knew where the pouch was hidden—if he did, why wouldn't he make a run for them as soon as he found out Greta died? Plus, if Mateo murdered Greta to get to the diamonds, why not kill Reynold, too? Cut off another tie."

Cam's hands jittered in frustration. "Whether or not Mateo killed her, my guess is that Reynold thinks he did. Of course, when I saw them together at the Laundromat, they weren't arguing. So maybe they made nice. Or maybe they were in on Greta's murder together." Cam paused, then said, "The text message. The big score. That makes sense now."

"Mateo found a buyer for the diamonds?"

"Exactly," Cam said. "Mateo finds a buyer and tells Reynold he needs to move fast. Only Reynold doesn't have the diamonds so he texts Greta, asking her to meet him on the street at one thirty in the morning. The perfect time to crack her skull and eliminate her from the picture."

"Who does that?" Kacey asked. "Reynold or Mateo?"

"Maybe both of them," Cam speculated.

"Maybe," Kacey said, still wary. "But I keep coming back to the fact that you found the diamonds on Tuesday. And Greta died on Friday night. Why would anyone kill her if they didn't know where they were hidden? And if either of them knew, why were they still buried in the cemetery three days later?"

Chapter 24
Monday, September 28

"If you're so into the maple leafs, I suggest you buy a Canadian flag," Yulian Barkov said. He sat on the top step of the porch, his back facing Cam and Emma and they stepped outside.

A pinch of nerves shot up Cam's back. "Mr. Barkov, I'm not interested in your business," Cam said. "Besides, I have my seven year-old here with me."

Barkov didn't turn. "You were interested yesterday."

"Daddy, can we go?" Emma asked. "I have school!" She was dressed in a long-sleeved shirt, denim skirt, and black tights.

"Sweetie, just give me a couple of minutes to speak with this man. I know you just ate breakfast, but go into the kitchen and you can have a few of the pita chips you like. In the pantry."

"Daddy, I need to go!"

He kissed her forehead. "Just a couple of minutes, I promise."

The girl scuttled inside and Cam shut the door firmly behind her. He turned his attention to Yulian who had risen and turned to face Cam, one foot planted on the porch, the other a step lower.

"How dare you come to my home," Cam growled.

"How dare you try to bring down me and my business. I have ears everywhere." Yulian smiled broadly, his eyes wrinkling. "What are you after?"

"Nothing anymore," Cam said. "Listen, my mother was a suspect in Greta Astor's murder. I was trying to do anything I could to help her."

"Including pointing the blame at me?"

Cam leaned back against the front door. He wanted to be able to twist the knob and slip inside as fast as he could if necessary. "Honestly, I don't care who the chief arrests, as long as it's not my mother. But the police found something out last night that took her off the hook, so I'm done. I promise."

Yulian shook his head. "A little late. The police are going to come down on me hard after they speak with Grady and Johnny. Not for murder, of course—I had nothing to do with that. But you, my friend, have made my life difficult. And I don't take well to difficulty."

Sweat dripped down Cam's temples despite the chill in the air. "What now?" he asked. "Are you going to shoot me in cold blood?"

Yulian rubbed his hands together. "Of course not, Mr. Reddick. You have a daughter who needs to go to school. But you remember my associates from the other night, right?"

Cam nodded.

"They do what I ask. And I ask all kinds of things. Not that I expect to be arrested for buying and selling gold coins, but if it comes to that, my associates will request that you forget any conversations you had at the pawn shop yesterday."

Cam fidgeted. He was supposed to go to the police station and make a written statement as soon as he dropped off Emma.

Yulian seemingly read his mind. "And anything you've said already about it will have been a lie. You were simply trying to cast suspicion away from your mother. And you regret that decision. It's as simple as that. I imagine Grady and his young shopkeeper and

Mr. Johnny Chiu will either decide that they have terrible memories or are liars as well." Yulian laid a hand on a porch post. "Understood?"

"Yes," Cam murmured.

* * *

Laminate "knotty pine" walls and steel gray doors— the Rusted Bonnet village police station blended the best of cheap and dirt cheap. At noon, wedged into a narrow upholstered chair in the waiting room, Cam scanned a copy of *American Snowmobiler*. A bottled redhead flipped pages of a dog-eared King James Bible behind the station's front desk.

Five minutes into an article about deep powder in Minnesota's Iron Range, Kacey trudged into the station behind Reynold Cornell and an officer in uniform. When Reynold saw Cam, a look of confusion passed across his face, then he promptly spat on the epoxy floor.

Kacey shot Cam a wink and was gone, passing through the door to the interior of the station.

Ten minutes later she returned. "Mr. Reddick, can you please come this way?"

Cam followed her to a windowless room, barren save for a rectangular table and four chairs the color of aluminum foil. Kacey handed him a set of forms and a pen. "Can you fill these out, please?" she said formally. "One statement for each of your conversations yesterday, the one you had with Mr. Lucky Moncrief about Mr. Yulian Barkov and the other with Mr. David Bielak about Mr. Reynold Cornell. Officer Davis will be just outside the door should you have any questions." She looked over her shoulder at a young African American woman with a short bob and holstered handgun.

"Would you like some coffee or a glass of water?" Kacey asked.

Instead of answering, Cam whispered, "Are you going to interrogate Reynold now?"

Kacey just smiled. "I'll be back to check on you when you've finished," she said, turned, and strode through the open door. Officer Davis shut Cam inside with no more than his thoughts and an itchy forearm, thanks to an insatiable mosquito in the waiting room.

Cam focused on the task at hand, transferring his recollection about the exchange he had with Dave Bielak to paper in painstaking detail. The air inside the room begged for a humidifier—he regretted not taking Kacey up on her offer for a glass of water.

After twenty minutes, Cam finished his written discourse about Reynold and Bielak. He knocked on the door and Officer Davis collected his form.

"What about the other one?" she asked.

"I'd like to speak with the deputy about it, please."

The officer nodded and asked Cam to remain inside. At his request, she fetched Cam a drink. He spent the next forty minutes in the desolate box of a room scratching his arm and sipping lukewarm water from a plastic cup.

* * *

"Yulian threatened me," Cam said. "This morning when I was with Emma."

"What?" Kacey's face flattened as she set foam cups brimming with black coffee on the interview room table and sat across from Cam.

Cam filled her in and concluded by saying, "I think that stamp collector at Grady's must have tipped Yulian off. He probably figured to get another pricey one-center out of it."

"Is Emma okay?" Kacey asked.

"She's fine. She had no idea what Yulian was doing and I shuttled her inside before she could figure it out."

Kacey sighed. "You should've told me right away."

"Sorry," Cam said. "You had Reynold and then Officer Davis was standing right here when you gave me the paperwork."

"She said you didn't write a statement about what Lucky said."

"Not yet," Cam said. "I'm not just afraid for me, but for you and Emma."

"Well, I'd recommend that you write out the statement," Kacey said and managed a weak smile. "His goose is cooked as it so happens."

"He killed Greta?" Cam asked in disbelief.

"No, but Reynold told us what Yulian's been up to—the source of the money he's been laundering. Both through his snack food business and the gold coin scheme."

"Are you going to arrest him?"

"Yulian? Definitely. The chief is sending a pair of officers to pick him up now."

"Thank goodness. What's he been doing to bring in his extra cash?"

Kacey closed her eyes and breathed in deeply. Her thick dark hair was set in a short ponytail. The cut of her police uniform made her slender shoulders appear more boxy than Cam knew them to be. "I feel I owe you a little, Cam, but keep this between us, please."

He nodded.

"According to Reynold, Yulian's running a bogus check scam. It's quite ingenious, actually. He starts by sending out checks to thousands of people—it's easy enough to print them online—along with correspondence on letterhead from a fabricated law firm, indicating that the recipient's part of a large class-action settlement. He creates a website for the firm and dummy Internet articles on the settlement. Every time he runs the scam, he starts fresh—new firm name, new web information, and a different brand or company that's the subject of the class action. Yulian always chooses a big name—Cheerios, Home Depot, McDonald's. One that almost anyone who receives a check would've patronized. That way, no one wonders why they'd been selected. And most people won't pass up the chance to cash in on free money."

"The checks bounce?" Cam hazarded.

Kacey nodded.

"How does Yulian get money out of it?" Cam sipped his coffee—it tasted like cigarette ash.

"The day after he mass mails *settlement* checks, Yulian sends a follow-up letter from the same phony law firm. The second letter explains that a mistake was made—the recipient's still entitled to a settlement but only for half as much as was written on the check. It instructs the person to cash the check they received but to wire back half of the amount to a specified account. If they cash the check and don't wire back the appropriate amount, the letter says that they'll be penalized by their bank."

"And Yulian collects the fifty percent wire payments?"

"Yes. According to Reynold, in any given scam, Yulian sent out some three thousand checks for about two hundred dollars each—big enough for people to cash, but not so large as to raise any eyebrows. And he never made them for an exact amount—more like $198.47 or $201.16, because that's what people have come to expect from these class-action settlements. Of the three thousand checks, most would cash them and forty percent or so would wire half of the money back out of fear of receiving the threatened penalty. So every time he ran the scam, he'd net over a hundred grand. Then he'd simply pull the money out of the account in cash and close it down. If any of the authorities looked hard enough, Yulian was afraid that the cash could be tied back to him—even though he used a fake ID to set up the wire account—so he laundered it.

"Through his snack food business and by buying and selling gold coins."

"Exactly."

"Amazing," Cam said. "So if the people who were conned wired a hundred bucks to Yulian but cashed two hundred, they're still better off, right? It's just the banks that take the hit?"

"I doubt it." Kacey scratched her earlobe. "A week or two after a bad check is deposited or cashed, if the bank can't find an account to pull the money from—the drawing bank—then the check bounces. I can't imagine Yulian was writing checks from the account that was receiving the wires—more likely, there was no real account on the outgoing end. And when a check bounces, whoever deposited or cashed it is responsible—the bank deducts the amount from their account plus a fee. So the bank breaks even—or makes money from the fee—but the customers lose the two hundred they deposited plus the extra hundred bucks they wired and the fee they pay the bank for trying to deposit a bad check."

"Reynold Cornell gave you all of this information?"

"It was like taking candy from, well, you know. When we told him we had a credible witness who insisted that he tried to sell stolen diamonds, Reynold turned from tough guy to frightened turtle in a matter of seconds. The chief told him we knew that he and Yulian had been frequenting local pawnbrokers. At the mention of Yulian's name, Reynold saw an out. My guess is that the pair of them have worked together on any number of other scams. Reynold said, as far as he knew, Yulian didn't know anything about the diamonds. But he told us all about the check scam for leniency on fencing charges. Unless we find out that he was in on the murder, of course."

"Which I suppose he denies," Cam said and raked a hand through his close-cropped hair.

"Of course. He claims he didn't even know the diamonds were stolen—Greta told him they were left to her by her grandmother when she passed on. And she needed to sell them to support her invalid mother back in Germany. Only Granny didn't leave any certificates of authority, so reputable jewelers wouldn't touch them."

"Quite a tale. Do you believe him?"

"Was Reynold dumb enough to fall for a story like that? Possibly, especially if he was enamored with Greta."

"Why wouldn't she just sell them on eBay or Craigslist?"

"My guess is that Greta was worried about the feds monitoring repeat high-dollar sales on those sites, so instead she had Reynold play the part of puppet."

"The list of names I found in her stuffed skunk."

Kacey nodded. "The six stooges. Potential flunkies to do her dirty work. Reynold was probably the most appealing—he has a real job, plus he's as good looking as Greta was, so spending time with him wouldn't raise any eyebrows. Reynold insisted that Greta didn't pay him. He offered to sell her grandmother's diamonds as a favor. Probably to get into her pants."

"Did he ever have the diamonds?"

"He says he never even saw them. I believe him on that front. I think those diamonds went from Ginsberg Jewelers to the Woodland Cemetery. Obviously there's a step or two in between that we're missing, but my gut tells me they never left the state of Ohio." She put her cup to her lips, then set it back down. "Reynold said he scoured lowbrow jewelry shops and pawn dealers looking for a taker. After striking out at place after place, he strong-armed Dave Bielak to give him the contact information for Mateo Olivia. Mateo's fee was ten percent—which Greta agreed to pay. But according to Reynold, Mateo was still talking to his black market contacts, looking for a buyer."

"What about the 'big score' message he sent to Greta?" Cam asked.

"He stuck to his guns—he says he didn't send that message or see Greta after she left the Stagger on the night she was killed."

"Someone lifted his phone?"

"That's his story."

Chapter 25

Becka Blom and her mother, Malika Njoroges, looked strikingly similar, right down to their dimpled chins and matching gold nose studs. Shortly after Cam left the police station, Becka finally contacted him—they had returned to Rusted Bonnet. Cam asked the pair to meet him at Peachy Kleen.

Becka handed him the keys to Montana and slumped into the center of a vinyl couch. She buried her face in her hands. "I'm so sorry," she said in a muffled voice. "I'll understand if you want to fire me." Cam could see tears streaming out from between her fingers.

He sat beside her and laid a hand delicately on her back. "It's okay, Becka. I know the whole story. And no, I don't want you to go anywhere."

"Mr. Reddick, we will repay you for use of your vehicle, for miles traveled as well as time lost," Malika said with careful diction in the Queen's English.

Cam looked up, then stood. "That won't be necessary, ma'am. I'm just happy you've been reunited."

Malika smiled. "It is such an amazing thing to see my daughter. All grown up. So beautiful. So polite."

Becka sniffled. "I can't believe I'm here with you. I feel incredibly happy, but sad at the same time. We missed so many years together."

Malika sat beside her daughter and placed a wrinkled hand over her knee. "Many years were lost, but we now have all of the years ahead. I feel blessed."

Cam collected the thoughts that had been lurking at the back of his mind. "Ms. Njoroges, I don't know what your plans are, but if you and Becka decide to stay in Rusted Bonnet, I'd like to offer you a position as a housekeeper with my company." Cam wasn't certain he could scrounge up enough work for another full-time cleaner, but he also didn't want to lose Becka to New York. Or Kenya. Besides, he reasoned, with another full-time staffer, he could spend less of his own time cleaning and more time marketing Peachy Kleen's services.

Malika's ebony eyes radiated with a beatific glow. "Yes, Mr. Reddick. I would like that very much, and I will provide you with an excellent reference from my employer in Queens. My daughter and I are most grateful for your generosity."

Becka stood abruptly, threw her arms around Cam, and kissed his cheeks. Cam flushed at the touch of Becka's lips. After a second, he awkwardly pulled himself out of the hug. *Missy is a lucky woman,* he thought to himself.

Becka looked at her mother. "I told you how nice he is, Mama."

"Yes, a very nice man, Afya," Malika agreed.

* * *

Tuesday, September 29

If I could just jump without falling, Cam thought, *I could touch the clouds.* With one boot planted firmly on either side of Jasmine Devlin's roof ridge under a low blanket of heavy gray billows, his sentiments ping-ponged between infinite freedom and abject claustrophobia.

Jasmine lived in a World War II-era brick ranch tucked into the shadow of a once magnificent, but now weather-beaten, Edwardian. On the other side of her perfectly pruned front yard, rose bushes climbed brown latticework to form a visual barrier against the gravel lot of the village recycling center.

Jasmine had asked Cam to clean the inside of her chimney ahead of the upcoming winter. As a male member of the housekeeping trade, he was routinely asked to take on less traditional tasks—mold remediation, insulation installment, plumbing, and now, chimney sweeping. Guided by his natural instincts and YouTube videos, he always said yes, not willing to let business slip through his fingers.

Cam connected a four-foot fiberglass rod to a square wire brush, raised it overhead like Ben Franklin hoisting a kite toward the heavens, and thrust it firmly down the chimney. He vigorously scrubbed black creosote from the interior walls while methodically lowering the rod. When he could reach no further down, Cam screwed a second fiberglass rod to the end of the first and pushed the brush deeper, then added a third, sweeping downward until the brush touched the stone base of Jasmine's fireplace with an agreeable *thunk*. Satisfied, he pulled the twelve-foot length of rod and brush out and repeated the exercise three more times.

A light rain began to fall as Cam stripped off his Kevlar gloves and face mask. He screwed the cap back onto the chimney top, tossed his equipment and gear to the ground, then briskly climbed down from the roof.

"Good thing you called," Cam said to Jasmine, folding up his ladder. He replaced his boots for sneakers on her front porch. "You had quite a bit of gunk in there. You must use the fireplace a lot."

"I certainly do enjoy a nice fire during the winter months," Jasmine said, holding open the door. She was dressed in a shapeless knit sweater over gray sweatpants cinched at the ankles.

"I just need to take off the plastic I put over your fireplace doors then clean out everything that I swept down the chimney. It shouldn't take more than twenty minutes."

He followed her through a narrow hallway to a prim living room. Faux gilding covered the wooden frames of every chair, table, and mirror in the room. Cam gently moved several pieces of furniture into the hall and laid a plastic sheet over the floor in front of the fireplace, then slowly removed the sheath covering its doors.

"Thank you for being so careful," Jasmine said. She sat on the edge of a chaise lounge, her back ramrod straight. "I certainly don't want any soot to get on the furniture." She patted the white fabric beside her.

Using a toy beach shovel, Cam scooped a combination of ashes and creosote from around the fireplace grate into a heavy-duty trash bag. "The décor in here is marvelous," he observed. It wasn't his style, but Jasmine had clearly spent a significant amount of time putting the room together.

"My one bit of luxury," she said. Despite crimping, muddy brown hair fell flat against the sides of her face. "You can never be too careful with money, especially now."

"It doesn't seem like the economy is ever favorable," Cam said without turning around.

"That's certainly true—Addison and I learned firsthand."

"How's that?"

"My sister and I tried our hand in a little business venture a couple of years ago, before you moved back to the village. You didn't know?"

"No," Cam said.

"We opened a boutique on the north end of town— Amore Gifts and Treasures. But we didn't last long. Mind you, I never had grand visions. I just wanted a place to wile away some of my lonely hours, talk Italian and French culture with my patrons. And maybe bring in a little extra money. One can only earn so much as a librarian."

"What happened?" Cam asked, continuing to shovel refuse from the fireplace.

"A combination of things, I suppose." Jasmine sighed heavily. "I should've taken a small-business class before starting. Between the lease, inventory, and advertising costs, we needed a pretty sizeable loan. And I completely overestimated the number of paying customers we'd have. There was good foot traffic for the first two weeks—people always flock to a new shop, but our goods were too upscale for the villagers. We'd have ladies fawn for an hour over a Limoges porcelain box, then walk out the door with nothing more than a tin of English breakfast tea. If we were *lucky*."

"How long were you open?"

"For about a year. Addison wasn't working at the time, and she put in at least eight hours a day. I spent every waking minute I wasn't at the library at Amore. I suppose the only good thing that came of it is that my sister and I grew closer. But the bank debt is killing us."

Cam turned and caught Jasmine with a roguish grin on her face. She quickly flipped it into a frown. He shifted his attention back to the fireplace, then asked, "How much are you and Addison in the hole?"

She didn't equivocate: "We owe fifty thousand to Bank of America. It would've been sixty, but I found a man who deals in European curios to buy our inventory."

"He wouldn't happen to be from Cleveland, would he?" Cam asked with abandon.

"No," Jasmine replied calmly. "What a strange question. He was from Thunder Bay, Ontario."

* * *

"It's about time," Samantha Krause grumbled to Kacey when she and Emma arrived at Peachy Kleen. Samantha and Cam had been crafting a supply order in the bull pen.

Emma ran to Cam and jumped into his arms. He twirled her in the air.

"Daddy, who was that man at your house yesterday?" Emma asked.

"No one, sweetie," Cam said.

"I have a feeling nobody here is going to see him for a very long time," Kacey said, then mouthed, "The judge denied Yulian bail," to Cam.

Kacey set Emma's backpack on the floor and turned her attention to Samantha. "About time? I told Cam I was bringing Emma by after school let out."

Samantha shook her head with apparent frustration. "No, no. It's been nearly a week since I called Chief Leftwich. He promised someone would investigate and be in touch with me. But I've heard nary a word."

Kacey leaned a hip against the wall. "Investigate what?" she asked.

"The incident at the Bear Claw!" Samantha looked at Emma and lowered her voice. "In the restroom."

Kacey put a hand to her chin—a silent question mark.

"How could the chief not have told you?" Samantha asked in disbelief. "There's a criminal running amok!" She took a short breath, then whispered, "Someone put shoe polish on the, um, seat in the ladies' room. Had I not laid down one of those paper covers I would have sat right in it!"

Kacey laughed, then covered her mouth. "Sounds like a high school prank," she said.

"Perhaps, but it was traumatic," Samantha huffed.

"I'll see who the chief assigned it to, Mrs. Krause," Kacey promised. "Any chance you could play with Emma for a few minutes while I talk to Cam?"

"I would love nothing more," Samantha said. She strode over to Emma and asked, "How about a game of Battleship?" Cam kept a selection of board games in Peachy Kleen's storage room.

Cam led Kacey into the breadbox and closed the door to the tiny space. He offered her the single chair and sat on the desktop. The smell of Kacey's moisturizer, redolent of sweet vanilla, filled the space between them.

"Did you know that Jasmine and Addison Devlin have bank debt?" Cam asked.

"Not in particular, but it doesn't surprise me," Kacey replied. "That store of theirs flopped."

"It gives her a reason to steal diamonds."

"I suppose," Kacey conceded. "But money could be a motive for just about anyone, whether they're in debt or not." She played with the straps of her purse, then added, "Yulian admitted to typing up the love letters from Dutch to Greta."

"Nothing like an arrest to squeeze a guy."

Kacey nodded. "I'll make sure to tell the prosecutor who draws Yulian's case. We'll see if he tacks on any charges for that. Either way, Yulian's going away for a long time."

"So is Dutch in the clear?"

"Not completely, but the chief has backed off of him as his main suspect. He's turned his attention to Jahi Shalabi. Bernie thinks Shalabi was in cahoots with the delivery driver, Ray Brewer."

Cam scratched his chin. "If they were in on the theft together, why would Shalabi tell me about him?"

"That's the same thing I said to Bernie. But he wants me to hunt down every lead."

"Make sure you dot your *P*s and cross your *Q*s, right?"

"Something like that."

"Shalabi told me he didn't know what happened to Brewer."

"He was easy enough for me to find." Kacey grinned. "The man has a record. Property damage. Apparently, he got upset with an Applebee's hostess in Akron. Kicked a plate-glass window and shattered it. I spoke with Brewer's probation officer this morning. He's living in a trailer with his mother in Sylvania, Ohio—that's just over the Michigan line. Delivering Domino's instead of diamonds."

"Quite a step down," Cam said. "I wonder why."

"I asked the probation officer. Apparently, Mr. Brewer realized that the diamond wholesaler didn't pay well enough for him to live on his own for the long run, so he moved home to mommy dearest. And Sylvania was too far from his delivery route."

"Are you going to see him now?"

"Yes. Thank you for taking Emma. I'm not sure if I'll be back before her bedtime."

"No problem, I can drop her off at school tomorrow morning before work."

* * *

Dinner with Emma consisted of fish sticks and canned corn—*the divorced daddy special*, Cam thought. As he was scooping chocolate ice cream into plastic bowls patterned with potbelly pigs, Cam heard a knock.

He left Emma on a kitchen stool and opened the front door to see Elena clutching a half-empty bottle of gin. "I need a drinking partner," she slurred, then added, "And I-I can almos' guarantee if it's you, that you'll be g-getting lucky tonight."

Cam took a step back. "Thank you for the … offer," he said apprehensively, "but my daughter's here and she's spending the night." Elena wasn't beautiful, but he found her self-assurance alluring. Fortunately, Emma saved him from having to test his willpower.

"How about I come back in a lil' while? After she's asleep."

"I don't think that would be the best idea," Cam said and slowly started to push the door closed.

"Maybe you'll change your mind." Elena winked at him, then wandered back down Cam's porch steps and over to her own.

After finishing their ice cream and three chapters in Emma's Judy Moody selection, Cam tucked his daughter into bed and headed back downstairs. Forty pages into the latest installment of John Sandford's Prey series, he heard a light tapping at his door.

Cam peered through the peephole. Elena again, this time without the bottle. *He would not start a physical relationship with his new neighbor*—not only because she had been drinking but because his feelings for Kacey were so uncertain.

He opened the door and said quietly, "Elena, Emma's still here."

She stepped toward him and laid a palm against his chest. "But she must be asleep by now." Her breath smelled of pine needles. Gin.

"I still can't do it," Cam said, standing his ground.

"Boo on you. So maybe you could make me a cup of coffee? Sober me up."

Despite his better judgment, Cam took a step back, allowing Elena inside. "You have to be quiet."

Elena put a finger to her lips and giggled. She followed Cam to the kitchen. He ground Columbian Arabica beans. So much for quiet.

"Drinking on a Tuesday night?" Cam asked.

"Please don't judge me," Elena said. Her speech wasn't as slurred as it had been an hour earlier. She sat atop the same stool Emma had perched on to eat ice cream. "I had a bit of bad news is all."

"Sorry. What happened?"

"Just some family squabbles. I'd rather not talk about it if you don't mind."

"No problem," Cam said. "Do you need some sugar?"

"Is that a come on?" Elena deadpanned.

Cam hesitated.

"Sweet'N Low, if you have it," she said, rescuing him from a response.

"I do. Cream?"

"Sure, why not? Tatum told me the county's going to bury their au pair tomorrow." Elena blew a wisp of hair from her eyes.

"Really?" Cam was surprised Kacey hadn't mentioned it to him.

"Apparently they couldn't locate her parents over in Germany."

"Does that mean there's no ceremony?"

"Just something simple graveside from what I understand. The county's allowing the McRaes' minister to say a few words, though Tatum told me she didn't know Greta's denomination. She said she'd send an e-mail around with the details."

"I haven't checked mine in a few hours," Cam said and poured steaming hot java into two mugs, then added sweetener and dairy to Elena's.

"Will the coffee keep you up?" Elena asked.

"No, I don't have a problem with caffeine." Cam flipped on a buccaneer's smile. "I have a problem without it."

Elena snorted.

"I can't believe no one could find her parents," Cam said. "You'd think she'd have to list emergency contacts with the au pair agency."

Elena shrugged. "Do you have any idea if Greta's boyfriend will be out of jail in time to make it to the cemetery?"

"My ex, the deputy chief, told me Reynold has a hearing tomorrow, but I don't know what time."

"Hmm," Elena said cautiously. "That guy makes me nervous."

"You know Reynold?" Cam asked.

"I've been to the Stagger Inn a couple of times. In fact, I was there on the night Greta died."

"What? Did you tell Chief Leftwich?"

"He didn't ask. Is it important?" Elena sipped her coffee.

She sounds remarkably lucid for a woman who had been drinking so heavily, Cam thought. "What time did you get to the Stagger that night?" He could feel his Adam's apple throbbing.

Elena tipped her head to one side. "I arrived at about ten forty-five, I think."

Cam played back the timeline in his mind. Reynold, joined by Addison, took his last cigarette break from ten thirty to ten forty-five. The text from Reynold's phone had been sent to Greta at just after eleven. Cam's mind jumped. Could *Elena* have stolen Reynold's phone? He brushed off the thought—suspicion was riding roughshod over his mental faculties. Elena didn't even know Greta.

"Did you happen to notice whether Reynold left the bar area around eleven o'clock?" Cam asked.

"I don't remember," she said. "I was engrossed in a conversation with a birder who was passing through town."

Cam pulled a stool to the other side of the kitchen island and sat across from Elena. "A birder?"

"Someone who watches birds. This guy photographs them, too. He went on and on about lens speeds and teleconverters."

"Did you speak with Reynold?"

"Not that night. The birdman bought my drink. Plus, the few times I looked down the bar, Reynold was talking to some guy. He looked pretty excited. Reynold, that is. The other guy's face was stone cold."

Cam blew hot air into his hands. "Did the man he was speaking with have dark hair and dark eyes? In his early forties?"

"Yes, yes, and yes," Elena said, her eyes opening wide. "Do you know who he is?"

Cam nodded. "Mateo Olivia."

Chapter 26
Wednesday, September 30

"Ray Brewer isn't smart enough to mastermind the theft of twenty-six diamonds," Kacey shouted in Cam's ear over a bitter wind cutting through the trees surrounding a nondenominational cemetery in Lia's Notch—an ink spot on the county map just northwest of Rusted Bonnet. Majestic paper birches towered above the burial grounds, honing the wind's tones to sharp whistles. A smattering of people stood in small clusters around a freshly dug hole, waiting for the minister.

"How smart would he have to be?" Cam shouted back, certain that no one could hear him other than Kacey. "All he had to do was switch the real diamonds for fakes before making the delivery to Ginsberg's."

"I'm not saying that he wasn't involved. But unless he's a terrific actor, he didn't plan the heist. The man couldn't even remember the routes he ran for the wholesaler. He said the GPS did the thinking, all he did was drive. And it seems unlikely that he was paid off to make the switch—that trailer was disgusting." Kacey made a face. "It had that smell a trash can gets a few days after you trim chicken fat."

"Maybe his cut's sitting in a bank account until the heat blows over."

"Doubtful. The theft happened a year and a half ago. I can't imagine anyone choosing to live in squalor for that long."

"How about his mother?" Cam asked. "Did you meet her?" He pulled the hood of his Paddington coat over his head.

"Marleen Brewer. Barked like a seal. Stands to reason—she smoked at least three Pall Malls in the half hour I was in their trailer."

"Could she be the brains behind the theft?" Cam asked.

"I doubt it. She wasn't much sharper than her son, and she seemed genuinely surprised that diamonds had been stolen from a client on Ray's route. You should have seen her eyes light up when I told her."

"Like a Christmas tree?"

"More like the Grinch shoving the tree up the chimney." Kacey laughed. "She had these wild yellow eyes. Caked with blue mascara."

"He hadn't told her about the theft?"

"To be honest, I'm not sure Ray even realized any diamonds were stolen."

"But Sheriff Lackey questioned him, right?"

"Yes, after he found out the diamonds they recovered from Erin Mack were fake. But the sheriff told me he would've had a more informative conversation talking to the man's GPS."

* * *

Greta's burial was less well attended than her remembrance gathering: Tatum and Dutch, Addison Devlin, a man in a suit whom Cam assumed was a county official, and two young women whom he recognized as local nannies. Reynold Cornell hadn't made it to the cemetery.

A gray mustachioed minister stood under a tent-sized umbrella at the head of Greta's grave. Hard rain and biting wind transformed his ninety-second stock-in-trade eulogy to a series of bleats in Cam's ears.

A pair of heavyset men in lime-green parkas lowered the closed wooden casket into the wet ground, followed by the minister tossing on a symbolic handful of dirt. The gaggle scattered to their cars as soon as the minister turned his back on Greta's body. Cam and Kacey stepped forward and peered down into the grave. Rainwater had already begun to turn the earth around Greta's casket to mud—Cam imagined worms, slugs, and sundry insects slinking through the hinged joints. He shuddered.

"Are you okay, Cam?" Tatum asked. She had crept to his side, her umbrella just underneath the one he held over himself and Kacey.

"I'm fine," Cam said, turning his head and watching Dutch briskly walk toward a new model Silverado. "Just cold. And a bit sad." He paused, then added, "I was surprised no one could find her parents. I wonder if her family and friends back home have started to worry about not hearing from her." Cam's thoughts shot to Becka Blom's mother—not knowing what happened to a child who had disappeared must have been torture.

"We scoured her e-mail account and even her phone records," Kacey said, staring down at the casket. The wind had begun to abate, but the rain remained steady. "We didn't find any correspondence to Germany. I have a feeling she ran away from home."

Tatum muttered to herself and clutched the collar of her black trench coat, pulling it tight around her neck.

"What was that?" Cam asked, knowing full well that her grumbling hadn't been intended for his ears.

Tatum wiped a bead of rain from her cheek with a gloved hand. "I said that I got what I deserved. I went through a reputable agency for Scarlett. Our new au pair."

"Greta's agency wasn't on the up-and-up?" Cam pressed.

Tatum laughed, then coughed. "I put an ad out on Craigslist. Almost all of the responses I received were garbage. I was just about to fork over the money for an agency when Greta called."

"Is that legal?"

Tatum raised a hand in the air. "Why not? Besides, Greta seemed perfect—so polite and refined."

"Did she have references?" Cam asked.

"I spoke with a woman in Cleveland. She told me that Greta was wonderful with her children."

Cam started to respond, then stopped. *So Greta had been an au pair in Cleveland.* He asked, "Did you ask her why Greta was looking for a new position?"

"Absolutely not. That would have been déclassé." She harrumphed.

"Do you recall the name of Greta's reference?" Kacey asked.

Tatum looked past Cam at Kacey, who was shivering in the cold. "I do," Tatum said. "Her name was Leslie Crutchfield."

* * *

"Back to the Crutchfields," Cam said. His breath fogged a patch of the Malibu's windshield the size of a stove burner. Kacey sat in the passenger's seat, staring out at the rain, which had picked up its fervor. Her cruiser and a pickup were the only other vehicles left in the cemetery's gravel lot. The truck belonged to the men in lime green, who had the unenviable task of refilling Greta's plot with saturated earth.

"T. L. is the dead father," Kacey replied. "Dr. Crutchfield is Thomas William, correct?"

"That's right," Cam said. "And his wife's name is Leslie. I heard Tom call out her name when I was at their house."

"So it's possible that there's more of a Crutchfield connection than just the location of the buried diamonds."

"And I was starting to doubt that Greta ever lived in Cleveland." Cam drummed his fingers against the wheel.

"The problem I'm having is that my instincts aren't directing me toward any of my suspects."

"Have faith, Kacey. You'll get him by hook or by ladder."

Kacey shed her boots, bent her knees toward her chin, and planted socked feet on the dashboard. "I think I believe Reynold—that he was being used by Greta to find a fence. Could someone else have preyed on him as well—used him to send that text to Greta?"

"I suppose. My new neighbor Elena said she was at the Stagger on the night Greta died. Apparently, Mateo Olivia was there. And we know that Addison shared a cigarette with Reynold in the parking lot. Either of them might have been able to talk him into it."

"Or swiped his phone and sent the text on their own."

"Right."

"You've been spending quite a bit of time with Elena," Kacey said.

"She's good company." Cam wrestled himself out of his coat and tossed it in the back seat. "But not my type."

"Hmm."

"Addison needed money—to pay off bank debt," Cam said, not wanting to dwell on Elena. "And she was at the McRaes' home shortly after Greta died, culling through Greta's clothing. She could have been looking for the address I found. And, of course, she wanted Greta's job and boyfriend."

"Plus Greta embarrassed her sister," Kacey added. "She has a whole menu of motives. For Mateo, killing Greta would be purely financial, *if* he knew where the diamonds were hidden. Kill Greta and take the diamonds for himself. One hundred percent is better than just a cut for fencing them. I'm planning to bring Mateo in today for questioning." She unwrapped a stick of Juicy Fruit and popped it in her mouth, then said, "I've been thinking more about Dutch. He had the opportunity to kill Greta, but no good reason to, as far as I can tell. Plus, if Greta died from a blow to the head, not a fall down the stairs, his opportunity to hide a trip wire doesn't hold any weight."

"Bernie moved from Dutch to Jahi Shalabi as his prime suspect, right?"

Kacey nodded. "He convinced Chief Lackey to let him to talk with Shalabi—Bernie's making the drive to Cleveland right now."

"And Ray Brewer is too dense to be at the top of the suspect list?"

Kacey nodded.

Cam jumped in his seat as a bolt of lightning cracked the sky. The men in green parkas pitched their shovels to the ground and bolted for the safety of their truck.

Kacey, unperturbed by the lightning, said, "That leaves Tatum and Jasmine. But I have no reason to suspect Tatum of anything. Besides, after Greta crashed down the stairs, she was in the closet with her children until the police arrived. So she couldn't have cut the cord from Greta's ankles."

"Unless she and Dutch made up that story about her hiding ahead of time," Cam corrected.

"I suppose that's true," Kacey allowed. "Last but not least is Jasmine. Sure, she was in debt and was not pleased with Greta after the stunt she pulled in the chess competition. But I just don't see it in her."

"Plus, she's built like a scrawny chicken. I don't think she could've carried Greta's body up the stairs."

"I'm not sure I agree with you there. Greta didn't weigh much and the killer's adrenaline would've been running high."

"So what's next?" Cam asked.

Kacey clapped her hands together. "Find Mateo Olivia. Hopefully between my interview with him and Bernie's with Jahi Shalabi, we'll learn something new."

Chapter 27

"That woman is like manna from heaven!" Samantha Krause thumped down onto the bull pen sofa beside Cam.

"Who?" he asked, setting down an appointment book and propping his feet up on a box of Clorox bleach jugs.

"Who do you think? Malika!" Samantha crammed her chubby bare feet onto the box next to Cam's. "New York City gets a bad rap for being dirty—can't be the case if everyone there cleans as well as she does."

"I don't think housekeepers clean the streets or subways," Cam commented. "Besides, Malika lived in Kenya for most of her life."

"Well, that explains it then. She has tricks up her sleeve that I've never seen."

"I suspect she didn't always have access to the kinds of supplies we do."

"The more elbow grease, the better the shine." Samantha held out her forearms and admired them—Popeye's rather than Olive Oyl's.

"Well, I'm glad she's working out." One day into the job and receiving praise from Samantha Krause was no small accomplishment.

Cam stood and straightened his slacks. "With Malika on board and Becka back, I have more time to work on finding new clients." With the exception of her mother, who decided to call her by her given name, Afya, Becka had decided to continue to go by the name she'd known for most of her life. "Did anyone from the police department get back to you on the shoe polish you found in the Bear Claw's restroom?" he asked.

Samantha clucked her tongue. "Some *newbie* came to see me last night. He couldn't be more than three months on the job if you ask me. Green as a shamrock and his uniform didn't even fit—too large on him by far."

"Perhaps he lost some weight?" Cam ventured.

"Not likely. He was eating a French cruller the size of a hockey puck when he knocked on my door."

"A hockey puck's not that large." Cam snickered.

"Oh, you know what I mean!"

Cam wasn't quite sure what she meant but kept the sentiment to himself. Instead, he asked, "What did the officer have to say?"

"That it must have been teenagers pulling some sort of prank. Of course it was a prank! That's just the point." She slapped her palms against her thighs. "The chief and Kacey should've been tasked to find the culprit."

"I'm sure they would have taken up your cause if they weren't so busy looking for Greta's killer," Cam said.

"I suppose," Samantha grumbled, adding, "Murder is *such* an inconvenience."

* * *

"So Bait, who killed Greta Astor?" Cam dropped a microwaved pea, skin peeled, into the fish tank.

The pea dropped like a rock. Bait lunged after it. The fish had developed a bloated swim bladder—likely from over imbibing on flakes—causing him to lose control of his buoyancy and flip onto to his back. The little fish continued to right himself, but every time he succeeded, physics bested his efforts and upended him seconds later. Cam found that a green pea or two set the fish's bladder straight, at least temporarily.

"It could've been almost anyone," Cam said, then added, "That service today was sad. No family at all. How could she just estrange herself?" Cam grimaced, realizing that his own life had run a similar course. He had abandoned Kacey and Emma and, to a large part, even his mother. Sure, they knew where he was living, but other than sending an odd check to Kacey and calling his mother on her birthday, he had all but disappeared from their lives for years.

He turned his focus back to Greta—according to Kacey, her phone didn't have any record of calls to Germany. She probably bought a new one after moving to the States, he decided, and never called overseas. Cam dropped a second pea in the tank. It settled alongside the first, which Bait was feverishly nibbling on.

Unless Greta never lived in Germany. He had only Greta's word that she had grown up in Europe and moved to Cleveland to be an au pair before coming to Rusted Bonnet. Sure, Tatum had spoken with her reference—Leslie Crutchfield—but the voice on the other end of the line could have been a friend. Or Greta herself.

If Greta Astor wasn't who she said she was, what was she doing in Rusted Bonnet?

A second later, Cam snapped his fingers. He didn't know her real name, but he knew exactly who she was.

* * *

"Jahi Shalabi, please." Cam cradled the kitchen telephone between his chin and shoulder as he reached for a pen. He took a strange comfort in maintaining a landline phone.

After a moment, a gruff voice came on the line. "Yes?" Cam recognized Shalabi's voice and could figuratively feel anger bubbling through his terse salutation.

"Jahi, this is Cam Reddick. We met on Saturday night at the club in Bowling Green."

"I remember," Shalabi rumbled. "All too well. Some cop from up in Michigan—Leftwich—just gave me the third degree for an hour. Man, I've gone through this garbage so many times. I had nothing to do with those diamonds, and sure as hell didn't kill anyone."

"Did he show you a picture of the girl who died up here in Rusted Bonnet?" Cam asked.

"Your sister, right? Why should I tell you?" Shalabi hissed. "That bonehead all but accused me of murdering her."

"That seems to be his style," Cam said coolly. "You're not the only one he's accused."

"You?"

"My mother."

"Better her than me," Shalabi said, his voice dripping with rancor.

Cam waited a beat, then tried again. "So did Bernie Leftwich show you a photo?"

After a pause, Shalabi said, "He did. And it's Trisha, that's for sure."

"Trisha? Not Greta?" Cam asked, his excitement growing.

"Trisha Richland."

Remembering the newspaper article about the robbery, Cam breathed with deep satisfaction. His revelation was spot on—Greta had changed her name when she moved to Rusted Bonnet. He had been prepared to text a newspaper photo of Greta to the jewelry store manager, but that was no longer necessary. Bernie Leftwich was brighter than he'd thought, not that it would point him directly to the murderer.

"And Trisha is who exactly?" Cam asked, already certain he knew the answer.

"Not your sister, right?"

"She's not," Cam admitted.

"Everybody's lying and pointing fingers, yet I'm the suspect." Shalabi laughed. "What do I care. I didn't do anything wrong. Trisha was my sales clerk. The one who tackled Erin Mack."

* * *

"It was smack in front of my face the entire time," Cam told Bait. "Erin Mack held a knife to *Greta's* throat, forcing Jahi Shalabi to open the safe holding the diamonds."

Bait was struggling to float upright despite having devoured both peas. *In another hour, he'll be back to his old self,* Cam thought.

"So the question is, how did Greta—Trisha—get the diamonds if Erin Mack swallowed them." Cam tapped his foot. "That's not right. Erin Mack swallowed a glove full of cubic zirconia. Greta must have had the real gems the entire time."

Cam stepped into his kitchen and chose a Dr. Pepper from an assortment of cans in the refrigerator. He popped the top and headed back toward the fish tank. "So let's play this out," he said. "Jahi Shalabi receives a shipment of diamonds at Ginsberg Jewelers, delivered by Ray Brewer. He locks the diamonds—the real deal—in the safe, intending to catalogue them a day or two later. Greta, as one of the sales clerks, would probably have an idea of when the shipments came in. So at some point between Shalabi locking them in the safe and the following afternoon when Erin Mack wielded a knife in the showroom, Greta swapped the real diamonds for fakes.

"The delivery was only made one day before the attempted robbery, so Greta must have had a stash of cubic zirconia stones. She could find out the number of real diamonds delivered and replace them with an equal number of replicas. With enough cubic zirconia, she could even try to match up the cuts and sizes." He took a sip of pop. "And she'd know Shalabi was lax about checking the stones as soon as they were delivered."

Cam set the Dr. Pepper beside Bait's tank. He cleared his throat and started to pace. "It doesn't smell quite right to me, either. Someone *killed* Greta. And in my story, I don't see a motive for murder. I think Reynold and Mateo only came into the picture after the fact, once Greta decided she needed to turn the diamonds into real money. Did she even know anyone from Rusted Bonnet eighteen months ago?"

Cam tapped on the side of the tank. "Do you need another pea, buddy?" Bait ignored him. "You're right. Two is plenty. We just need to give your scaly little body time to recover." Another thought sprang into Cam's head. "Sheriff Lackey told Kacey and me that no one other than Shalabi and Ginsberg himself could open the safe. So Greta couldn't have made the switch before Shalabi arrived at work, unless she had figured out the combination."

Cam rubbed his hands together. "What am I missing, Bait?" He left the fish and moved to the center of his sectional. "Is there any chance Greta's murder had nothing to do with the diamonds ... No way—there has to be a connection."

Cam knew he should get to Peachy Kleen before dusk—he'd let his scheduling responsibilities lapse. But it was hard to *think* there, even in the breadbox, especially when Samantha was stomping about in the bull pen between jobs.

Five minutes later, head in his hands, he said out loud, "Erin Mack." Cam stood and glided—socks over hardwood—back toward Bait's tank. "I need to find Erin Mack. If Greta stole the diamonds, it's too much of a coincidence that Erin tried to rob the store on the same day. Plus, if Greta had figured out a way to switch the real diamonds for cubic zirconia, why would she tackle Erin Mack? She'd be better off letting Erin get away—no one would have known the stolen diamonds were fake until Erin tried to fence them." He grunted in frustration.

"And then there's the latex glove—Erin Mack brings a latex glove with her to a robbery. Why? And she wasn't wearing them on her hands to mask fingerprints." *Was Erin so smart that she thought of every contingency, including getting tackled?* Cam shook his head. "Swallowing the diamonds couldn't help her in the long run—she was in police custody. So why do it?"

Bait bobbed up and down at the top of his tank, his swim bladder problem apparently subsiding.

An instant later, Cam punched a fist into his open palm. "Because she needed *time*. Erin was working *with* Greta to give her *time*. Time for Greta to get the real diamonds out of the store with no one suspecting her. I wish I could see the video footage from the robbery." His heart thudded as he mentally played out the scene. *Greta—the sales clerk—tackles Erin Mack, positioning their bodies to block the security camera and Shalabi from seeing their hands. Perhaps for only a few seconds, just long enough for Erin to slip the pouch of diamonds that Shalabi handed her—the real ones from the safe—into Greta's pocket. A prearranged performance, practiced to perfection because Greta didn't know the code to the safe. Then as they wrestle on the floor, they shift their bodies back around for the benefit of Shalabi and the camera. Erin Mack makes a show of taking a stash of cubic zirconia stones she had brought with her, dumping them into the latex glove, and swallowing the whole package. When the police arrive, they have two eyewitnesses' accounts—Greta and Shalabi—and video backup of Erin swallowing a glove full diamonds. No need for the cops to search the jewelry store or its employees. Greta probably had the real diamonds in her pocket the entire time she was speaking with the police.*

Cam drained the rest of his Dr. Pepper. "Erin didn't act alone, Bait. Greta was just as much a part of the robbery as she was. They would have to assume that Erin might spend some time behind bars, but not too much—the prosecutor couldn't prove that she stole real valuables."

So why was Greta killed? "Greta moved to Michigan and changed her name from Trisha," he said. "In fact, she created a whole new identity. That's why Kacey couldn't find any relatives in Germany. Greta's probably an American, which is why she didn't have any European stuffed animals.

"But moving may not have been part of the original plan. At least not Erin's. Let's say Greta was supposed stay put, as Trisha Richland the jewelry sales clerk in Cleveland. When Erin was released, they'd sell the diamonds and split the proceeds. But Greta double-crossed her, changed her name, and fled the state. When Erin got out of prison, both the diamonds and Trisha were gone. *That's why Greta was murdered.* Are you listening to me, Bait?" Cam locked eyes with the goldfish for a split second. "Find Erin Mack and you've found the killer."

Chapter 28

And Erin Mack was surprisingly easy to locate once Cam put his mind to it. His subconscious mind that is.

Before dinner that evening, he had called Kacey and walked her step by step though his breakdown of the robbery and its participants. She agreed with his deductions and had promised to hunt down the security tapes—if the Cleveland sheriff's department still had them. They didn't expect to see Erin pass Greta the diamonds—Sheriff Lackey wouldn't have missed it— but rather, confirm that their bodies obscured the camera long enough for a transfer as they wrestled on the jewelry store floor.

Neither of them had been able to pin down Erin Mack's true identity while on the phone. But just hours later, lying on his California King knee deep in a REM cycle, Erin Mack's face appeared to Cam. Not the face in the photo Sheriff Lackey had shown him in Cleveland. Not exactly. At the time, he thought that Erin looked vaguely familiar but he couldn't place her. Now, realizing that Erin Mack must have killed Greta, the nether regions of his mind filled in the blanks. A light touch of the scalpel, colored contact lenses, hair coloring, and a moderate change in weight—the woman's face he had been shown in Cleveland mutated into one much more familiar to him. A woman who lived in Rusted Bonnet. Only under a different name.

* * *

Thursday, October 1

Cam spent Thursday morning tracking down two people and peppering them with questions to confirm his supposition. The first was Reynold Cornell—he had been released on his own recognizance—and the second, Tatum McRae.

Satisfied with their responses, Cam set to work on baiting a snare. A fingerprint trap so simple that Emma could have concocted it—comprised of a friendly invitation to lunch at the Bear Claw, a glass of lemonade, and a surreptitious request that the waitress leave the glass on the table until his suspect departed.

Once Cam's prey left the diner and backed out of the parking lot, he lifted the glass with a napkin. His plan was to walk it across the street to his Malibu in the Peachy Kleen lot and surprise Kacey at the police station. He'd hand her a neat little package—Erin Mack's Rusted Bonnet identity and the lemonade glass with prints surely to match those from Mack's Cleveland case file.

Chapter 29

Cam never saw the knife coming. It was pressed to his throat less than a second after he shut the drivers' side door of the Malibu.

"Get back here and lay flat on your stomach," commanded a familiar voice from behind him.

Cam froze momentarily, then he tried to twist his neck, but the flat side of the knife pressed harder against his skin.

"Slowly," the voice said and pulled the knife back a few inches.

Cam did as he was told—sliding into the back seat, his eyes locking with hers, then flipping onto his belly. She jumped onto him, a knee digging into his lower back, then stuffed a gag into his mouth. She bound his hands behind his back with a length of rope and tied his feet at the ankles. She dug the keys from his pocket.

"You really need to start locking your car door, Cam," she said and climbed in front. The parking lot behind Peachy Kleen was empty. She turned and rolled him onto the floor of the back seat then threw a blanket over the top of him.

"Those fingerprints you took from my lemonade won't match Erin Mack's," the woman said and started the engine.

Cam tried to wriggle his wrists but they wouldn't budge. He grunted.

"I had dried super glue on my fingertips," she said. "You're very easy to read. The only reason I came to lunch was to see if you were on to me. Your eyes gave you away—they were all nerves."

Cam squirmed on the floor as the car lurched into gear.

"You were much more nervous than when we drove to Grand Rapids or Bowling Green."

* * *

"I don't want to kill you," Elena said. "One murder was plenty for me, but I have no choice. I can't imagine you've told anyone that you've figured out I'm Erin yet, given your little ruse, so I have to shut you up before you do."

Tied to a chair in Elena's living room, blinds drawn, Cam was trapped in his own personal Navajo-styled hell. She had ungagged him, but warned that screaming would only quicken the route to his last breath.

"I know I made a mistake," she said, "by telling you that I was at the Stagger on the night Greta died. I was trying to point a finger at the Cuban, of course."

"Mateo," Cam said. "Did you know him?"

She shook her head. "No, but I overhead Reynold talking with him about trying to find a buyer for the diamonds. I had been planning to text Greta from Reynold's phone anyway, with a made-up reason for her to meet him after his shift."

"And once you overhead Mateo and Reynold, you knew a 'big score' text would all but guarantee that Greta would come outside at one thirty."

"Exactly." Elena sat on the sofa across from Cam, a kitchen knife in her lap.

"Did you leave the bar and come back to swipe Reynold's phone?" Cam asked. "Because Greta and Addy were there."

"Trisha, not Greta, as you well know. They came in soon after Mateo left. I saw Trisha before she saw me so I tucked myself into a booth behind a pint glass and a newspaper. Plus, the Stagger's dark. Besides, I've changed my appearance quite a bit—the manager from Ginsberg's didn't recognize me dancing ten feet in front of his band."

"That was pretty brazen."

"More of a test. Or maybe just a lark."

"Then you *borrowed* Reynold's phone?"

"That's one word for it," she said and smiled. "After Trisha left, Reynold stepped outside for a cigarette with Addison. He came back in at about ten forty-five and went straight to the storage room, probably to toss the phone back in his locker. It took all of thirty seconds for me to slip in from the door by the ladies' room to the kitchen. Reynold didn't even bother to lock his locker. No that it mattered, I'm pretty handy with a bobby pin. And passcodes to an iPhone are even easier—two minutes on YouTube can teach you to bypass any code. Fifteen minutes after I sent Trisha the big score text, I went back in and deleted her reply. Easy stuff."

Cam grumbled. "I can't believe I brought you with me to investigate when it was you I should've been looking at the whole time."

"I was happy to make the trip with you to Grand Rapids to track down Jasmine's story. At the time, I didn't think much of your detective skills. But when you wanted to go see Shalabi, I'll have to admit I was worried you'd gotten that far. You were shrewder than I originally thought. That's why I tried to push you to look harder at the Cuban. But I wasn't sure if you bought it or not. In fact, I got so paranoid that I followed you this morning."

"I wish your instincts weren't so good," Cam said.

Elena smiled. "You spoke with Reynold about seeing me at the bar that night, yes?"

"He remembered you being there, sitting by yourself at a nearby table, not with a birder."

She sighed. "After talking with Reynold, you went to the McRaes' house. Why?"

"I wanted to ask Tatum whether you spent a lot of time alone in Greta's room after she died. She told me you wanted to redecorate for the new au pair. I imagine you were looking for the diamonds or any hint of where they might be."

"I came up empty. But you didn't, did you? What did you find that led you to Cleveland?"

"A notepad stuffed into a plush animal. Tatum also told me you'd never been in the house at the same time as Greta—you said you needed quiet to 'visualize' the home's décor, and that meant no distractions from the children or their au pair. She also said that on one of your first visits you suggested tearing out the carpet runner and refinishing the hardwood on the staircase. So you must have had a good, close look at the stairs."

"When I saw the nail hole on the top step, it gave me the idea to make Greta's death look like she had fallen, or, if the police looked more closely, would implicate Dutch."

"But in your haste to escape after pulling Greta's body down the stairs and letting out a shriek, you didn't completely cut the nylon cord from one of Greta's ankles."

"No one's perfect." Elena smiled wryly.

"Are you going to kill Reynold and Tatum, too? Seeing as how I asked them about you this morning."

"No," Elena said. "And I won't kill the waitress at the Bear Claw, either, if you're worried. I imagine you asked her before we met for lemonade to save my glass—a strange request. After you disappear, I have no doubt your ex-wife and the chief will come down hard on me. But I'm not coming back to be found."

"So go!" Cam shouted. "Leave me tied up and get as far as you can as fast as you can."

"Shh. Do you want to be gagged again?" She stood and laid the knife against one of his cheeks. It felt cold. "You're a different story, Cam. You're too good at detecting, will have too much motivation to find me, and have too much time on your hands. You'd find me eventually and I don't want to look over my shoulder forever."

"But the police will find you if you kill me. Reynold and Tatum and the waitress will all come forward."

"They will and they'll all point to me. That's why I'm not even going to try to make your death look like an accident. I need to get rid of you and flee. But they won't catch me. The chief isn't completely stupid and he'll figure out that I'm Erin Mack, but he's not clever enough to coordinate a nationwide manhunt, at least not one that will succeed after I change my name and appearance again. Your ex will want to track me down—you are her child's father after all—but it's your daughter who will keep her from doing it. She can't go traipsing across the country looking for me week in and week out and care for a young child. Eventually, she'll give up."

"You're not really going to kill me right here in your own living room, are you?"

"Definitely not," Elena said. Her eyes looked feral. "I'll wait until it's dark and take you somewhere else. It was risky enough getting you from the car in here." She glanced at a wall clock. "Another five hours."

"Can you at least make it painless?" Cam asked. "Maybe stuff a bunch of pills down my throat."

"That's one option," Elena said. "Another is to bash your head with a rock, like I did with Trisha. It doesn't matter one way or another to me. My only concern is that no one finds your body. At least not right away. And I have the perfect spot for that."

"A better one than the bottom of a staircase."

She sighed and walked toward the kitchen. "I didn't want to kill Trisha," she said over her shoulder. "When I met her that night in the driveway, I confronted her about fleeing Cleveland, of course, but then I simply asked her where the diamonds were. Begged her to tell me in fact."

"You just happened to stake out a hole in the floorboard and bring twine and a nylon rope with you?"

"A girl has to have a Plan B." Elena returned with a glass of water. "Plan A was to get her to tell me where the diamonds were so we could split the proceeds."

"Or murder her and take them all for yourself," Cam said.

She put the glass to his lips and he drank. "It crossed my mind, seeing as how she double-crossed me," she said. "But I wasn't going to do it."

* * *

"How did you and Greta meet?" Cam asked. The minutes to dawn seemed to tick by at the speed of a mollusk marathon. His wrists, still bound behind the chair, were raw from rubbing skin against rope for so long.

"Me and Trisha," Elena corrected. "It's a funny story. We were both trying to hustle the same guy." She disappeared into the bedroom, but kept speaking. "Trisha, of course, used her looks. She could convince almost any man to do anything for her."

"Like Reynold fencing the diamonds?" Cam said.

"I imagine," Elena replied. "But in this case, she just used her beauty to draw his attention. It was her con that reeled him in."

"I feel like I've heard about more cons in the past two weeks than in my entire life," Cam mumbled.

"I can't hear you," Elena shouted back. "Trisha was a pro," she said loudly. "I was just an amateur trying to convince a stranger to buy me dinner by pretending that

I'd forgotten my wallet at home. I offered to write the guy a check if he'd pay my way because I had my check book, but the restaurant manager wouldn't accept it. Of course the check would bounce, but I'd be long gone by then."

"Did the man bite?" Cam asked.

Elena strode back into the room, dressed in black jeans and a dark crewneck sweater. "I never had the chance to find out. Trisha was sitting at the bar next to him and spotted my hustle before I even had a chance to finish my pitch. She scared me off, but asked me to stick around. In retrospect, I think she already had the diamond scam in mind and needed a woman who was naïve but eager to learn the con game to swallow that cubic zirconia. Trisha should've gone into psychology. She told me once that the key to any good scheme is to pinpoint a person's emotional void and offer to fill it. A con artist excels by making her mark feel like a special snowflake."

"So Greta had something more grand going on with the man at the bar?" Cam asked.

Elena sat back down, and brought her knees together. "Trisha," she said with a smile. "Yes. A mid-length scam. This one spanned two nights and she had close to a dozen flunkies playing parts. She picked her mark the same way I picked him—a middle-aged man at a relatively respectable establishment and dressed well enough to have money, but looking somewhat down-on-his-luck, too. His jacket a little wrinkled, his hair a bit mussed. Trisha has a couple of drinks with him and gets him talking about his sob story.

"After a while, she pulls out a deck of cards and shows the man a couple of quick slight of hand tricks. *Not just a young and pretty face*, the man thinks. But he's no dummy. *Why's she interested in the likes of me. I might buy a pretty girl a drink or two, but I'm not getting conned.* 'What's your angle here?' the man asks, thinking himself to be shrewd. It's then that Trisha admits that she rigs card games for a living. She says that the world is full suckers and you're either a fisherman or a fish. 'But you caught on quickly,' she says. 'You must be a fisherman.' She laughs and orders another round of drinks.

"He agrees, of course, that it's hard for anyone to put one over on him.

"'Like that girl who wanted you to buy her dinner,' Trisha says. 'She surely wanted to write you a bad check in return.'

"'Exactly,' the man says with a wink. 'I picked up on that right away.'

"Trisha doubted that he did, but says nothing of course. She goes on to tell him that she's in a bit of a bind. 'See, I have this poker game set up for tomorrow night. Only it's a two-man con and my normal partner went and got himself tossed in the pen for selling dope. Crazy that it's still illegal here, right?'

"The man nods, then says 'Any chance I can help? I know my way around a poker table.'

"Trisha told me the best cons make it seem like it's the mark's idea. Just like she made me think that *me going to jail* was my idea, not hers." Elena laughed.

"What a farce. Anyway, Trisha tells the guy that her partner's job is easy—whenever she taps the table he just has to go 'all in' on the hand. She stacks the deck and handles the rest. But she couldn't possibly use him. She just met him.

"At this point, the man is begging her for a chance. Doubtless, it seems so much more glamorous than his neighborhood game in a suburban basement with Tostitos and salsa.

"'Nothing personal, but there's no way I can trust you,' she says. 'The stakes are too high and I hardly know you.'

"'But you approached me,' the man countered.

"'To see if you'd fall for a twenty dollar con here at the bar,' she said. 'But you were too quick. You spotted me as a fisherman before I could even set the bait, let alone reel you in.'

"'Which is why you should let me help. You said you do most of the work. What kind of cut does the partner get?'

"'Thirty percent,' she said. 'I'll tell you what. I know of another game tonight. Small potatoes. A five hundred dollar buy in. I can front you the money if you don't have cash on you. We'll call it a test. Are you game?'

"The man readily agrees and Trisha leads him to the back room of another bar where a small game is just getting started. Trisha hands the man five hundred in cash—a bound wad of fifties and the game goes precisely according to plan. Each time Trisha furtively taps the table, the man pushes all of his chips into the middle of the table, no matter his hand. After two hours, Trisha and the man are the last standing and call it a night. They had taken four other men for a ride and split two grand—at thirty percent, the man has a fresh six hundred dollars to his name."

"I think I see where this is going," Cam said. "The next night, Trisha didn't loan him the buy in money, did she?"

Elena laughed. "Definitely not! On the first night, she made sure he had ready access to a large amount of cash. Not many people have twenty grand sitting around, but on a weekday it was easy enough for the man to liquidate a sizable chunk from his 'rainy day' brokerage account. Trisha said there would be another three players the following night, all putting up twenty large. So a total of a hundred grand in the kitty. The man did the math—he'd bring twenty as would Trisha, leaving sixty thousand for the taking. And thirty percent of sixty is a cool eighteen thousand. After seeing how easy the trick worked that night, he was chomping at the bit."

"Except this time he lost?"

"You got it, friend. The first night, Trisha paid off some stiffs to lose on purpose and the following night another three to have one of them win. The deal being that Trisha comes back and collects the mark's twenty grand after he goes home."

"And because it wasn't Trisha who beat him, he probably never even knew he'd been conned."

"Exactly. The set up the second night isn't in the back room of a bar, but in the dark kitchen of a boarded-up restaurant downtown."

"Did Trisha play it off like she made a mistake?" Cam asked, intrigued. "Said her finger must have slipped as she was stacking the deck."

"Not even. When they leave, she blows up at *him* and accuses *him* of going in too early. Said she hadn't tapped yet, She's never partnering with an amateur again and on and on.

"'I swear I saw you tap,' the man would plead. 'It was dark, but I'm sure I saw you twitch. Why are you so mad?' he'd shout. 'I just lost all of that money. I can't just blow that kind of dough without feeling it.'

"'Well, I'm sorry you lost it,' Elena would say, softening. 'But it took me two months to line that game up and I needed the money from those clowns. I'm going to have to move back in with my mother.'

"And the two would part ways, the man feeling nothing but pity for Trisha and twenty thousand lighter."

* * *

Elena zapped Cam a mug of tomato soup, which she fed him, then explained that she had to leave him alone for a while "to make burial arrangements." To make doubly sure he wouldn't get away, she dragged Cam and his chair into her bedroom, blindfolded and gagged him, tied the chair to a bed post, and told him she was wedging another chair under the door handle on the outside of the room.

Try as he might, Cam couldn't wriggle free from his bindings. *Think*, he pleaded with himself. *If he could just get himself to the window, maybe someone would notice him.* But the zip ties around his wrists didn't budge and the more he strained, the more they cut into his painfully tender wrists. *No, he thought, he had to convince Elena to let him go.*

But he didn't give up the physical struggle either. By the time Elena returned two hours later, Cam had managed to tip himself and the chair onto its side.

She removed the blindfold and gag and dragged him back into the living room, still in the chair. "We're all set," she said. "And I picked up a few over-the-counter goodies to give you a peaceful passing."

"Thank you," Cam rasped.

She put a glass of water to his lips and he greedily drank it down.

"How did you find Greta?" Cam wheezed. "After you got out of jail."

"Trisha? That was easy. Actually, I was lucky, too. As astute as she was, Trisha didn't cover her tracks well enough. To get the nanny job with the McRaes, she needed a reference."

"Leslie Crutchfield," Cam said.

"Yes. At least that's the name Lallie gave me."

"Lallie?"

"Eulalia Grant. She's a woman down in Cleveland who Trisha and I used for a few small jobs we pulled. The diamond heist was our biggest, but not the first."

"What was her role in the Ginsberg robbery?" Cam asked.

"Nothing. It was too complicated."

"Passing the real diamonds to Trisha while you wrestled on the floor and swallowed the fakes?"

"You are clever," Elena said. "Plus, we didn't want Lallie getting a full third or coming after us once she found out how big the score was. But when Trisha decided to double-cross me, she called Lallie to play the role of former house mistress, Leslie Crutchfield."

"So Trisha never knew Leslie for real?"

"Not that I'm aware of. Trisha gave Lallie a disposable phone and told her that when a call came in from a Tatum McRae with a 248 area code, she was to pretend that Trisha, who now called herself Greta, had been her children's German au pair. She gave her three hundred bucks and swore her to secrecy, in case anyone ever asked.

"But when I got out of prison and realized that Trisha had fled, Lallie was one of my first calls to see if she had heard from her. Lallie stonewalled at first, but when I flashed a pair of hundreds at her, she caved. Lallie gave me Tatum's name and recalled her having a metro Detroit area code, so Trisha was fairly easy to find, even going by the name Greta."

"It's interesting that Trisha used Leslie Crutchfield's name. She's a real person."

"I know. According to Lallie, Trisha said she and her husband were customers at the jewelry store."

"She certainly leaned on the Crutchfield name," Cam said.

"There's something else?"

Cam smiled. "Untie me and I'll tell you." He looked up at a brightly colored wall hanging.

"Fat chance," Elena said with a laugh. "But tell me and I'll give you some chocolate. I have a bag of mini Snickers bars."

"I'm worse than a dog," Cam said. "A fine last meal I suppose."

Elena bounded into the kitchen. *She seems chipper,* Cam thought.

"Leslie Crutchfield's father-in-law died about two years ago and is buried in a cemetery in downtown Cleveland," he said. "That's where I found the diamonds."

"In his grave?"

"Nearby," Cam said. "He died not long before you robbed Ginsberg's."

"Leslie or her husband probably mentioned it to Trisha when they were looking at jewelry," she said. "It probably gave her the idea of hiding the diamonds there."

Elena unwrapped a Snickers and popped it into Cam's mouth. The combination of chocolate and caramel had never tasted better to him.

"And how did you find the location?" she asked.

"It was a little circuitous, but the notepad I found had some clues."

"She should have just told me where the diamonds were," Elena said. "She'd be alive today. And you'd be happily scrubbing up after other people and on your way to reviving your marriage."

Cam smiled, unclear how Elena had made the leap about his relationship with Kacey. "I wouldn't have gotten so involved if you hadn't dumped a bucket of nails in front of my mother's house," Cam said. "I assume that was you?"

Elena pushed a second Snickers into Cam's mouth. "Yes, but I had no idea whose place it was at the time. I was watching the McRaes' house the morning after Trisha died."

"You mean the morning after you killed her and tried to make it look like an accident," Cam said through a mouthful of candy.

"Semantics. There was a lot of police activity, obviously. I called on Tatum that morning to see what was happening, using the interior decorating pretext, of course."

"Of course," Cam said.

"When she told me about the bit of cord tied around Greta's ankle, I was steaming mad at myself. But it also calmed me a little. After I took off the previous night, I realized that I didn't have both knotted pieces of cord but I had no idea where it was. I was pretty frantic at the time."

"You can work on your demeanor when you off me," Cam grumbled.

"I will!" Elena grinned. "I like you, Cam. It's a pity that you have to go away."

"Can I charm you into keeping me alive?"

"Not a chance. Anyway, when Tatum told me about the darn rope I left around Trisha's ankle I knew any chance of her death being deemed an accident was out. I had rubbed that twine around the post in hopes that the police would look to Dutch if they were after a murderer. Or Reynold for that matter seeing as how I used his phone. So I found a farmhouse and dumped out a pailful of nails, figuring it would add more credence to the trip wire angle. I never thought the chief would suspect the person who lived in the house of murder."

"Like you said, he's not the most clever. Can I ask you a favor?"

"Let me guess, you want another Snickers?"

"Well, yes, but that's not it." Cam forced his eyes to tear, which wasn't a terribly difficult feat given the situation. "Can I call my daughter? I haven't always been such a good father. I've been working hard to change that and she and I finally have a relationship. Can I please just talk to her? Tell her I love her?"

Elena looked sad as she gently slid a chocolate chunk into Cam's mouth. She turned away from him. "I can't do that," she said. "It's too risky."

"She's six," he begged. "I just want to hear her voice one more time. You can stand over me. I promise I won't say anything."

"I'm very sorry. Now shut up before you make me change my mind." She waited until he swallowed, then stuffed the gag back in his mouth, ran into the bedroom, and slammed the door. He could hear her sobbing.

For the first time in hours, Cam saw a glimmer of hope.

She came back ten minutes later, seemingly composed and dressed in a black camisole and camouflage-print cargo shorts. Her eyes were bloodshot, but she was no longer crying. "Let's do this now," she said sternly.

Cam slumped in his chair, his flicker of hope snuffed. "My daughter," he tried through the gag.

"Shut up," Elena shouted and struck him in the back of the head with a palm.

"It's close enough to dusk," she said. "I'm going to untie you so that you can walk like a normal person to my car in case anyone is passing by. But I have a stun gun." She strode in front of him and waived a black rectangle in front of his face. It looked like an oversized garage door opener. "If you try to run or make a peep, I'm mowing you down. And then you get the knife, not the pills. Got it?"

Cam nodded and she removed the gag.

"Elena…" he said.

"It's Erin!" she interrupted.

"Sorry, Erin. I thought of a way out."

"What part of shut up don't you understand?"

"Just hear me out. You don't have to kill me, but you can still get away."

"You're going to promise not to search for me, not to hunt me down, right? No dice. It's too risky."

"No," Cam said. "I'll confess to the murder."

Elena jerked her head back, then seemed to recover. "That's rich."

"Seriously, Michigan doesn't have the death penalty. And I'd rather spend my life in prison than die—anything to see Emma again, even if she thinks I'm a killer."

"I'm not buying it." Elena set the stun gun on a coffee table and began to untie Cam's ankles from the chair. "As soon as you got to the police station, you'd tell them everything, not confess."

"I'll tape it," Cam pleaded. "Right here, right now."

"It's not 1986—I don't have a tape recorder."

"Your phone does. So does mine. I can record it on my own phone, write a note, and you can drop them both in front of the police station."

"In a bassinet, like an abandoned baby?"

"However you want."

"You'd just change your story later."

"But the chief would latch onto it. He's desperate to find Greta's murderer."

"The chief may not be the smartest, but if you change your tune, with everything else stacked up against me, the prosecutor won't bite. I'll have to run again."

"So run," Cam said. "That's what you're going to do anyway."

She finished loosening his feet. Cam rolled his ankles then stood up and did ten deep knee bends. "That feels good," he said.

"That's never going to work for me. Come on, it's pill city and a hole in the ground for you. And I changed my mind—I'm keeping your wrists tied. We'll just throw a jacket over them."

"Won't the guilt destroy you?" Cam asked. "Killing a little girl's father."

She grunted and picked up the stun gun.

"Greta was different," he tried. "She turned on you. I didn't. That wasn't cold blooded. You can justify that one to yourself easily enough. If you kill me, you'll never be able to sleep at night."

"I'm not looking forward to it," Elena said. "But that's life." She pulled a windbreaker from the closet, slapped it over his wrists, then grabbed her handbag. "I have all sorts of good meds in here—green ones, white ones, red ones." She tucked the stun gun into the waist of her shorts. "My car's right in front. Three steps down the porch and straight into the passengers' seat. The door's unlocked."

Elena nudged Cam toward the front door from behind. He steadied his nerves, knowing what he had to do.

He twisted the knob and stepped onto the porch, his eyes scanning the street. A single man dressed in flannel and denim stood with his dog on the corner—half a block to Cam's right and across the street. Cam could make out a plastic Mutt Mitt over his hand.

"Get into the car," Elena whispered in his ear.

Cam took a deep breath and a single step then shouted, "Help! This woman's trying to...."

He felt the jolt at the side of his neck. His head reverberated like frozen fruit in a food processor—one being shaken by a gorilla during an earthquake. He collapsed onto the steps in a heap.

He sensed Elena grab at his shoulders and try to lift him, then drop him. In a blur, she was gone. Cam strained to prop his head up. He saw her car shoot down the road and his head fell, his chin hitting the step with a thud. Seconds later, a terrier's tongue bathed his cheek and a throbbing pain coursed through his jaw.

"Bruiser, back up," a man's voice said. "I called 911. An ambulance is on the way."

Chapter 30
Friday, October 2

"Your jaw's cracked," Darby said.

Cam lay under a thin blanket in the twin-sized bed in his old bedroom. "What's in my mouth?" he mumbled, unable to part his lips more than a centimeter.

"Not as many teeth as there used to be. But a whole lot of metal and elastic. You're lucky it's not completely wired shut. The oral surgeon said four weeks, then comes the dental fine tuning. You'll need at least two implants."

"How am I supposed to eat?" Cam's head was throbbing.

"With a straw. Smoothies, lukewarm soup, anything run through a blender. The doc gave me a sample six pack of chocolate-flavored Ensure."

"Am I okay otherwise?" He tried to lift his head, but a bolt of pain forced it back to the pillow.

"You are. The stun gun didn't do any damage. But falling on your face sure did. I have liquid acetaminophen for the pain." She picked up a bottle from the nightstand, poured him a capful, and put it to his lips.

"It was Elena, my neighbor," he sputtered and drank the medicine.

"I know, dear. Kacey told me."

"Did she catch her?"

"She's looking. As is every other officer in the state."

"Where's Emma?"

"At school. It's almost noon. You've been in and out of a fog since leaving the hospital last night."

"Can you prop me up?"

Darby sidled to the head of the bed and arranged a pillow upright, then guided Cam up, one hand at his lower back and the other behind his head while he scooched. He pushed the blanket down to his waist.

"Thanks," he said and noticed a partially-eaten piece of blueberry pie on the dresser.

"I have to slurp for food for a month and you're eating pie?" he said with a laugh. *Ouch. I have to remember not to laugh*, he thought.

"Sorry, you were asleep." Darby said. "I never properly thanked you for getting me off the hook. You almost got yourself killed for me."

"Yes and no," Cam said. "At first I was just trying to clear your name. But once I got started, I couldn't stop."

"Well, you're clearly quite good at detective work. Plus, you've been spending a lot of time with Kacey lately."

Cam knew his mother too well to believe the comment was merely a flip observation. "She *is* the deputy sheriff," he said.

"I'm well aware." Darby lifted the spoon from her pie plate and held it up, contemplating her reflection.

Cam hesitated, then turned his mother's unasked question around on her. "Do you think I should ask Kacey if she'll start seeing me again?"

"Do you think you're ready for that?" She pointed the spoon at his chest. "If you and Kacey get back together, it has to work out—anything less could be catastrophic for Emma."

Cam stared at his mother, then looked down, his confidence plummeting.

"Listen," Darby said. "I know what a terrific help you've been to Kacey, and you *are* making tremendous strides personally. All I'm saying is don't rush it. I love that girl to death, and nothing would make me happier than seeing you two get back together. Eventually."

Cam smiled wistfully.

Darby contemplated her half-eaten dessert. "I wonder—do more people eat pie with a fork or a spoon?"

* * *

"You've been asleep for nearly three hours," Kacey said. She sat at the edge of Cam's bed.

Cam wriggled his jaw. "It feels a little better now than it did this morning. Did you catch Elena?"

Kacey beamed. "We did. She ran north, but the police in Cass City nabbed her. The dog walker who called 911 caught her license plate so we tracked her down pretty fast. She's already back in Rusted Bonnet in the lock up. Once she has a chance to meet with a defense attorney, we'll get started with her."

"That's wonderful," Cam said.

"The chief wants to get your statement. He can come here to take it."

"Can't you do it?"

"Given our history, the chief wants to do it himself—so there's no question of anything untoward."

"I suppose I can deal with him." Cam smiled. "Is Emma here?"

"Yes, your mother picked her up from school. They're in the kitchen making brownies. I'll get her in a few minutes."

"You didn't tell her what happened, did you?"

"Definitely not. I just told her that you fell on the cement and broke your teeth. And that you'll be staying here at the farmhouse for a few days while you start to recover."

"Thanks."

"No, thank you, Cam," Kacey said and touched his knee. "I don't think we'd have solved Greta's murder without you. I mean Trisha's."

"I highly doubt that. Are you charging Elena with premeditated murder?"

"Technically, first-degree, but it's basically the same thing. Plus kidnapping and battery charges for holding you hostage and zapping you."

"That was no bug zapper."

Kacey smiled, then sighed. "She wasn't even on our radar. To be honest, I don't remember the photo Sheriff Lackey showed us of Erin looking anything like Elena."

"There wasn't much there," Cam agreed, "Something behind her eyes more than anything." He leaned toward the nightstand and took a sip of water through a straw. "Once I figured out that Erin Mack must have come to Rusted Bonnet to track down her former partner, I realized that the suspect list was remarkably short. Actually, nonexistent. First, Erin was a young woman. That eliminated all of the men and Tatum, who's a bit older. Then I considered the time frame. The diamond heist was eighteen months ago, while Greta was still working at Ginsberg's in Cleveland."

"Trisha," Kacey corrected. "Originally from good ol' Dayton, Ohio."

"A long way from Dresden." Cam straightened up against the headboard. "At first I thought Addy or Jasmine might be Erin—either one could've taken a quick trip down to Cleveland for the robbery."

"But Erin went to prison for twelve months."

"That was my next thought. Both Addy and her sister were living here in the village the entire time Erin was locked up. It was killing me—I knew what must have happened but found myself plumb out of suspects."

"Then Elena Ramp appeared to you as a modern day Jacob Marley?"

"Something like that. As soon as she came to mind, everything fit like a glove to be tied." Cam stretched his legs out in front of him. "I had only her word of where she'd been living while Erin Mack was in prison. And she had access to the McRaes' home."

"That was smart. I should've figured that out," Kacey said and fingered a thin chain at the side of her neck. "I had to notify Trisha's parents this morning that not only was their daughter murdered, but she had been a jewel thief."

"Yikes," Cam said, bringing his knees to his chest.

"And then I told them her body was buried in a rural Michigan cemetery under a gravestone marked with the name Greta Astor."

"Double yikes!" Cam inhaled deeply. "I can't imagine how hard that must have been."

"It was definitely uncomfortable. I feel for the officer from Dayton who was there in person. He just put me on the telephone. Trisha's parents and sister will be here tomorrow."

"At least they'll have some closure. I suppose that's better than never knowing what happened to her." Cam slowly swung his legs off of the bed. "I need to stand up," he explained.

"Let me help you," Kacey said, letting him use her forearms to pull himself up.

He stood and put his hands on her shoulders. He felt Kacey's muscles twitch beneath her blouse. "You should be proud of yourself," he said. "I certainly am."

"We make a good team," she replied, then quickly added, "when it comes to detecting."

"We do." Cam folded his hands behind his back. "How about we ask my mother to take Emma for a couple of hours one night next week? You and I can go and celebrate. Even if I have to drink soup through a straw."

"Should we invite the chief as well?" Kacey's voice was timid. "It's his accomplishment as much as ours."

"No, I'd rather it was just the two of us."

"I was afraid of that."

"Sorry," Cam sat back on the bed. "I'm not trying to pressure you. I've just felt ... well, extremely close to you these past two weeks."

"So have I." She took a deep breath. "Okay. But don't tell Emma. I don't want to get her hopes up. But yes, let's give it a shot." Kacey smiled, then quickly shuffled out of the room.

Cam laced his fingers behind his head. Everything was getting better. One day at a time....

THE END

ABOUT THE AUTHOR

 Stephen Kaminski is the author of *An Au Pair to Remember*, the first installment of the Male Housekeeper Mystery series. He also writes the award-winning Damon Lassard Dabbling Detective books. Stephen is a graduate of Johns Hopkins University and Harvard Law School and serves as the Chief Executive Officer of the trade association representing the Unites States' poison control system and its fifty-five centers. He lives with his daughter and rescue kitty in the Washington, D.C. area.

Praise for the Damon Lassard Dabbling Detective Mysteries

"I didn't put it down until I finished it. It is well written. The characters are well drawn. The plot is positively diabolical. There is also a hint of romance. And there is humor. In other words, a perfect cozy. You DO want to read this book."

Kate Elizabeth Shannon, Author of the Brigid Kildare Mystery series

"What a treat! It's fast-paced with likeable characters. There's a wonderful blend of mystery and romance. If you are a fan of good old fashioned mysteries that keep you guessing until the last couple of chapters, this is the perfect book for you."

Socrates' Cozy Cafe

"Just when I didn't think there could be another unbelievable cozy mystery, I am proven wrong. I honestly don't believe I have ever read a mystery that dealt with such serious issues of depression, bullying, and retribution. I was so drawn into this story that I nearly read it all in one sitting. Damon was either diabolically clever, immeasurably stupid, or a splendid combination of the two."

My Devotional Thoughts

"Calling all cozy mystery lovers. Damon Lassard is the male equivalent of Jessica Fletcher in Murder, She Wrote. It has been long time since I have read such an entertaining yet at the same time thoughtful cozy mystery."

Cleopatra Loves Books (UK)

"If you enjoy cozy mysteries such as the Hamish MacBeth and Agatha Raisin series by M.C. Beaton and the Coffeehouse series by Cleo Coyle, you'll definitely enjoy your time with Damon Lassard."

Dreamworld Book Reviews

"This whodunit is a great read. Fast-paced and action packed, you will read it late into the night."

Shelley's Book Case